THE SKYWALKERS
JC RYAN

By JC Ryan

Rossler Foundation Mysteries

The Tenth Cycle

Ninth Cycle Antarctica

Genetic Bullets

The Sword of Cyrus

The Skywalkers

The Phoenix Agenda

The Rowen

Termination

Vinci Books

vinci-books.com

Published by Vinci Books Ltd in 2025

1

Copyright © JC Ryan 2015

The author has asserted their moral right to be identified as the author of this work in accordance with the Copyright, Designs and Patents Act 1988. This work is a work of fiction. Names, characters, places and incidents are the product of the author's imagination or are used fictitiously. Any resemblance to actual persons, living or dead, places and incidents is entirely coincidental.

All rights reserved. No part of this publication may be copied, reproduced, distributed, stored in any retrieval system, or transmitted in any form or by any means, including photocopying, recording, or other electronic or mechanical methods, nor used as a source for any form of machine learning including AI datasets, without the prior written permission of the publisher.

The publisher and the author have made every effort to obtain permissions for any third party material used in this book and to comply with copyright law. Any queries in this respect should be brought to the attention of the publisher and any omissions will be corrected in future editions.

A CIP catalogue record for this book is available from the British Library.
Paperback ISBN: 9781036700423

The EU GPSR authorised representative is Logos Europe, 9 rue Nicolas Poussion, 17000 La Rochelle, France
contact@logoseurope.eu

Chapter One

THE PROPHET

In the aftermath of 9/11 Western governments and their security agencies were in turmoil. Congressional oversight committees, news media and conspiracy theorists all demanded to know - how did this happen? Why did we not see this coming? What could we have done to prevent it? What can we do now? Investigations were conducted; findings and recommendations were made and heads rolled. Whether in public or in secret, consequences were felt.

To this day, only a select few people knew that the real findings of the investigations were dramatically different from the official conclusions reached by the government's 9/11 Commission.

The "chance" discovery of suspicious Wall Street activity prior to the attack, by a young whiz kid, shocked the CIA and FBI to their foundation. It took a beautiful twenty something old college psychology graduate less than an hour to rub their noses in the information that was there right in front of their eyes for years.

If they'd just bothered to look, she pointed out, they

would have seen the escalation of the sale of American and United Airlines stocks over the months prior to Al-Qaeda operatives hijacking the planes that would crash into the Twin Towers and Pentagon. What she showed them was put under wraps in less than an hour and she was offered a job with the FBI on the spot.

While he rattled the American military saber in public, eventually winning consent for his plan to root out terrorism, the president's instructions in private were unambiguous. "Do whatever it takes to make sure this never happens again."

Salome James, head of security at the Rossler Foundation for the past twelve months, top FBI profiler and analyst, recipient of the Congressional Medal of Honor for her heroic actions during the Sword of Cyrus crisis two years ago, was sitting at her desk, looking at The Prophet dashboard on her computer screen.

She was busy comparing month to month data on the "Calamity Indicator", as the operatives called the part of the dashboard that indicated suspicious activities. Deeply engrossed in her thoughts, she murmured, unconscious that she spoke aloud, "That red line has moved two clicks higher since last month." In the last six months it had been going in only one direction – up. At this rate it would trigger the alarm bell in another two months. *What is causing this continuous uptick? I have to take a closer look.*

The Prophet, the most sophisticated, broad-ranging data collection and analysis software on the planet, had been developed as top priority and in ultimate secrecy in the months following the embarrassing revelations by that whiz kid.

A smile played around Salome's lips as she remembered the day that had changed her life. She would never know where she got the guts to do it. It must have been the forwardness of her youth. How could she ever forget what it felt like to walk into the FBI's offices in New York City, into a room full of experienced and hardened FBI operatives and turned them on their heads. How their faces had turned red as she showed them in a fifteen-minute PowerPoint presentation that the financial markets actually "knew" about the eminent terrorist attacks for months before it happened. In hindsight, if they'd had The Prophet available to them before the attacks, the alarm bells would have gone off fourteen days before the attacks.

Now the Prophet had been developed to help security agencies identify imminent threats to security from terrorists, rival nations, and from internal weaknesses lurking inside the global economy. It had proven itself on many occasions. It was responsible when, a few years after it was developed, the warning signs of an impending terrorist attack were picked up and again three days later in London, when a plot to blow up ten US passenger jets was thwarted, leading to the arrest of twenty four Pakistani extremists.

Salome had been part of the project team that developed The Prophet and was still a foremost expert user of the system. But, over the years, she had also realized that it had some shortcomings. She'd discussed her ideas with superiors at various occasions but by that time complacency was firmly in place yet again and her requests fell on deaf ears. With no serious terrorist attack on home soil in more than ten years, no one could see the urgency to enhance the system.

Her point for enhancements should have been driven home when The Prophet failed to alert them of the looming Sword of Cyrus crisis. Had they made the enhancement she'd been campaigning for, they would have detected the threat months before it happened and not just forty days before D-day. But again, no one had wanted to see it as urgent.

Since her permanent relocation to the Rossler Foundation a year ago, though, she'd found that she had more time to organize her thoughts about the enhancements to The Prophet. Fortunately, there was no one better than Raj Sankaran, the Rossler's resident database and computer expert and paranoiac, to help her make those enhancements.

Chapter Two

FIND ME THAT FLYING MACHINE

"I'm telling you, the man's a crackpot."

John Brideaux looked at his colleague in disgust. "So you say, but he's found some very interesting artifacts for me. I say we give him a shot."

"Ancient flying machines on the moon? Ridiculous. If you want to spend your money chasing after myths and legends, fine. I'm out."

Brideaux sat with his elbows on his writing desk, his hands tented and tapping on his chin as he considered what to do. He had no problem funding Dr. Matthew's research himself, but he did have a special group of friends and colleagues who would be disappointed at the very least if he didn't offer them the opportunity. On the other hand, if there really was such a thing as an ancient flying machine and an example could be found, he'd want to be the one to own it.

He also didn't want to suffer being the laughingstock of his friends. If his recently-departed colleague was an example of the reception he'd get, then he'd just keep the idea to himself. Act boldly, keep his cards close to his vest. That was the way to handle this. Matthews' crazy little idea had better have some merit, though. Weighing his eagerness to own the rare and unusual against the potential loss, Brideaux came down firmly on the side of the rare and unusual. A small loss, for him, meant nothing at all. He had plenty of money - more than plenty if the truth were known.

Brideaux sent for Dr. Stephen Matthews right away. The time to act was now.

"Mr. Brideaux, thank you for seeing me." Matthews approached with his right hand out as Brideaux stood to receive him.

"Of course, Stephen. You've brought me some unique pieces in the past. I'm happy to hear you out. Where'd you get this idea of ancient aircraft?"

"It's simple, really. Recently, a closely-held secret from the US space exploration program was leaked. One of the moon rocks brought back by the Apollo 11 mission had a 10-inch statue of an angel embedded in it. It's been kept under wraps since 1969."

"Extraordinary!"

"Yes, I thought so. The statue bore a remarkable resemblance to a bronze angel guardian from a medieval cemetery near Rome, but the metal was quite out of the ordinary."

"I meant that the government could keep a secret for that long."

"Oh, quite. But, as I was saying, they couldn't determine what the metal was, until someone decided it was an iron compound, found only on the moon. Do you understand what this means?"

Bemused by Matthews' enthusiasm, Brideaux shook his

head, though he had a good idea what it meant. Someone had been on the moon long enough ago for the statue to have been completely encased in moon rock. But, let Matthews tell it--he was like a small child with a new toy to show off.

"Don't you see? Someone was on the moon, *thousands of years ago*. How did they get there if ancient man didn't have aircraft? Specifically, spacecraft. And there's more."

Brideaux sat forward. More?

"Ancient Chinese texts, from perhaps 2000 BC, refer to space flight, specifically to the moon. Other accounts, long thought to be myth, are surprisingly accurate. The kicker is this. Just before landing, on the last reconnaissance pass, one of the Apollo astronauts said he had just seen what looked like a structure. His description sounded very much like a structure that the ancient Chinese texts described as having been built on the moon! Many people heard the statement clearly, but when the segment was rebroadcast, the statement was no longer there. Eleven minutes had been cut from the tapes, but too many people had heard it. NASA denies it to this day, but it's been floating around in conspiracy circles all this time."

Brideaux waited until Matthews' breathless flood of words wound down. "What's your proposal, Dr. Matthews?"

"Two-fold. If ancient China had aircraft, chances are that there are wrecked ones, or fragments of wrecked ones somewhere.

"I'd like access to the Tenth Cycle library, to see if the technology was passed down from previous civilizations. Asian civilizations have always fascinated me. How they advanced so rapidly. Since the library was discovered, I've always wondered if they had a head start based on survivors from earlier cycles."

"Interesting. Well, as it happens, I'm in a position to help you with both of those requests.

"Thank you, sir! And as for the matter of my compensation..."

"Let's start you with a grant of $50,000. That should be adequate for now. We'll revisit it if and when you need to mount an expedition."

"Thank you, Mr. Brideaux. That's most generous, most generous indeed."

"Dr. Matthews, find me that flying machine."

Chapter Three

THE SPIDER WEB

Salome's desire to improve the Prophet was rooted in several facts. First and most distressing had been its failure to predict the Sword of Cyrus crisis. It was during that crisis that she'd met her husband and the cadre of Rosslerites who were now dear friends and extended family.

Second was her wish to protect her eccentric and brilliant husband, Roy, from the consequences of his tinkering with nanoscience gleaned from the Tenth Cycle library. Of course, what she thought of as tinkering had led to astounding advances in convenience and ease of the human condition. Roy's inventions ran the gamut from a tiny battery pack that needed only a few minutes in the sun to charge it for up to a year to improvements in waste treatment plants that had all but wiped out previously ineradicable third-world dysentery and hundreds of improvements in between. However, it had also been responsible for the development on the back of his work of nano-nuclear weapons by the Sword of Cyrus.

And finally, by extension and her own sense of duty, she

felt responsible for the well-being of her employers and indeed everyone who worked in and for the Rossler Foundation. Before her employment, despite expert security in the form of Luke Clarke, Sarah Rossler's uncle and former CIA agent, the Foundation had endured three major crises in the short time they'd been in operation. It was her mission to see to it they were prepared should another occur, and if possible, see to it that another *didn't* occur.

With that in mind, she first approached Roy with her idea to take matters into her own hands and have The Prophet enhanced. Brilliant as he was, though, Roy was no expert in data analysis, unless it had to do with his own research. As she'd anticipated, he suggested she approach Raj with the project, and offered to put in a good word for her with his friend.

So it was that she found herself in her office one morning with Raj attending her introduction to her project intently.

"Raj, before I tell you what I'd like to do and what I need your help with, I need to share with you some top secret information. I've received permission to do so, but you must swear never to reveal the information you're about to hear.

"All I can do is swear to stop you if you get into something I feel must be shared," he replied. "Will that do?"

Irritated, she nevertheless answered, "For now." Then she continued. "In my work, I've been using a tool that came out of my master's thesis. It uses various databases, including financial market data, aggregated personal data from major banks, parsed internet searches and a few more items, to…"

"Predict terrorist activity. You're speaking of The Prophet."

The Skywalkers

Salome rocked back in her chair, stunned that Raj knew of it, even to the extent of knowing the top-secret code name.

"Don't be so surprised. You know of my contacts."

She did. They'd made use of his network of computer hackers and conspiracy enthusiasts during the Sword of Cyrus incident. What surprised her was the extent of their knowledge, though in hindsight perhaps she shouldn't have been so taken aback. However, his next statement stunned her to the core.

"We're not the only ones who know about it, Salome. Why do you think there have been so many instances of terrorist attacks the Prophet *didn't* warn of? ISIS, al Qaeda, HAMMAS, all know about it. They've learned how to evade its detection. It needs updating to fill the gaps they're exploiting."

Shaken but undeterred, Salome took control again. "That's why you're here, Raj. I've been telling my FBI colleagues for several years this needs doing." *And if you'd said these things to Luke Clarke, my friend, it may have made a difference.* She didn't share that thought with him. 20/20 hindsight didn't make a bit of difference. What was done was done.

She went on. "You may already know some of this, but please allow me to tell it as I see it. The Prophet doesn't account for the actions of individuals with regard for company behavior. It doesn't know who owns companies behind the scenes. That means that company XYZ, for example, which let's say is a major gold producer, could be controlled by Company A owning 20% stock, Company B owning 25% and Company C owning 10%.

"There's nothing to give us a red flag when the CEOs of these three companies get together for a cozy chat in

Paris. By the same token, we don't know if those same CEOs together own small but controlling stock in XYZ's major competitor. Once they decide to take over, a handful of people could buy stock that's just below the threshold for The Prophet to notice, and vote their shares as a block. No one even knows that the company has just endured a hostile takeover, not even the company itself."

Raj was nodding the entire time, already ahead of her it seemed. "So what you have in mind is tracking the movements of the wealthiest men in the world and see if they are together or at least in touch."

"And women. Don't forget the most ruthless member of the Orion Society was a woman."

Raj nodded fervently, "I'll *never* forget. So you think there could be something like that? A bunch of people who are determined to control all wealth, for their own purposes?"

"Isn't it always? Behind every total take-over ideology is either religious extremism or greed. And often both. What do you think? Is there a way to detect this type of behavior?"

Raj answered confidently. "There's always a way. It may not be strictly legal."

"What do you have in mind?"

"We need access to their phone records, email, even GPS data from their cell phones. That way, we can see if there's a link between their movements and changes in companies such a group might be interested in controlling. Say, energy, financial, pharmaceuticals maybe. Definitely communications."

"How would you get that?"

"Better you do not know," he answered. And then in a comical parody of an SS officer, he leered and said, "Ve haf our vays." Regaining his serious demeanor, he asked if she had specific individuals in mind, or parameters he could use to build a profile.

"I have a few names, but let's go for parameters. That way, no one slips through the cracks. But Raj, we need a proactive system. Once they gain control of a company, we'd be hard-put to rewind. We need early warning if something is afoot behind the scenes."

"I know. What I am thinking is something like a virtual spider web. The way they are staying under the radar is by making small, slow, careful moves. I will build a net fine enough that any move at all will tug on the web. You will know something is going on long before it is complete. Even transactions happening in the background and without the notice of the markets will cause a ripple in the web."

"That's what we'll call it, then. The Spider Web. And Raj?"

He alerted, tilting his head to indicate he was listening.

"Don't get caught."

Far sooner than she expected, Raj was back to show Salome what he'd built. If she hadn't known better, she'd have suspected he was already working on it before they talked. With a few tweaks it was perfect for her purposes, and she embarrassed Raj with her praise.

She wasted no time in setting it to collect data on some of the companies she'd long suspected were being controlled by a hidden agenda. It took days for the data to come in, and when it was complete it was massive. But as soon as she started analyzing and looking at the reports, Salome picked up a number of suspicious-looking anomalies. Among the most alarming was her discovery that literally all satellite communications, internet service providers and telephone companies were in the hands of a handful of companies, each owning 15% to 25%.

As she dug a bit further and looked at the personal data of some of the CEOs of those companies, and then even further into some of the larger shareholders, it became obvious that what she'd suspected was true.

There were many puppet CEOs, and many wealthy and powerful shareholders hidden behind other companies owned by yet other companies. Prominent among them were the names of some well-known people; industrialists, old money, politicians; even the current president hiding about five levels deep.

Salome made a mental note to let Daniel know this president was no Nigel Harper. Of course, not many were the man Nigel Harper was. It wasn't surprising the incumbent might have shady things going on.

As she kept on digging into the personal and social interaction of some of those who seemed to have their fingers in the most pies, she learned that many of them, the so-called minority shareholders, were old buddies and in each other's company regularly. A few retrospective queries of the new databases compared to the history of share movement revealed a few strange bedfellows. Nothing that could land any of them in jail, but the big picture was certainly cause for serious concern.

Over the next few weeks Salome built a terrifying picture. Pharmaceutical and health companies, communications through all media (TV, newspapers, internet, telephones), energy where Tenth Cycle technology hadn't yet arrived, transport including airlines, shipping, rail and road transport, along with military contractors, big agro and big pharma, and technology companies; all were controlled by a handful of companies whose names showed up over and over. They were always in a minority shareholder position individually, but as a group the controlling interest was overwhelming.

Before she'd even finished the thought, Salome answered her own question as to the regulatory agencies. The SEC was headed by POTUS's crony. The UK had shut down their regulatory agency in the wake of the sub-prime mortgage debacle of the first decade of the century and replaced it with the Central Bank. That was a case of the fox guarding the hens if she'd ever seen one. The answer was the regulatory agencies were either blind or complicit.

The biggest problem was going to be how to identify the real people behind those companies. She had some names already but she suspected those were set up to take the fall if whatever the real powers were up to became known prematurely. It was going to take more time and effort to get to the bottom of it and to put tabs on all of them.

Her predecessor in the Foundation, Luke Clarke, was supposedly retired. Indeed, his wife, Sally, became irate if he so much as telephoned her. But because of his position in the family and his years of experience in the security game, Salome thought it was worth the risk of alienating Sally to get Luke's take on what she'd discovered. It was time to take her findings to him, or rather, ask him to come in and take a look.

Chapter Four

THERE IS NO STOPPING THIS

Daniel Rossler was at his desk as usual, in the physical plane. His mind, however, was far afield. When had the dream discovery of a lifetime become so unsatisfying? Outside his open office door, employees walked back and forth, going about their business. Momentous discoveries had been made in the Tenth Cycle library, and there were plenty more to be made, Raj assured him. The portion of data that had been translated was a tiny fraction of what was there.

It had even been more or less peaceful since the threat of mass annihilation from a rogue Middle Eastern cabal had been narrowly averted by the brilliant and untiring work of their own Roy James, now on permanent loan to the Rossler Foundation from CalTech. After the first few tumultuous years since breaking the Pyramid code, a couple of years' peace and tranquility was just what they all needed. And yet, Daniel couldn't help feeling that something was amiss.

Daniel remembered the world before 9/11, even though

he'd still been young. It had changed so much since then; now it was a world with so much uncertainty, violence and death, not to mention corruption and unhappiness. He couldn't help but feel that people were a lot happier before 9/11 than now. Except for the fact that his family, Sarah and little Nick, had come along after 9/11, he certainly had been happier in those simpler times. That attack had shaken his sense of security along with almost everyone else's.

It was true that technological advances had shaped the world in the last two decades. Though it was true the average person's life on that front had become better. But the scary thing was it seemed humanity was not adapting well to these technological advances. Especially in the realm of communication, people had been saying for years that technology was causing so many social issues.

People could not communicate properly anymore. The art of socialization, good manners and caring about fellow human beings had all but disappeared. Political correctness had become the norm to the point where everybody exercised their 'rights' without consideration for anyone else's. No longer did the masses recognize the concept that one person's rights ended when they impinged harmfully on someone else's. One person might exercise his right of free speech despite it being hate-filled - and don't you dare stop them or say anything about it – while another was shouted down for calling that to the attention of the crowd.

People did not lie anymore they only "misremembered" or "misspoke". They did not get fired they got "dehired", or "downsized". It had reached the point of the sublime ridiculous. Manholes had to be called "maintenance holes" because it would be sexist to call it a manhole. No one knew what the word du jour was for a person of color, because it changed so often, and yet most people never stopped to consider that there was no need to express a difference based on skin color. Why not just say 'that man'? Why did his color or ethnicity have to be called out?

Worse yet, people would get depressed and aggressive if they were not connected to the internet and in touch with friends and family 100% of the time. Studies showed that the majority would give up sleep, sex, money and food in exchange for being connected.

And yet, the internet, the media with the most potential for honest news and understanding of the world, had become one large scam or a place to watch funny videos that showed the same animal behavior for the entertainment of the masses. Historians warned that it was becoming the 'bread and circuses' that brought down the Roman Empire. But no one remembered their history, so the warnings fell on deaf ears.

Daniel's inner dialog had turned to these thoughts and similar ones more and more often, but he kept them to himself. They were depressing and worrying, but he didn't want them to infect his loved ones, or for that matter, his Foundation. He didn't know what the answer was, but he remembered the warning that came with the Tenth Cycle library. Indeed, he could hardly forget, because Sarah wouldn't allow him to. Maybe the library contained some wisdom that could be useful. He was mulling over hiring more translators to work through the library more quickly. Maybe a dedicated team to look for political and social information from the Tenth Cycle.

However, a welcome diversion in the person of Sarah's uncle, Luke, interrupted those thoughts.

"Luke, what a pleasant surprise. To what do we owe the honor?" After the Sword of Cyrus crisis, Luke's wife Sally had put her foot down and insisted he retire, again, and this time for keeps. It had been a convenient time, since Salome, the FBI profiler, who'd been seconded to the Rossler Foundation during that crisis had fallen in love with Roy James.

Luke and Daniel together had persuaded her to leave the FBI and take Luke's vacated position. One of the last favors to the Foundation that Nigel Harper effected was to have the FBI permanently loan her to them, continue to pay her salary and afford her all the privileges as well as the duties of a special agent. Her brief was to see to it that the Tenth Cycle library didn't fall into the wrong hands. Of course, Roy's presence may have had something to do with it.

"Salome has been asking me to come in and look at some data she's prepared," Luke said. "Thought I'd stop in and say hi, before meeting her in her office."

"Glad you did. Can you stay for dinner, after?"

"Not tonight, sorry. Sally's expecting me home. I'd take a rain check."

"Ok I'll have Sarah get with her to arrange a date that is suitable, and we might as well make it a party, get Ryan and Emma to join us. Sarah loves any occasion to get us all together, you know. And Nick will be in seventh heaven – his grandma and Aunt Sally spoil him rotten."

"Sounds good. Anything exciting on the horizon?" Luke, retired though he was, still had plenty of interest in anything controversial coming out of the Foundation's research projects.

"Not really. It's getting to be downright boring around here."

"Careful what you wish for, Daniel. Careful what you wish for."

Only an hour later, Daniel took a call from one of the Foundation's most generous supporters and trusted associate, John Brideaux.

"John, good to hear from you. It's been too long, my friend."

"Indeed it has, Daniel. And I hate to be calling just to ask a favor, after all this time, but as you know..."

"You're a busy man, of course. What can we do for you?"

"I have a friend, a gentleman who is well qualified, I assure you, who'd like to have a look around the data in your marvelous library, if that can be arranged."

"I'm sure it can. What's he looking for?"

"Well," said Brideaux, "That's a bit hard to explain. If you don't mind, I'd like him to explain it to your archivist, and if it's something that would interest you, I'm sure your man could explain it better to you."

"Fair enough. I assume you mean Raj, our data specialist."

"He'll do nicely," Brideaux answered. He said nothing about Raj's background, or indeed the fact that he knew almost everything there was to know about it. However, a man whose main goal in life was to prove that the US government had been covering up an alien landing on earth would be the perfect person to help locate any references to ancient flying machines, whether they were of earth origin or beyond. Brideaux had reason to believe that Raj would be easily persuaded to keep the project low key, as well. They'd have to trust one other person, a translator, but that would be easy enough with the right leverage.

"Who's your friend, if I may ask?"

"Dr. Stephen Matthews. Retired from University of Michigan a few years back. He's..."

"A bit of a crackpot." Daniel smiled, and the teasing tone carried through the phone.

"Quite, but he has made some surprising discoveries."

"Oh, he's welcome to do some searching. I'm not sure what he'll find that's relevant to his field, but Sarah will enjoy talking with him, I'm sure. And Raj is a bit of a crackpot himself, so the two of them ought to get along."

"Splendid," said Brideaux. "I'll send him over. And Daniel, thank you."

"John, after what you've done for us, I could hardly deny you such a small favor. We're glad to have him."

Salome greeted Luke with pleasure in his former office. The two respected each other as colleagues at the top of their respective professions, despite the agency rivalry between their former employers. Her spot-on profile of the man who'd put together the network of spies for the Sword of Cyrus organization had meshed perfectly with his knowledge of international criminals matching it. Together they'd cracked the spy ring in time for Roy's technological breakthroughs to avert the disaster.

"Luke, thank you for coming here. It would have been extremely delicate to bring all this to you at your home. How are you doing? Did you and Sally enjoy the visit to Ryan and Emma last night?"

"I guess he told you about it, right?"

"No, he didn't tell me. It's all here in front of me on my computer screen." Salome watched Luke as she dropped this bombshell.

Satisfyingly, his jaw dropped, and then he frowned.

"Salome, you'd better explain that. Are you keeping tabs on me? That's not okay."

"Oh, Luke, don't worry. That was just my way of driving a point home. This isn't about you. Let me explain."

"Please do." Luke's tone was still cool, but he was listening. Her next words set him straight.

"Can I assume you know about The Prophet, Luke?"

"Oh, of course! That was your baby, wasn't it? Sam Lewis filled me in on it. Said you created quite a stir when you walked into the FBI offices with your theory about 9/11."

"It wasn't a theory, Luke. It was all there to be read, by anyone who was paying attention. Problem was, no one was paying attention. And now the problem is there are gaps, and it's happening again."

Luke sat forward, stunned. "Do you mean to tell me there's another planned attack on American soil?"

"No, no. At least, not like that. What I mean is, no one's paying attention to things that matter, just like back then. I've pointed this out to the powers that be in the agency, but budgets are tight and they won't listen."

"What do you mean, things that matter?" Luke queried.

"I've suspected for a long time that if we'd been tracking certain people, for example, the wealthy families that made up the Orion Society, or the Sword of Cyrus, we'd have known about their underground associations long before they became a problem. You know as well as I do that wealthy people hide their wealth by acting through shell corporations; companies that own companies that own other companies, with puppet CEOs to hide behind."

"Sure. Anyone who watches movies knows that. What's your point?"

"Well, to make a long story short, I gave up on trying to

get the FBI to enhance The Prophet, and enlisted Raj." She continued by explaining the changes they'd made, telling him he didn't want to know when he questioned how they were getting some of the data.

"The little parlor trick I pulled by telling you what you were doing last night is nothing. I also know you stopped at the grocery store before coming here, and that you made an ATM withdrawal. I'll give you a demonstration of just how far-reaching it is in a minute, but first, look at these."

Salome had gathered and organized her data carefully. Only she could have read the truth in it until she'd organized it. Now she handed Luke chart after chart showing relationships that should not have existed, corporate takeovers that made no sense and other evidence.

After looking at the first chart, Luke raised his gaze to Salome, one eyebrow raised. "You haven't copied this straight from a fringe lunatic manifesto?"

"Nope. Verified and traced all the shell corporations myself. Every major bank in the US is owned by a handful of European aristocrats who are all related to each other by birth."

"Why haven't the antitrust regulations been triggered?"

"Come on, Luke, you know the answer to that. It takes special access to some deeply-buried information to put it together. Security agencies have it, but they're all busy monitoring for terrorism these days."

"Oh, of course. And why exactly do you have it? Never mind, don't answer that."

Salome smiled. "Here. Take a look at this one. I think you'll find it particularly interesting."

After Luke read it, he again fixed a stare on Salome. This one wasn't so friendly. "Why in heaven's name would you have done this?"

"To convince you it was possible. Don't worry, Luke, you'll walk out of here with it, and I didn't read it. Your financial records, passwords and browsing history are all safe. I did the search myself."

"How did you even get this stuff?" Luke's face was still red. If this stunt hadn't permanently ruined their relationship, Salome would be relieved.

"One organization has been quietly buying up the interests of all the major search engines. That organization could easily compile this type of report on every adult in the world, save those who have never accessed the internet at all. The implications are grave. With even a fraction of the information in that report, they could ruin you if they wanted. And it gets worse. Universal medical records. I haven't found any way to crack those, but if someone does, look out."

She didn't want to continue, seeing a vein on Luke's forehead throbbing, but she had one more thing to say. Luke tilted his head, obviously expecting something else.

"Given the breadth of the population that's on the internet, they could shift world opinion in hours, determine the outcome of elections, bring down the stock market, whatever they wanted. And no one would be the wiser." Her quiet words conveyed a threat so sinister that it clearly stunned Luke, even though he was a seasoned ex-CIA agent.

"And who is it?"

"That's where the threat lies, Luke. I haven't been able to penetrate their identities, and I'm not certain what they're up to. Whatever it is can't be good."

His brow furrowed, he gave his assessment. "Okay, I buy that something's going down, but what?"

"Do you remember all that hullabaloo about a New World Order that the conspiracy theorists used to spout?"

"Sure," he said. "I was there. You were just a sparkle in your mother's eye."

"Not even that, but there's something to the saying that those who forget their history are doomed to repeat it. I know it wasn't just fringe lunatics, and the people behind the scenes might have been more successful had the time been right. They didn't prepare well enough, and the movement collapsed. But a few of the leaders had made some serious money. They went underground. I believe what we're seeing here is a resurgence. I haven't even shown you what I've discovered about communications. The same thing's happening there, worldwide."

"That isn't good news for the Foundation. Anytime since its inception, when there have been powerful groups with an agenda that isn't in the public interest, the library has been a target for acquisition by stealth or by force. What's your proposal?"

Salome drew a deep breath. "I believe there's no stopping it. This sneaked up on us and isn't on the radar of government agencies yet. Furthermore, we can't trust any agency now not to have been compromised. The Foundation, critical staff and the database all have to go to ground. In other words, hide until it's over, or until we can form a resistance movement."

"You can't be serious! Where would such a large group hide, these days?"

"That's what we need to find out."

"Well, good luck convincing Daniel of all this. You're not thinking of handing him a report like you just handed me, are you?"

"Are you kidding? That would be worth my job. And, I

think we have some time. I don't see anything on the *near* horizon that would trigger a crisis. But I believe in being prepared. And I was hoping you'd help me."

"Me! No, you don't understand, Sally would skin me alive."

Salome laughed. "Surely it isn't all that serious."

His dark look made her think again. "You just don't know."

"I'll try to do it on my own. But I reserve the right to tell him you agree with me."

"You're going to get me killed, I swear. Sally's had it up to here with conspiracies. But, okay, I'll help if I can. What's going on in the library these days?"

"Nothing out of the ordinary. The in-house staff is still digging through the energy and medical sections, but we keep a tight lid on that nowadays. Anything exciting is licensed only to well-trusted companies to develop before rolling availability out to everyone. We constantly monitor those companies to see that they stay trustworthy. All that was tough to get through the board, but after what happened two years ago..."

"Yeah, that did bring some folks up short, didn't it? Keep me posted if anything comes up. Maybe Sally's cooking will send me to the grave happy and well-fed long before anything breaks."

"You wish." Salome laughed. "So, what do you suggest?"

Luke thought for a few minutes before answering. "Well, for one thing, you've definitely uncovered something, but damned if I know what it is yet. And we don't have much time to figure it out. I'd say that Doomsday clock they keep is at about five minutes to twelve o'clock. So, here's what I'd do. I'd go ahead and bring Daniel up to speed, and see if his friendship with President Harper is such that he can bring it up with the incumbent and try to get our old agencies working on it."

"Luke, remember that the president is a beneficiary of whatever this is."

"Yes, but I'm not at all sure he's bright enough to understand he's part of a conspiracy."

Salome snorted. Political commentary wasn't part of her brief, though she agreed with Luke's assessment.

He went on. "It looks like they're waiting for something. Because frankly, with the assets they already have, they're poised to take over most of the world any time. The only thing I can see holding them back is the security forces of the governments they'd likely target. Until they find a way around that, or find a way to get those forces behind themselves, we've got some time."

"Okay, thanks, Luke. I'll take your opinion under advisement, and I'll keep you posted. You're sure you don't want your job back?"

"As sure as I'm sure I love my own skin and wouldn't risk Sally's wrath." He left laughing, with Salome echoing. But, when he was gone, she sobered instantly. Her path still wasn't clear.

Chapter Five

THE PREPPERS

Salome did know that she didn't want to bother Daniel with a problem until she had a proposal for a solution. In her world, people who brought problems without suggested solutions didn't last long. Since she'd already discussed it with the only person she dared to that was part of the security world, she needed a problem-solving person to talk to next. And, she had the perfect candidate - her husband. Even though it wasn't his area of expertise, Roy was pragmatic and never failed to impress her with his grasp of any subject that caught his attention.

"Roy, have you ever wondered about preppers?" She knew the answer. It was one of his many obsessions, and an interest he shared with Raj.

"What do you mean, wondered?" he asked.

"Do you think they've got the right idea? I mean, what if they didn't think of everything? Or manage to store enough to get through a crisis?"

"I'm sure they have the right idea. Does your question

mean you're finally willing to do what Raj and Sushma do? At least as far as food storage goes?"

"Maybe. I'm more interested in what a truly prepared person would do. Like, would they have somewhere to go where other people couldn't find them and take what they have?"

Roy put down his fork and regarded his wife fondly. "Well, if they were smart, they would."

"What would that look like? I mean, where could you go these days that no one could find you? And what would you have to take with you?" Salome could tell from Roy's expression that she'd introduced a subject she could mine for as long as she wanted. For him, it was better than TV or a movie. More like a video game; one where he could build an imaginary world and make it as perfect as possible. One thing she knew about Roy was that it would be created down to the last, tiny detail. Even the nano-detail. She was so caught up in her strategy that it took her by surprise when he answered with a question of his own.

"Salome Catherine, tell me what you're getting at. I know you well enough to know when you have something on your mind. Spit it out."

Uh-oh. He'd caught her out, and the use of her middle name was ominous. She only ever heard it from her mother when she was in trouble. Looked like Roy had picked up on that. With no other choice, she once again launched into the explanation she'd given to Luke.

When she was finished with that, she wrapped it up with why she'd brought up prepping. "The only solution I can see is for the Foundation to go to ground, or prepare to, so when whatever this is happens, we're not in the line of fire."

Roy nodded as she spoke, giving her the space to fully explain before he said another word. When she finally stopped speaking, he was ready. "You know what would be fun?" he said. "Finding a perfect spot right around here, or close enough that we could actually pull it off. Man, Raj would freak out. He'd be so jealous!"

"That would be fun," she agreed.

Roy was so taken with the idea that he started looking online at topographic maps and Google Earth that very evening, marking promising spots. Before long, his office was cluttered with large-format printouts that were cluttered with X's marked in red pen. When Salome went to remind him to come to bed, she stopped at the door, taken aback. What the heck?

"Roy, what are you doing?" She started picking up the large sheets of paper to make a path to him.

"Stop! You'll mess up the order," Roy said. "I'm printing out maps of likely spots."

"But, why wouldn't you just save them electronically?"

"Because...well, it was supposed to be a surprise." For a moment he seemed downcast, and then his expression bounced back to his usual happy demeanor. "We're going camping. For our vacation. Off the grid."

Salome was used to guarding her expression. It was so easy to hurt him unwittingly, especially when it took her a few minutes to catch up with his enthusiasms. "Camping? Oh, that sounds...fun?" *Camping? What was he thinking?* Neither of them had what one might call survival skills.

"To find the spot. Don't tell me you've forgotten already?" Roy said, already beginning to look downcast.

"No, no, baby, of course I haven't forgotten. I was just surprised you'd already... Never mind. I think it's a brilliant idea. When do you want to go?

"Well, I've got several spots to explore. I just need to calculate the most efficient way to travel, and then we'll need a list of gear, and I guess we'll have to buy it and ..." Roy paused for breath.

"That's lovely, dear. We've got lots to do to get ready. But let's go to bed now. Tomorrow's a work day."

Roy had been absorbed in his work, but looked up at her when she spoke. What she was wearing made him forget all about what he'd been doing and eagerly follow her to their bedroom. Being worshiped that way could go to a girl's head.

Chapter Six

FOUND THE EIGHTH CYCLE

Within a week of Brideaux's conversation with Daniel, Matthews was ensconced in a guest office with a full complement of office equipment. Daniel sent Raj to meet with him to get an idea of what he wanted to find.

"This is between us, right?"

"Well, unless translation is required," Raj hedged.

"I understand that a translator will be provided under a non-disclosure agreement."

"Uh, I don't know anything about that, but if that's what Daniel said, I'm sure it's true," Raj said.

Matthews cleared his throat. "Here's what I'm looking for, then. You're aware, I'm sure, that some of the hieroglyphics in the pyramids and other ancient artifacts have depicted flying machines."

Raj leaned forward eagerly. "Yeah, and I've always wondered about that."

"You and many others. I happen to believe that the ancients depicted what they saw. However, since the Tenth Cycle library was discovered, I've wondered if some remnant of the population from the Tenth Cycle didn't survive and pass on some of their knowledge. Even artifacts from before the cataclysm. It would explain a lot."

"Like that spark plug," Raj said, referring to an object found in ancient strata in California.

"Precisely. So, what I'm looking for in the library are plans for such machines, especially any that would resemble the representations we know of from our own distant past. There has to be a link between the actual technology and its survival into our cycle."

"That's fantastic, man! What I need to do is get the index for transportation ready for processing. I'll have that for you tomorrow."

Matthews blinked. "You can be so sure?"

"Dude, I've been looking for something like this on my own, in my spare time. I've got the calculations done on the right area, just need to plug them in and run the algorithm. I'll talk to Daniel about assigning us a translator as soon as I have it running."

Matthews smiled. It was going to be very satisfying, working with someone who had the same enthusiasm for the project as he did. He would have to remember, though, not to give any hint that he was actually hoping to find some reference to a location where he might actually discover one of the artifacts itself.

The process of running the algorithm was more tedious than Matthews had realized. He assumed, as did most people unfamiliar with the inner workings of the library, that there were indexed printouts of the text. Nothing could have been further from the truth, although headway had been made in storing electronic text on powerful servers. The process of running iteration after iteration of Fibonacci numbers as skip sequences on the tens of thousands of numbers calculated from the dimensions of the stones within the pyramid took time.

Even with super-fast computers that had taken advantage of Roy's nanotechnology discoveries within the library, the amount of data was so monumental, no pun intended, that waiting for a process to finish was like watching grass grow. Or so it seemed to Matthews. While he waited for his computer to spring to life with the raw, unedited data, he took the time to get to know the famous linguist, Sinclair O'Reilly, who headed the translation department.

"This process is incredible, sir. I understand you did the first calculations by hand."

"Not by hand, no," Sinclair answered. "Though the computers we used eight years ago were primitive, compared to the tools we have now. Sometime it seems it's been twenty years, not eight."

Sinclair turned away, and then back. "Oh, I'm assigning my best employee as your translator. Daniel mentioned you'd need his assistance full-time."

"Thank you. Indeed, I shall. That's most kind of you."

Matthews wasn't a linguist himself, but he quickly learned and memorized certain characters and groups of characters forming words and concepts in the Tenth Cycle script. That way, he could scan the text rolling down his monitor for sections that contained potentially interesting information. Once he identified them, he handed off those sections to the translator for a quick synopsis. In this way, Matthews was making quick progress through everything Raj could supply him.

He'd been working in his guest office quarters for several

days already and had identified some information to further explore, when his eye caught a reference to the word 'cycle' among other words he didn't recognize. It didn't make an impression at first. He was looking for words like 'machine', 'craft', 'flying', and variations of them, especially in close proximity to 'air', 'sky', 'heaven' and the like. It was only when he started seeing 'cycle' with increasing frequency that it registered.

Several years ago, an obscure reference to the Ninth Cycle made it clear that the Tenth Cycle civilization were not only aware of earlier civilizations, but had studied at least the one just previous to theirs. A Ninth Cycle city deep within an extinct Antarctic volcanic caldera had become a tourist destination for the Tenth Cyclers, in fact. However, no one had found references to even earlier civilizations, other than those implied by the numbering system the Tenth Cyclers had imposed.

Matthews hadn't thought about it before, nor was he aware that anyone else had. But, there must have been a reason, one involving evidence, that the Tenth Cyclers named their own civilization the Tenth Cycle. If that evidence existed, very likely it would be recorded somewhere in the library, of course. If so, did Raj, who was most familiar with the extensive index, have any ideas where the Tenth Cyclers might have stored the annals of the earlier civilizations? Matthews thought, perhaps not, or there would have been news stories chronicling the discovery. Was it possible that he was just now making the discovery?

The key lay in the words around 'cycle'. While suppressing his natural excitement, Matthews still wanted to know more about this section, and he wanted it now. He called to his translator, working in an adjoining office with an open door between them.

"Mike, can you come take a look at this right now? I just need a couple of words clarified."

Mike appeared at his elbow. "Sure, Dr. Matthews. Point at the ones you want to know."

Instead, Matthews pointed at one that he was sure meant 'cycle,' and asked Mike to verify that it did.

"Yes, that's cycle, all right. Will that be all?"

"No, Mike, have a closer look. That word is all over the place on this section. Could you look at the words just before and after, and give me an idea what this section's about?"

"Sure. Do you mind if I borrow your chair?"

Matthews got up so Mike could get a closer look. The young man's next utterance was encouraging.

"Wow." He said nothing else as he continued to scroll. Matthews waited patiently at first, but after the next "wow", could contain himself no longer.

"What is it?"

"See these words?" Mike pointed.

"Yes, but I don't recognize them."

"They're numbers. Most of them mean ten and a few mean nine. But this one," he said, pointing to the screen, "means eight."

"Do you mean that the section could refer to the Eighth cycle?" Matthews controlled his excitement with difficulty.

"Yeah, it looks like it does. Wow, I've never seen anything about the Eighth cycle."

Now Matthews was unable to control his voice, which came out harsher than he intended. "Well, what are you waiting for? Tell me what it means, man!"

"It looks like it's just pointing to other reference points where there's information about the other cycles. Raj would know more about that than I do."

"Then we must get Raj here, at once."

Matthews' urgent call to Raj summoned the data specialist to his office within a few moments. As soon as the translator had given Raj the coordinates within the index, he was able to sign up to his intranet account and pull up his records from Matthews' workstation. It was the work of only a few moments to begin scrolling the text from the Eighth Cycle references. Both Matthews and Raj waited tensely while the translator read off the gist of what they'd found. And then, Raj ran for Daniel's office.

"Daniel," he cried, skidding into the inner sanctum like a kid on a pair of those old-fashioned shoes with tiny rollers in the soles. He was moving so fast that if he hadn't steadied himself by swinging around the doorframe with one hand, he'd have careened into the opposite wall.

Daniel looked up, startled and then alarmed at the expression on Raj's face.

"Raj, what the hell?"

"Eighth Cycle. Daniel, we've found the Eighth Cycle!" He had no more breath to explain his meaning, but Daniel caught on.

"Tenth Cycle records about the Eighth Cycle civilization? Is that what you've found?" He got out of his chair and rounded the desk to pound Raj on the back, unwittingly hampering the other man's ability to catch his breath. Raj nodded, unable to speak because Daniel was knocking the breath out of him every time he caught one.

Daniel stopped pounding Raj on the back and stood straight, wearing his astonishment in the lines of his open mouth and widened eyes. "Raj, do you know what this means?"

Raj nodded again, then shook his head no. He thought he knew what it meant, but wanted Daniel to articulate it.

"If they have records of the Eighth Cycle, they may have them for all the others. We'll have historians and archaeologists begging for access! Who knows what we may learn that has been forgotten in the depths of time?"

That was pretty much what Raj was thinking. And if that was the case, he was going to need several more assistants.

Within days, news of the discovery had been reported to the board and selected universities. Matthews, of course, reported it directly to his employer, John Brideaux. True to his previous generosity to the Foundation, Brideaux called Daniel to offer to support the research for up to six months.

The Foundation offices took on a new buzz. In-house translators worked on assignments chasing down references to Ninth or Eighth Cycles, now that they knew where to look for them. Researchers went to work scanning newly-translated texts for anything that would benefit the current, or Eleventh Cycle, civilization. Sarah had a small group specifically looking for anything that would help calculate how many years had passed in the Eleventh Cycle, her eye as always on the approach of the end of the cycle and how a civilization-destroying cataclysm might be avoided.

With all this activity, it wasn't surprising that it took only a matter of a few weeks for the next bombshell to be discovered in the texts.

No one could have predicted what it was, but the Rosslers were in a perfect position to find it plausible when it was found.

Chapter Seven

A SHORT SECRET EXPEDITION

"JR, how do you feel about another archaeological expedition?" Daniel dropped the question into a lull in conversation in the canteen, where he, his brother, and a few of the close friends that formed the core of the Foundation were having a coffee break, along with Stephen Matthews.

"Sign me up! Where to this time? The Himalayas? The Amazon jungle?"

"Not such an exotic location, I'm afraid. Stephen here has found a reference to coordinates where a hardened facility from the Eighth Cycle was concealed within a geological feature right here in North America."

"No kidding! Where?"

"Seems to be in one of the side canyons branching off from the Grand Canyon."

JR's countenance fell. "Man, we can't mount an expedition in there. It's a National Park."

"No, it's all arranged. We have the financial backing from an old friend of the Foundation, John Brideaux. He's sponsoring Stephen's research here and now he's also used his influence to get you into the Park with permissions we normally couldn't get."

"This will be just you and Robert, as far as anyone knows, two buddies having a bit of a vacation backpacking in the canyon. We've secured special permits for you. You guys go for a couple of weeks, check it out, and report back. If you find anything, we'll cross that bridge when we come to it."

"That's a lot of ground to cover in two weeks," JR objected.

"Oh, didn't I say? We have specific coordinates, thanks to the work Summers did to translate Tenth Cycle references back in the day. You'll start by dropping into the canyon with one of the mule tours, but instead of accompanying them back up, you'll be on foot for the rest. You'll follow a map we've had made to a side canyon just a few miles upstream, but after that you'll have to keep your eyes open. Chances are the entrance is high on the canyon walls, after so long."

"Hey, that actually sounds like fun," JR remarked.

Salome spoke up. "Chances are there's nothing left. I mean, look at the ruins in the desert southwest, like Mesa Verde. Only about 1,500 years old and crumbling when they were found. We're talking fifty to seventy-five thousand years for this facility. It would be a miracle if you found anything at all, much less anything major."

"Salome's right. This is precautionary only. After some of what's happened in the past few years, we're a little smarter and a little more cautious with information like this."

"I suppose you've already checked with my wife."

"Yes. She's attending a medical conference next week, says it's the ideal time for you to go have some fun."

"I guess I will, then." JR grinned, his boyish good looks somehow the perfect complement to his freakishly tall frame. "When can I tell Robert?"

"Come back to my office with me, and we'll tell him together. Stephen please join us, we could use your input in the planning."

When Robert arrived, he found Daniel, JR and someone he'd seen around the halls lately but hadn't yet met already convened. The first thing Daniel did was introduce him to Stephen Matthews. Then he explained the reconnaissance mission they were asking him to undertake with JR.

JR didn't at all object to the outing. In fact, he thought it would be fun. He did have one question, though. "How the heck could a big archaeological site, or even a small one, have escaped notice in the Grand Canyon? Wasn't every inch of it explored and mapped already?"

"Well Dr. Matthews here found some controversy. It seemed someone had reported that the Smithsonian was concealing the existence of ancient relics found in the Grand Canyon, and there was an Egyptian connection." Daniel's explanation was as puzzling as it was surprising.

Robert countered, "Let me see if I understand this correctly. The Tenth Cycle library came from the Great Pyramid of Giza, and now there was at least some evidence that maybe Eighth Cycle people had left something similar in the Grand Canyon?"

Matthews handed him a printout of an old article. "Read

it when you have time, but in summary what it says is some miner, back in the early nineteen-hundreds, found what looked like hieroglyphics, and a big city or something, down one of the side canyons. Here's the weird part, though. It looks like the whole thing was covered up by the Smithsonian, and the area is off limits now. I am still wondering why they'd do that."

JR, not to be outdone, chimed in with his two cents. "If this were true, then several generations of archaeologists have been denied the opportunity to study what could have been the key to some of the mysteries of North American archaeology all along. Egyptian visitors over 5,000 years ago? Or an ignorant man, stumbling on an Eighth Cycle city and mistaking it for Egyptian?" For the normally genial and joking JR, this was a scandal, and he let the others know it.

But Daniel had what he thought was the explanation. "Rumors of concealed finds being secreted in the Smithsonian's maze of underground storage rooms have been rife for years. Lots of people, Raj included, believe them. Somehow, the stories have always been passed off as hoaxes, and the Smithsonian has never been called to account for them."

Matthews added, "Well here's the thing, there were supposedly artifacts taken out of the site and stored at the Smithsonian. I wonder what the chances are that we could somehow manage to have a look at them. The connection between the Egyptian link to the Tenth Cycle and this is too much of a coincidence for me. The guy who discovered this thought it meant Egyptians had visited North America. I'm wondering if it wasn't Egyptians at all, but Eighth Cyclers."

JR agreed, saying, "Well there's one thing I have come to accept since I started working for the Rossler Foundation. Nothing is too weird to be true and I wouldn't be surprised to learn there are more secrets in the dusty basements of the

Smithsonian than anyone realized. We all know how inconvenient information about the more secret of the holdings could be buried and marginalized as conspiracy nut hoaxes."

"There seemed to be consensus, then." Daniel interrupted the speculation and said, "Ok enough of that. We have an expedition to plan and launch."

Chapter Eight

TENT, CAMPFIRE COOKING KIT

On the Wednesday morning before JR and Robert were to set off on their trek, Daniel glanced at his Director of Security and gestured for her to come in and sit down. She closed the door behind her and did as he indicated.

"Roy and I want to go on a little trip. Just a getaway. We're thinking about a week. With JR and Robert off exploring, it seems to me that this is the best time for me to be gone. After they get back, assuming they find something, all hell's going to break loose, and I don't know when I'll be able to get away. Sorry for the short notice, but will it be ok if we take off next week?"

"That makes sense," Daniel said. "But, shouldn't you have a deputy in place before you take time off? Have you hired a second in command yet?"

"No. I've been looking. I was wondering if you could persuade Sally Clarke to let Luke come watch the store for a week."

"Oooh, you want me to live dangerously, is that it?" Daniel laughed. "I'll get Sarah to ask. If worst comes to

The Skywalkers

worst, maybe we can pull in Sam Lewis for a week, if we can find him. Last I knew, he was fishing in the Catskills."

"There's a thought. Is there time? I'd really like to leave Saturday morning, if you can spare me."

"I'll work it out. You and Roy go have fun. Sarah and I will hold down the fort until everyone's back."

"Thanks, Daniel. This means a lot to me."

"Don't mention it. You and Roy haven't taken any time off since you got back from your honeymoon. High time you used some of that accrued leave."

After Salome left, Daniel sighed. A little more notice would have gone a long way, but he was glad that Roy and Salome were going to get a break. They'd both been working too hard for too long. One of these days he was going to have to surprise Sarah with a vacation. He'd use the excuse of finding out if Sally was up for some babysitting when he called to suggest that Luke come in for a week to take over Salome's duties. He had no doubt that Luke would love it. It was Sally that he and Luke both feared. Daniel laughed, startling a passerby. Sally was all of five-foot-three, a fearsome monster if there ever was one. Images of her sweet face while reading little Nick to sleep replaced those of Luke, who always feigned terror when he talked about Sally bullying him. Daniel couldn't help but roar with laughter again.

As usual, Roy had been absorbed by his project, supremely unaware that Salome at least couldn't just up and go off on a vacation. Salome was certain the thought never occurred to him. In fact, he probably shouldn't have done it without advance notice either, but as the star researcher on staff, he'd get away with just about anything he took into his head to do.

Salome walked over to Roy's office and gave him the news that their vacation had been approved.

"Oh." Roy blinked. "Thank you for handling that."

"You're welcome. You promised to make a list of what we needed to buy. Have you done that?"

"Oh, yes, let me see, where did I put it?" Roy pawed among the mess of papers on his desk, before patting his pockets and coming up with a folded piece of paper and handing it to Salome.

"Tent, campfire cooking kit...Roy, I've never cooked on a campfire."

"Oh, then, uh, maybe we'd better get a kerosene stove instead."

"Okay. Let's see, sleeping bags, kerosene lantern..." Salome's voice trailed off as she read the list. But when she looked at her husband's happy expression, she decided it would all be worth it, and maybe it would be fun.

Salome got on the phone to locate a rental SUV, and by noon on Saturday, they had stuffed everything into it and were on their way north, up I25 toward Bighorn National Forest in northern Wyoming. From there, Roy had traced the most efficient route he could through promising areas in Montana and Idaho. He'd used both mountains and forested areas as his criteria. The week would be spent mostly in driving and quick reconnoiters with satellite images and topographical maps to guide them into public lands.

Technically speaking, they would be trespassing, but the areas were so remote that Salome didn't think there'd be a problem. Only when it came to proposing a large compound where the Rossler Foundation could burrow in and hide would that become an issue. And if it came to that, Salome didn't want their whereabouts to be broadcast through public records. Or private ones for that matter.

Like the secretive separatist organizations that occasionally fell afoul of the ATF department, they'd be outlaws. But if it came to that, the government would be the bad guys this time. Salome had every confidence that the Rossler Foundation needed this backup plan, but getting it approved by a small, core group without alerting the board and government agencies from the national to the local was going to be tricky. She was going to look like a conspiracy nut, like Raj, but the safety net would be worth it. At least Raj would be on her side.

"Roy, did you say anything to Raj about what we're doing?"

"No, should I have?"

"No, just wondering. I know he and Sushma have a hideaway of sorts somewhere in Nevada. Have you ever talked to him about that?"

"Not really. Just what to have if you want to disappear for a few weeks."

"Hmm. And what if you wanted to disappear for a few years? If my doomsday scenario ever happens, God forbid, we will need a hideaway for quite a few years if not longer."

Chapter Nine

ELIGO RARUS

They called themselves Eligo Rarus, which means 'selected few', but of course they'd elected themselves to the designation. It came out of the rumored Billionaires' Club of the early years of the century. When the bottom dropped out of the economy in the first decade, about one percent of entrepreneurs somehow ended up with all the money, leading to a backlash against 'one-percenters'. Eligo Rarus was formed from the top one percent of them, maybe a dozen or so to begin with. Attrition had brought them down to six, who were obscenely rich on a scale that even the rest of the obscenely rich couldn't begin to imagine.

They met via private satellite secure link every two weeks to discuss world events and take actions in their mutual interest. And they had an agenda.

For as long as the group existed, these six had been accumulating shares in key industries such as communications, transport, banking, pharmaceutical, medical, technology and other key industries worldwide. They were shrewd enough to hide what they were doing – very seldom would they buy controlling shares, and never in their personal names. Instead, the acquisitions were always through companies that owned companies that owned yet more companies - hiding themselves five, six or more levels away from the front, the public eye and any security screens.

By now, between them they owned stakes in or controlled pretty much everything that had an impact on human life on this planet including water. Through their holdings they controlled politics in every democracy in the world – they decided who gets elected and who not, they decided which companies were going down and which ones were making a profit. They could drop the share values of a company in a matter of minutes and then buy up what they wanted at rock bottom prices or just destroy the company because they did not like it.

During the latest meeting, they talked about elections happening in the UK and, in a few months' time, Germany. Already they had decided the outcome of the UK election. The Tories will be in, and Lady Spencer (distant family of the late princess Diana) will be the new prime minister. As for Germany, the front-runner was entirely unsuitable. Soon, embarrassing revelations about his infidelity would surface. When his campaign was already reeling, more rumors, this time regarding his father's role during World War II and the family's suspicious rise to wealth would deal the death blow. The preferred candidate, Uwe Meinhardt, would then sail into office on a backlash.

Next they turned their attention to a new up and coming internet search engine. Already, it had cornered ten percent of the search market, in just the last six months. After making the decision whether to simply shut them down or to own them, the decision was to own them by funding the venture capital they sought. Afterward, Eligo

Rarus would divert traffic to them from the existing search engines so they would become popular quickly. Once they were making money, an IPO would be proffered, so Eligo Rarus could step back and let other companies take up the shares, funding the company going forward. Obviously, their own hidden companies would own the control as always.

The most interesting point of discussion was an update about the Eighth Cycle discovery by the Rossler Foundation. The Eligo Rarus had been keeping their eyes on the Foundation since it was formed a few years ago and considered it a prime target. When the time was right, they planned to move in and take over that Tenth Cycle Library, but for now they were happy to just observe and let others pay for it.

Now there was a new asset. Without mentioning how he came by the idea, one member opined that it would be nice if the Eighth Cycle discovery could lead them to the answer they'd been looking for; how to swiftly subdue all world governments with little bloodshed and put everyone under one government. What a blessing would it be to humanity if that day arrived. The day when there is one government, one currency, no war, no religion, no suffering, no terrorism, food for everyone, global and efficient health services, housing, happiness and peace. Of course, there would be no mention of individual freedoms. The cost of the Utopia they envision would be acquiescence to the greater good.

Yes, it was a prerequisite to becoming a member of Eligo Rarus. Apart from being the richest of the rich, they were expected to be a humanitarian and promise to devote their time, resources and effort for the good of humanity. Atheism was also required. There was no place for religion in the Eligo Rarus worldview; it had just caused too much trouble in human history. Already a meme with this outcome in mind was circulating on Eligo Rarus-controlled social media. It stated: If all religions preach peace, why can't all religions maintain peace? Christians, Jews, Muslims — all had contributed to millions upon millions being killed in the name of religion. And that must be stopped.

By the end of the secret meeting, they all had their assignments.

Chapter Ten

SPICY FOOD AND CHEAP TEQUILA

JR and Robert Cartwright, the Foundation's geology consultant, also set out on their journey on Saturday, first driving to Denver International Airport and then boarding a flight for Flagstaff, Arizona, where they'd rent a vehicle to drive to the park. The men were good friends, having survived two hazardous expeditions in Antarctica together. Their gear was well broken-in, minimal as the parameters of the trek required.

Because they would be on special permit in the back country of a National Park, they would have to pack out everything they brought in, including their own waste. Between the heat at the bottom of the canyon at mid-day in May and the need to move fast, they were traveling light, taking nothing but the clothes on their backs, toiletry necessities, a supply of sunscreen that JR's physician wife Rebecca insisted upon, a few changes of underwear, dried survival food and their cameras. Water would be filtered from the Colorado River with a tiny apparatus using a nano carbon filter and some other technology that JR didn't understand, provided courtesy of Roy James' prolific lab.

Bivouac would be under the starry sky, with a rock for a pillow at best, unless the night were unseasonably warm, in which case they'd be able to use their outer, long-sleeved shirts to cushion their heads from the hard ground. Temperatures would range from a high of around ninety degrees Fahrenheit during the day to a low in the mid-fifties at night. During the day, the relentless sun would make the temperature feel much hotter than it was. At night, the dry air would have the opposite effect, exaggerating the feeling of cool on their skin. This would not be a comfortable trip in any sense of the word.

JR carried a satellite phone, and Robert had a complex survey tool designed for back country exploration by a company that had licensed some of Roy James' nanotech inventions. With it, he could pinpoint their location with a high degree of precision using the GPS system, as well as measure distance between one point and another. It would record their trip automatically, and when the data was downloaded, draw an accurate map directly to whatever they found. It would also measure and precisely map the interior of a structure or even a cave, in three dimensions.

Each man carried a one-thousand foot coil of climbing filament, a core of nano carbon thread, another of Roy's toys, wrapped in a nylon sheath, super light and stronger than any old-technology climbing rope had ever been. They also each had a supply of tiny nano steel pitons and a small rock hammer. If they used them, the pitons would have to be removed as they descended and carried out with them as well. However, both men were well-versed in free-climbing techniques, so they wouldn't use either the filament or the pitons unless it was absolutely necessary. Nevertheless, they'd be less destructive to the environment. JR blessed their access to Roy's numerous gadgets each time he hefted his backpack. Just the weight reduction alone was astounding.

The mission was to find the coordinates they'd been given and survey the canyon walls on both sides of the narrow defile for any sign of man-made structures or caves that might hold such structures. If they found anything, no matter how insignificant, they were to measure and photograph it, leave it in situ and return with their report. It was simple enough, but required the skill and strength that the men brought to the mission. Despite the hardships they expected, both men looked forward to the challenge, and set out with good cheer. They wouldn't be able to speak of their objective until they had left the others in the mule tour group behind and were alone.

The flight to Flagstaff was uneventful, but because of the timing, the itinerary included an overnight stay there before they drove to the South Rim of the canyon the following morning. JR and Robert decided to indulge in the spicy cuisine of the region, a fusion of Mexican and Native American that threatened to blow Robert's ears off, to JR's amusement. Washed down with a couple of margaritas and some mariachi music, the meal promised to be their last bit of fun for the next ten days.

The following morning, JR picked up their rental vehicle for their drive, while Robert did his best to recuperate from overindulging in both spicy food and cheap tequila from the night before. Next time, he'd listen to JR when he recommended a top shelf margarita instead of the standard one.

Chapter Eleven

TO THE CANYON

JR was disgusted that he hadn't thought this mule expedition thing through. He could only imagine what he looked like on the back of his long-suffering steed, with his legs canted out at an odd angle due to the fact that there wasn't a single saddle available with a long enough drop to the stirrups to accommodate his leg length. At 6'10", JR's was in the ninety-nine point ninth percentile. He should have been used to nothing fitting him, but he just hadn't thought about what it would mean on the back of a mule.

What he needed was a Percheron, or some other really tall horse. Of course, a saddle for it with extra-long stirrup straps would be nice, but at least his knees wouldn't be jutting out. Looking over the side of the narrow trail, just wide enough for his mule without his knees sticking out sideways, JR figured there wasn't a horse in the world stupid enough to take that trail. Even the mule had to have blinders on, which may have been the reason it kept scraping JR against the cliff that rose from the other side of the trail.

The Skywalkers

They should have hiked it. If he'd had any foresight, he'd have volunteered to walk in front of his beast, instead of perching comically on its back. The poor mule was already taxed, as JR, though fit and slender, weighed in at two-hundred and thirty-four pounds. It probably would have appreciated the break.

JR looked over his shoulder at Robert, on the mule behind him. "How's it going?"

Robert wasn't a short man, though he often told JR that he felt short, standing next to his mate. Nevertheless, he cracked a grin every time JR looked back. JR would never live this down, and what was Robert doing? Was that a cell phone? He wouldn't dare take a photo...oh, man! JR turned forward again, making plans to get hold of that phone and delete every photo of himself he could find, as soon as they reached the bottom where he had some room to maneuver.

JR never thought about the time when none of this would have been a joke. That first expedition to Antarctica, when he'd met Robert and all of them almost died had both changed his life forever and saved it, ironically. Before that, anger had consumed him. He didn't even remember why he'd been angry, he just was. The war, his fiancée leaving him, leaving school. All of it and none of it. But once he learned Rebecca cared for him, it seemed to melt away. One day he was angry, and the next a little mad, until the time came that he wasn't even a little stressed, under normal circumstances.

Of course, people trying to blow him and his family up, that stressed him some. But that was all behind him. He was incredibly lucky to be riding this crazy mule down this crazy trail, with a crazy best friend behind him taking photos that would probably end up on Facebook, if he didn't get that phone away before Robert found some signal. When he added it all up, this was a fine day, and there was an adventure ahead. What could be better than that?

And the best part was there were no secret societies plotting against them this time. No more Orion Society with their spies in government agencies; no more Sword of Cyrus looking to end the civilized world in nuclear violence. This was going to be fun, after he got off this dratted mule and he and Robert could strike off on their own. The way he'd always wanted it, two buddies looking for archaeological mystery. The only thing better would have been if Rebecca were with them. On the other hand, there was something to be said for boys' night out. Too bad a six-pack or so wasn't in the weight budget.

Robert didn't know when he'd had a better chuckle. JR looked like something out of a Disney cartoon up there, swaying from side to side with the mule's gait and those legs sticking out at a crazy angle. Every now and then he yelped when his left knee made contact with the wall on that side. The bloke was going to have a sore knee, though. Robert hoped it wouldn't be bad enough to slow them down.

Aside from the amusement he took from the comical scene before him, Robert was enjoying this ride immensely for the rich geological interest. Imagine, a mile-deep canyon, cut by the Colorado River through three of the four geologic eras. The significance was staggering, and the sights enthralling. Robert had never been here before, though of course everyone in the civilized world knew of the Grand Canyon. The opportunity to do what he was doing - and get paid for it - was amazing.

If he'd had his way, he'd be taking samples from the

The Skywalkers

strata as they descended. Naturally, it was forbidden. If everyone did that, the canyon would be wider than it already was within a year or two. Besides, others had already done it. He didn't need to. And if he and JR found what they hoped to, his name would be made twice over. After Paradise Valley in Antarctica, another significant find at his age would be unbelievable. Working with the Rossler Foundation had been the best decision of his life, despite the dangers he'd faced.

By the time they reached the guest ranch at the bottom, Robert was wishing he'd done a bit more conditioning on the back of an animal before taking the trip. His backside would be stiff and sore for a while, he reckoned. Unless the walking loosened him up. JR didn't look to have fared much better, as he was limping, more on the left side than the right. His knee must have really taken a beating.

After their permits were examined by rangers at the guest ranch, the two men waited until everyone was occupied with something before slipping around a corner in the canyon wall. It was part of their restrictions that they make sure no one saw them going into areas not generally open to the public. Their plan included getting far enough away from populated areas that no one could spot them making camp, before night fell on this first day. It was a tall order, since the canyon was narrow enough to block the light early in the afternoon at this time of year.

They walked for an hour, figuring that they'd made a distance as the crow flies from the ranch of about three miles despite having only a rudimentary trail. Robert figured that JR made up for obstacles with that long stride, as if he wore seven-league boots. He, on the other hand, had to scramble around or over many of them. He was ready for a break.

"How long d'you think we can keep going, mate?"

JR, several strides ahead, had to turn around and ask Robert to repeat himself. When he did, JR looked surprised. "Until full dark, right?"

Robert sighed. At this rate, full dark couldn't come fast enough for him. But, ever practical, he objected. "Better save enough light to set up a bivouac, isn't it?"

"Oh, I guess you're right. Another half-hour, say?"

"Sounds right. Let's go, then."

By eight p.m. on Saturday evening, the two friends were sound asleep, oblivious to the spectacular night sky.

The upside to their early night was that both JR and Robert were wide awake by the time the sun rimmed the lip of the canyon above them with gold. They'd filled their Camelbaks with filtered water from the river the night before, so their morning routine was quick. By around six a.m., they were picking their way around dark shadows beside the river, while the sky became lighter and lighter as the sun rose higher.

The GPS device showed they were two, maybe three miles from the ranch site as the crow flew, so they talked in normal tones, though they didn't shout as sound carries far in such an environment. Their map showed they had a good ten miles to go before turning off into the side canyon where the coordinates in the Library had been plotted. If they didn't encounter any obstacles in the nature of impassable areas beside the river, a day's vigorous hiking might bring them to that point. If they had to tack away from the river to go around something big, then it depended on how quickly they could get back to the more or less direct route.

The Skywalkers

It was strange, down in this canyon, that the air wasn't colder this early in the morning. At the top, yesterday morning, it was chilly, around forty-five when they started down. The day warmed up, but now JR realized that it was also because they'd been at an altitude even higher than Boulder's at the rim, nearly 7,000 feet above sea level. Descending to the canyon floor brought them over 5,000 feet lower. No wonder. Today, it was warming rapidly. They'd planned as well as they could for the extremes of temperature, so it wasn't going to be a problem, just something to occupy his mind as he trudged along ahead of Robert.

He was dodging any vegetation that he saw in time, so as not to damage any bit of the ecosystem in which they were intruding. Putting a big hiking boot down between a tiny plant of some sort and a flat rock, he froze when the distinctive sound of a diamondback rattler started.

"Robert, stop."

"What is it?" Robert asked.

"Rattler. I'm going to let him settle down before I move. Don't come any closer."

JR strained to see the reptile, but colored as it was to blend into its desert surroundings, he couldn't spot it. Then he realized it must be under the rock. How odd. He thought they liked to sun themselves on top of rocks. A full minute passed before the snake relaxed and stopped rattling. When the sound stopped, JR snatched his foot back, the movement setting off the danger signal again.

"Guess we'd better go around that," he remarked, sounding calm though his heart was hammering in his chest. Logically, he knew that his thick leather boots would have protected him from a low strike. His nervous system wasn't having it, though. As far as his adrenaline was concerned, he'd dodged a bullet. Indeed, a snakebite out here would be something of a disaster. They had a snakebite kit, but getting back to civilization for antivenin would be tricky. JR resolved to scan further ahead from now on, though that wouldn't have helped in this case. He just hoped any other snakes out here weren't the crazy kind that hung out under rocks instead of on top of them.

When he'd retreated to Robert's position and struck out to give a wide berth to the rock, Robert remarked, "I've never seen a rattler."

"You're lucky." JR had seen plenty of the poisonous reptiles of the continent, from the cotton-mouth moccasins that he'd encountered as a boy fishing in North Carolina, to the more deadly coral snakes of Florida. Rattlers, of course, were everywhere. JR hated each and every one of them, as a species and as individuals. His heart was still racing from the harmless encounter with the diamondback.

"Well, we've got a few fairly nasty ones back home," Robert answered. "Not rattlesnakes, though. At least they warn you. Now, the death adder, he'll ambush you."

JR turned an incredulous look on his friend. "Cut it out with the snakes, man. They give me the creeps."

"Heh, just like Indiana Jones, mate?"

"Something like that," muttered JR.

It was in the afternoon of the second day that the GPS warned them the side canyon was nearby. Both men had been focused on the ground ahead of them since the snake encounter the day before. Now they looked up, scanning the seemingly-impenetrable walls for a crack or crevice that would lead into a side canyon. When nothing presented itself as likely, they looked at each other, baffled.

It had to be around here somewhere. There was no question the GPS device was highly accurate. But in the afternoon shadows, it was possible they'd missed something. The only thing to do was to start right next to the wall and move alongside it. Surely the opening would be easy to spot that way. The men had come to one of the many spots where the bottom of the canyon on both sides of the river was only yards wide between the river and the canyon wall. If they didn't find the side canyon on this side of the river, they'd have to cross the treacherous body of water and explore the other side in the same way.

The Colorado is deceptively smooth in long stretches. Rapids ranging from Class 1 to Class 10 are spread out along the river from Lee's Ferry to the Diamond Creek take-out, some 225 miles downriver, with many existing within the Grand Canyon. In places where the river looks smooth, there are often undertows that can pull a man down and keep him down until they spit him out hundreds of yards downstream, often lifeless. It is not a river to swim across.

Chapter Twelve

I'M ALMOST CERTAIN IT IS

Salome was sick of the car by the time she and Roy reached the small town of Buffalo, Wyoming more than five hours after leaving Boulder at noon. Her delight at the charm of the little town nestled in the foothills of the Bighorn Mountains was contagious. Even Roy looked around with pleasure. What impressed Salome the most was the green. In Boulder, even though it was late spring, snow was still likely. Salome had expected desert landscape all the way north into Wyoming and into Montana.

Instead, they were gazing at vistas of forested hills, snow-capped peaks that might have inspired the 'purple mountain majesties' of the song. Salome nearly forgot their mission in her desire to stay right there and explore the lakes and mountains of Bighorn National Forest. They decided to stay in town for the night, both a little daunted by the complications of their camping gear. In the morning, they'd do what they could to explore the back roads. Salome began to realize that the task to find somewhere that no one ever went would be more than a two-week jaunt. Unless

The Skywalkers

they stumbled on somewhere early on. This wouldn't be it. Too many people knew of this hidden beauty to expect to find a secluded area.

The next day brought confirmation of her fears. No matter how small the road they turned down, there was traffic. Maybe only a little, but she was looking for somewhere they could be the only car on the road for an hour or more. They explored for several hours, then reluctantly left the area and headed toward the next town north, Sheridan, where they'd again get off the main road and explore in the north end of the National Forest.

If they didn't find anything suitable there, they'd go on to Billings, and then turn west toward Gallatin National Forest, dipping back into Wyoming to travel through it toward Bozeman. Salome couldn't explain to Roy exactly what she was looking for, but she'd know it when she saw it. It needed to be a spot where a nearly unnoticeable road went, unimpressive where the smaller road left the larger one, but leading to an area where they could build a compound that, though unobtrusive, would house around a hundred, maybe more.

Hard decisions would have to be made about whom they could shelter. More than a hundred, and it would be too easy to find them.

Salome mentioned her concerns to Roy. The area needed to be heavily wooded, to shield their buildings from satellite imagery. It wouldn't be perfect; the satellite cameras were too good. Ideally, she was looking for a heavily wooded area on the sides of mountains that would be accessible only with four-wheel drive, on roads that were barely used.

"What about a cave," he responded.

"That would be even better, if we could find one that isn't on the grid as a tourist attraction. Even a small one, where we can retreat if a hostile force did find the compound."

She'd seen some likely areas on the topographical maps, comparing them with satellite images Roy had printed out. It appeared there were some areas on the images so deep in shadow that they could hide almost anything. Unless that meant the land was so steep they couldn't build on it, those were the best bets. All of them were in the Gallatin National Forest, though, so it was worth exploring Bighorn, simply for the closer location.

They drove in companionable silence except for the brief moments when one or the other had another thought about the requirements for survival they must take into account. Salome was impressed as always with Roy's thoroughness. He had an entire list of his own inventions that would be helpful, like the water filters JR and Robert had taken on their jaunt, only much bigger, the reverse-engineered lighting from Paradise Canyon in Antarctica, and more. He had plans for others he hadn't yet had time to build, and some things they expected the environment to provide if they were lucky, like geothermal energy.

They'd fallen silent for a while, when, out of the blue and totally off topic, Roy asked, "Do you think it's possible to make love in a tent?"

Salome smiled. "Oh, I'm almost certain it is. Let's find a camping spot and find out."

Chapter Thirteen

NO INTELLECTUAL CURIOSITY

Having reached the canyon wall, JR and Robert decided to use an old strategy, one they utilized in Antarctica while seeking an exit from Paradise Valley. This time, they'd go an agreed distance, JR walking back toward the way they'd come and Robert going further along the wall. The GPS should have been accurate to within a couple of yards, but there was no indication of a side canyon here that they could see. They agreed to go a mile, each in their own direction, then turn around and meet back in the middle to report findings.

As it happened, though, they were still within easy earshot when Robert found it. A narrow fin of the lowest stratum hid the entrance to the canyon from view. Since they hadn't been separated for more than three or four minutes, he halloo'd for JR to turn around and join him. JR let Robert take the lead as they slipped into a crevice that met all the criteria of a slot canyon. The walls were carved in fantastic shapes, but overhead there was only a tiny sliver of open rock. Looking down from a plane, no one would ever see it.

No wonder it wasn't on any maps except the one that the Rossler Foundation cartographer drew from the description and coordinates in the Tenth Cycle library. Even the obscure reference was vague. The Tenth Cyclers hadn't found the spot, either; and yet, someone had known of it. It was a mystery best left to the translators, but at least they'd found what might lead them to the Eighth Cycle facility. From here on out, they'd have to go slowly and keep a careful watch. There was no description of what they were looking for. JR could only hope they'd recognize it when they saw it.

They'd been walking and sometimes crawling in the slot canyon and Robert was several yards ahead of JR when he gave a shout of surprise. JR hurried forward and found Robert teetering on the edge of a drop-off that opened into a much wider corridor. The floor of the wider area was at least twenty feet below.

"How the heck was this formed?"

Robert answered him with an absent mutter. "Had to have been some kind of shifting, but this is the wrong kind of formation for that. We're standing at the bottom of nearly a mile of sedimentary rock, and the water level of the river is above that floor. Why isn't it full of water?"

"I don't know. Maybe because the river's about a quarter of a mile away by now?"

"These strata are porous. The water should find its way here."

Both men considered the implications of the dry bottom of the canyon. "Well, it doesn't look like it's in any danger of flooding. Let's get down there."

Robert studied the surrounding walls some more, then shrugged. "Might as well."

The drop-off wasn't as sheer as it had seemed to JR when he first saw it. It was an easy scramble for both of them, and as they turned to look back where they came from, they realized it would be an easy climb back up as well. From the floor of the crack in the rock, they could see no way out except back the way they came from. It was an eerie feeling, being closely surrounded by cliffs over a mile high. JR had the uneasy sensation of waiting for the walls to close in and crush them. Robert didn't seem worried though. He was already heading for the opposite end of the crack in the earth. JR quickly followed.

About a quarter mile from where they'd climbed down, the crevice took a sharp turn away from the direction JR thought the river lay, and immediately opened into a wider segment. Robert consulted his GPS. "It should be along here somewhere. Look up, all the way to the top of the walls, make sure we don't miss it."

JR scanned upward from where he stood, wondering how they'd ever see an opening if it were hidden the way the slot canyon that led them here had been. To add to the difficulty, the sun had sunk far to the west much earlier, and it was now deep dusk in their narrow spot.

"Let's make camp for the night. We'll be able to see better in the morning."

"Good point."

It was then that they realized, both dropping their jaws in unison. They were miles from water. How would they survive the next day without going back to the river? It was a little like the old riddle about the fox, the chicken and the corn, only instead of having to figure out how to get all three across the river, JR and Robert would have to figure out how to make it any farther than they'd gone if they had to continually go back for more water.

By the time they'd discussed the dilemma, it was too dark to see the climb up to the slot canyon, so they decided to conserve what little water they had left, and go back to the river the next morning for more.

JR was restless, his brain working on a different solution instead of allowing him to sleep when the moon rose, flooding his resting place with light. Despite the dilemma that they weren't sure they had a viable solution for yet, he was deeply content. The silvery light made it almost as light as day, and fell on the rock in a palette that was both monochromatic and variable enough to discern the different layers. A glint of light off something that was moving caught his eye.

"Robert."

A muffled oath responded.

"Robert, are you awake?"

"I am now," Robert said, sitting up and glaring at JR, whose attention was on the wall nearby. Robert followed his gaze. "Is that...?"

"I think maybe."

"I didn't see that before."

"Neither did I, till the moonlight hit it. How can we mark the spot? We'd kill ourselves trying to get there tonight."

"Agreed. Let's see if this little toy will do something about it."

Fumbling with the GPS, Robert found a mode he thought would work. He aimed it like a theodolite at the glimmer of light and pressed the record button. Then he set it carefully on a flat spot, aimed in the same direction. With any luck, he'd be able to duplicate the vertical and horizontal angles in the morning, and they'd be able to locate their water supply.

"Dude, you said the water would find its way through." JR's crow of delight rang off the nearby walls.

"Yeah. Let's just hope it doesn't all find its way through at the same time. Could I get some sleep now?" Robert asked.

"You don't really think...?" But Robert was already asleep. JR cast a suspicious look at the trickle of water. Surely that wouldn't flood even a fraction of the box canyon they found themselves in, would it?

It was still dark at the bottom of their box canyon when JR woke with a jerk. He'd fallen asleep with his eyes fixed on the trickle of water that would mean, he hoped, that they wouldn't have to backtrack for the precious fluid this morning. He rolled over to see if Robert was awake yet, then sought the spot where the water had been last night. No joy. With no light glinting on it, he couldn't see it. He didn't panic, though. Robert's combination GPS-surveying device had the coordinates, he thought.

Thinking about water made him thirsty, but he was cautious enough not to gulp the remaining water in his Camelbak. Just a sip would have to do until they knew whether they could take advantage of the artesian trickle above.

"You're up bloody early, mate," Robert said, from his sleeping spot a few feet away. He'd rolled from his back to a propped-up position and was watching JR scan the canyon wall. "Breakfast ready?"

JR grinned. "You bet. Bacon, waffles, scrambled eggs, whatever you want."

Robert snorted. "I think I prefer this dry energy bar, thanks."

JR shrugged and opened his own energy bar. "Your loss."

Getting an early start was a good thing, since they still had to either climb to the water or backtrack to the river. As soon as it was light enough to see what they were doing, Robert started climbing, but soon came to a sheer rock face. He set a piton, then dropped the filament through it to JR to belay, and continued his climb. He was close to eight-hundred feet above the canyon floor when he reached the seep.

Robert set his feet and leaned back in his harness. This was going to take a while. The trickle of water was just that. Now that he was close, he could see the desert varnish--the dark stain that flowing water creates on sandstone--indicating the seep was permanent. It flowed through a tiny flaw in the rock, nothing more than a crack, and spread out as it dropped until it was nothing more than a wet area of sandstone. Robert assumed it evaporated rapidly when the sun hit that portion of the canyon wall, which was why it never reached the bottom.

To fill the Camelbak was going to take some ingenuity. Fortunately, he had that. Praying that it wouldn't backfire, Robert set a piton at the bottom of the crack and watched to see if the water would flow along it. He heaved a sigh of relief when it did. Now to hold the bladder of the backpack where the drips that were forming on the end of the piton would fall into it. At the rate it was going, he estimated he'd be hanging here for at least an hour, to fill both packs. He blessed JR's foresight in emptying everything but the bladders from the packs. They were going to be heavy enough with just the water.

As he waited for the bladders to fill, Robert occupied his mind by speculating about the source of the water. There was no doubt it was above the highest level the river would reach, even in flood season. Naturally, Glen Canyon dam above them on the watercourse would regulate flooding this far south, but it wasn't an issue. This was ground water, thankfully filtered through nearly a mile of porous sedentary rock, so there'd be no need for their water filter to be sure of purity.

Robert was also curious about something else. This box canyon was an impossibility. Unless there were a turn up ahead that led out below the level of the floor where he and JR had slept last night, there was no way for natural processes to have carved it. The Grand Canyon was carved by the river, supplemented by wind. Even the slot canyon that led here could have been a leftover from an earlier time, long before the dam, when the water level of the river was perhaps higher. But, the canyon being 20 feet below, with no apparent outlet at the other end, that was impossible without geologic shift, and that didn't happen in such a small, localized area.

He was still thinking about it when he returned to the floor of the canyon, but he thought he had the answer.

"JR, we're close."

"What makes you say that?"

"This canyon. It can't be natural. Something the Eighth Cyclers did made it subside."

JR stared at him a moment. "You mean, we may not find anything?"

"Not necessarily. I can think of several reasons. But unless I miss my guess, this facility we're looking for is under our feet somewhere. We just need to find a way to get down to it."

Before they went any further, JR suggested they set up a grid, at least in theory, since they really had no way of marking one off physically. If they were looking for something underfoot, rather than an opening in the canyon wall, they needed to focus on a small area at a time and thoroughly explore it before moving to the next. It was time to survey the canyon, make sure there were no turns in the walls hidden by close perspective and shadows, like the slot canyon had been. But first, JR tried the satellite phone, hoping to let Daniel know that they were in the right area. Unfortunately, without a repeater at the top of the canyon rim, he'd have to have some luck hitting an Iridium satellite directly overhead. But, there was no luck today. The call wouldn't go through, with no satellite signal detected.

The two men set to work, using the small device that Robert carried. After a few hours, they had a digital two-dimensional map of the canyon, which proved to be only a quarter-mile wide on average, and less than half a mile long, in an irregular shape that in no way resembled a modern building's footprint. Though light reflected into the canyon, it was too deep and the walls too steep to admit sun at any time other than right at mid-day. From this, JR concluded that any light source they found in the facility would likely not be solar-powered, assuming the canyon hadn't subsided in the fifty-thousand years or so since the Eighth Cyclers built it. Robert had stated his assumption was they had deliberately sunk it to conceal it. It was a good a guess as JR was willing to make, so they were operating on that theory.

The question was, how did the inhabitants get here? Not to mention the supplies it would take to build what was described as a hardened facility. That surely implied it wasn't carved out of the living rock. Furthermore, the effort required to remove enough material from underneath to both build a facility and sink it to this level would have been staggering. JR and Robert discussed the various ways it might have been done as they began walking the virtual grid, beginning at the right of the drop from the slot canyon and up against the wall it dropped from.

"They could have built it above ground and then sunk it," JR said.

"I guess fifty-thousand years could have created this solid-looking canyon floor, but I wouldn't expect it to be this even. We should be able to discern the shape of the building, with the edges of the canyon floor several feet at least below the middle."

"Oh, I guess you're right. But maybe they dug just under the footprint of the building."

The mental picture was so ridiculous that even JR admitted it was far-fetched. Of course, the whole thing was far-fetched. However, after the revelations from the Tenth Cycle and the discovery of a tropical paradise enclosed in the caldera of a dormant volcano in Antarctica, far-fetched had become the new normal. The explorers had to agree that if there were a facility here, and it was in fact Eighth Cycle people who built it, they weren't likely to understand the technology.

JR stopped to wipe sweat from his forehead. "You know what?"

"No, what?"

"We'll figure it out when we find the damn thing, so let's just work."

Robert laughed. "You have no intellectual curiosity." He ducked as JR aimed a playful swipe at him from three yards away. "Hey, even your arms aren't that long."

The pair worked diligently until it was too dark again to see anything. Cursing the lack of foresight that left the nano lights Roy had reverse engineered from Paradise Valley at home, they once again went to sleep long before the moon crested the canyon rim to shine its light on the key to their puzzle.

Chapter Fourteen

WHERE DO WE FIT INTO ALL THIS?

Luke grew more concerned about what he was seeing in Salome's Spiderweb while he was minding the farm, so to speak. Once he started watching it every day, he decided it had been a mistake to let Salome leave without filling Daniel in. Never one to second-guess himself, he nevertheless approached Daniel with a lead-in, both to ease into it for Daniel's sake and to protect Salome from any backlash.

He chose a moment when he ran into Daniel in the canteen. "Hey, Daniel, I was going to come to your office after my break. Want to grab our coffee and have a little pow-wow?"

"Sure. What's it about?"

"Let's wait."

Ten minutes later, a patently curious Daniel seated in front of him, Luke took the bull by the horns. "Daniel, did you ever hear about an FBI project called The Prophet?"

"You mean, besides the ones in the Middle East who keep prophesying my downfall?"

Luke chuckled. "Yeah, besides those."

"No. What is it?"

Luke filled Daniel in, philosophizing that if Raj and his cronies already knew about it, the Top Secret status was moot. He got a kick out of describing Salome's role in its creation, when she was barely out of diapers, as he put it.

"Interesting, Luke, but what's on your mind? You weren't just coming to my office to tell me old news, were you?"

"No. What I need to tell you is what Salome has done with it, with Raj's help. She's been trying to get the FBI to update it for years, and with good reason. What her enhancements have revealed looks very much like a conspiracy by a handful of companies, maybe just a handful of individuals, to control every major industry you can think of."

"Wow, you mean, buy up shares in the biggest companies?"

"No, I mean buy up shares in *every* company. Total control, Daniel."

"What? You can't be serious. The FCC and FTC..."

"Are unaware of it. The shell corporations are so numerous and the relationships between them so vague that it isn't visible. Until Salome traced them, that is, on a hunch. Without that hunch, no one would think to look."

As Salome explained to him, Luke now explained to Daniel what was happening and how. Minute activities, many layers deep, by companies that were all but invisible in the markets, but resulting in rich and influential individuals seizing virtual control by banding together to control their shares as a block. The difficulty in tracking it, without the tools Salome had brought to bear, including the one only she and Raj had access to. "But Luke, I don't understand.

Why won't the FBI listen to her? Or the CIA, for that matter?"

"Who knows? Maybe they don't want to be embarrassed again, or maybe they're receiving orders to let it go. I did tell you that our current fearless leader is implicated, didn't I?"

Daniel shook his head at the disrespect he heard in Luke's tone for the incumbent president. Not that he didn't agree. The man was no Nigel Harper. But a criminal? Well, it had happened before.

Luke went on. "She says she's given up, and I agree she should. It's hard to know who to trust anymore. But, her trip isn't what it seems. She's planning for disaster."

"So, where do we fit into all this? Assuming it's true." Seeing Luke about to protest, Daniel hurried on. "I have no doubt it's true, I'm just stunned at the speed of the developments. How long has this been going on?"

"It's hard to say how long. But I can answer your other question. The history of this Foundation shows that any time there's a powerful group of bad guys out there, they are watching you closely. I'd say the Foundation is a prime target, especially now there's evidence of another huge find."

"Won't they already have an idea, from Salome's searches, that we are trying to find them?"

"It's possible. But I understand she used a variety of hacker techniques to mask where the searches were coming from, as well as using some obscure search engines she didn't think had been compromised yet. The big three or four she's been avoiding for months."

"Why didn't she bring me her concerns herself?"

"It was all pretty circumstantial. I didn't believe her

myself, until she showed me something that almost caused me to strangle her."

Daniel's eyebrows went up in astonishment. That hadn't sounded like a joke.

"She had about thirty seconds to explain, Daniel, and she took a huge risk, but nothing less would have convinced me. This is bigger than just telecom companies. She had a dossier on me that had things even I didn't know. It also included my bank accounts, investment accounts, passwords, the contents of my will..."

"You're not serious!"

"I am. There simply wasn't anything but circumstantial hints here and there. How she ever got onto it is a mystery to me. But it did convince me. There are forces moving behind the scenes to completely dominate finances, communications, industry, hell, even world opinion. I've never seen anything this big before."

Coming from a retired CIA analyst, that was a shocking statement. The next one was even more so.

"Salome believes the Foundation needs to prepare a place to go to ground. Somewhere that a core group of people can literally hide from what's coming. That's what she and Roy are doing; finding the place."

Daniel was, as his brother would have said, gob smacked.

"My own employees don't trust me?"

Luke's voice was a little gentler when he answered. "That's not it, Daniel, they respect and admire you, especially Salome and Roy. So much so that she won't put any half-baked idea in front of you. You need to know she has your best interests at heart. And you need to be ready to listen to what she has to say when she gets home."

Daniel dropped his head a bit as he nodded. "You know,

I was just thinking about something along these lines, the other day when you dropped in. I'll listen. Thanks for paving the way, Luke."

"Any time, Daniel. Ryan and I thought you must be something special from the time Sarah brought you home like a prize. You've become more than that to me, though. A good friend, as well as my nephew-in-law. I'd do anything to protect what you've built here, even stand up to Sally."

Daniel smiled. "That's a huge compliment, Luke, and I feel the same way. Let's just hope no one takes over the world between now and the time Salome gets back. But, if they do, we can always sic Sally on them."

Chapter Fifteen

DO YOU KNOW HOW TO PITCH THE TENT?

Roy and Salome had decided against camping on Sunday night after all. In the first place, it had gotten too dark to see a good spot, not that they'd know what a good spot looked like, Salome reflected. In the second, both were a little daunted by their new equipment. She'd asked Roy if he had ever been camping before.

"As a kid, sure," he answered.

"Well, do you know how to pitch the tent, and set up the stove and everything?" she asked.

"No, not really, but how difficult could it be? Do you? "

"Me?" she'd asked. "Not a chance! I'm a city girl, remember?" In fact, she'd grown up in a loft in Manhattan, the daughter of a fashion designer and an English professor who were rather surprised to find Madame Professor pregnant again at the age of forty-five. Neither had ever expected to have more children after their son, the brilliant but pathologically shy brother Salome had used as a model to get inside Roy's defenses.

Fortunately, Salome had been a brilliant child herself and her parents were as proud of her accomplishments as they were of her brother's, before their deaths in a small-aircraft crash on the way to a fashion show in Chicago. From her father, she'd inherited an impeccable taste in fashion, and from her mother a precision in speech that often made people think she was a stick-in-the-mud, until they discovered her sense of humor and her passion for life. Neither had ever taken her camping.

Faced with fumbling in the dark to get their camp set up, they decided instead to go on and drive to Billings, spend the night in a hotel, and get an early start in the morning.

By afternoon on Monday, Salome was grateful for the early start. The Gallatin National Forest was going to be it, she'd known it since they entered the wooded hills.

"Look, Roy. The mountains here are higher and more massive than in the Bighorn. This is our place, I just know it."

In addition, the woods were denser, and there were tiny dirt roads leading off in a maze that would be hard for anyone looking for something like a hidden compound to navigate.

In fact, she and Roy had been wandering on them for hours. "It's lucky we ended up with this SUV," he remarked. Some of the roads were little more than tracks made by a few off-road enthusiasts looking for a picnic or camping spot, apparently, for they led nowhere. After back-tracking on several of these, Salome knew what she was looking for. Around mid-afternoon, she spotted it, a faint track with a log-and-chain barrier across it. Hanging on the chain was a sign that said 'Road Closed'.

"Roy, take that one," she said.

"But honey, it's closed."

"Just drive around, love. There's no fence. It's just to discourage traffic."

Muttering that he was indeed discouraged, Roy drove off the road, dodging a large boulder, and went around the sign. "Now what?"

"Just follow it to the end."

To call it a dirt road would have been elevating it to an honor it had never deserved. The track was rough, barely visible in spots, and long. To Salome's delight, it all but disappeared as it led around an outcropping of granite and into a narrow corridor through densely-spaced trees, finally opening out into an area that had little underbrush. It was as if the tree canopy above had deprived any lower-growing plants of the sun they needed to thrive. A carpet of evergreen needles, with pine-cones scattered here and there, blanketed the bare soil.

"This is perfect," Salome cried. She clapped her hands in delight, like a child. Roy got out of the SUV and stretched, cramped from long hours behind the wheel. She went to him and hugged him, her arms around his waist. "Isn't it beautiful, love?"

He looked around, and his eyes took on a soft look. "Almost as beautiful as you."

Salome giggled, a trait that she usually suppressed when working. "Flattery will get you anything you want," she said.

Roy grinned his boyish grin.

It would be full dark early, under these trees. And it was far too late to make their way out of this secluded glen and to a hotel. Camping it was, and she needed the light to figure out the stove and other gear they'd brought. She bent down and picked up a handful of the pine needles. Surprisingly, there was bare dirt only a few inches down. The needles were dry and brittle, so they'd have to clear a wide spot if they were going to have a campfire, which she wanted for the light and warmth even though they had a Coleman kerosene stove to cook on.

"Roy, love, could you clear a spot about ten feet in diameter, so we can have a campfire?"

Roy looked around. "Babe, ten feet isn't enough. A spark would send this whole area up in a blaze. Can you do without a fire tonight?"

How disappointing. A campfire would have been romantic. But, Roy was usually right about anything he stated like that. "Yes, I guess so. Want to help me set up the tent?"

He came to join her at the back of the SUV, looking in dismay at the jumble of gear they'd shoved in, hurrying to get on the road on Saturday. "Where is it?"

"It's in there somewhere. A big canvas bag, remember?"

"Oh, yeah. Damn, I'm going to have to unload the whole kit and caboodle. Why don't you try to organize it somehow, as it comes out?"

"Sounds like a plan."

As Roy brought out item after item of food, a Port-a-Potty, the kerosene stove, cooking utensils, sleeping bags, a deflated air mattress and more, Salome dutifully put them in separate areas according to their function. The tent was the last thing to come out.

"That wasn't very good planning, was it?" Roy asked, his face red from the effort of reaching into the vehicle and dragging stuff out.

"I don't know how else would have been better. We need all this stuff, right?"

"I think so. I guess we'll see."

Roy picked up the heavy bag with the tent in it and walked a few yards away. He dumped the contents on the ground and began fumbling with short metal tubes.

"Wait, love, shouldn't you read the directions?" Roy could build a nuclear weapon in a kitchen with a Swiss army knife, though. Surely he must be able to pitch a tent and get a gas stove working.

He looked at her incredulously. "I'm an engineer, remember?"

Salome considered it the better part of valor to let him do it, noting where he laid the pamphlet with directions, for when he gave up. Meanwhile, she set the stove on a short folding table and took out the directions for lighting it. 'Hmm, pump this thing, oh, wait, I need to connect the kerosene bottle. Where is it? Oh, here, inside the stove. Screw the connector on here. Okay, now pump it ten times and press the red switch. Where's the red switch? Well, that's a stupid place for it.'

Salome sat up, swept her hair into a knot that wouldn't last long without a barrette, and tried again, now that her hair wouldn't catch fire along with the cook ring. She pumped again, then reached around the other side of the stove for the igniter. A flame leapt up, almost singeing her nose, and Salome shrieked, jumping back and falling over as the stool she was sitting on lost its balance.

Roy was at her side immediately. "What the heck?" he asked, looking down at her.

"Help me up," she said, her dignity ruffled. "The stove exploded at me."

The Skywalkers

Roy helped her get to her feet and looked at the stove. "It doesn't look like it exploded."

"Well, it tried to burn me." Roy shook his head.

"Hey, it's going to take both of us to put this tent up. Could you help me?"

Muttering unladylike curse words at the stove, Salome started to go with him, then hesitated. "Wait, let me get some water on to boil. I'm not lighting that thing again tonight."

When she'd put on a pot of water, Salome went over to where Roy had laid out the tent. He'd staked the corners down in a neat square, and the rest of the tent lay crumpled in the middle, waiting for the poles to slide through the loops that would erect a cozy little canvas room for them to sleep in.

"Tell me again why we didn't get one of those nylon things that you just throw in the air and it comes down as a tent," she said.

"Because they aren't very roomy," he explained, for the third or fourth time. "We wouldn't have been able to get the air mattress in it. You said you didn't want to sleep on the bare ground."

"Oh, yeah," she said. She hadn't counted on a four-inch bed of pine needles. "Okay, let's do this. What first?"

Roy held up a more-or-less U-shaped assembly of metal tubes, a straight center tube connected to two end tubes with a bend at the connecting end. "This one goes across the top, through the loops, to hold up the roof," he said. "Then there are some for each of the corners. This one has to go in first."

Salome looked at the assembly of tubes, and at the straight seam at the top of the tent. "Shouldn't we put the middle part in through the loops and then connect the sides?" Without saying it, she was thinking that for an engineer, he hadn't quite grasped the concept. Any woman who'd ever hung curtains on a rod knew you couldn't turn a corner while trying to thread something onto a straight rod. Maybe it was just too simple for his mind.

"Oh, uh, I guess you're right." Roy disconnected one side tube from the straight top part and had Salome hold up the last loop on one side, while he threaded the tube through the first and middle loops. Holding the middle of the straight tube, he skirted around the tent floor and swapped places with her, attaching the second side while she held up the middle. He stepped back. "There, that wasn't so hard, was it? You can let go now."

As soon as she let go, the whole thing collapsed, knocking one of the side tubes out of its socket.

"Huh." Roy scratched his head. This wasn't as easy as it looked.

After a few more attempts, they managed to get the top stabilized while they worked on the corners, and then Roy's first mistake came back to haunt them. With the floor staked down, it was impossible to properly stretch the top corners of the square tent. But, as soon as he pulled the stakes, the center pole at the top collapsed again. Salome was ready to tell him to forget it, they'd blow up the mattress and sleep in the back of the SUV, when they finally, by trial and error, got the tent up. She resisted kicking one of the poles in the certain knowledge that if she did, the whole thing would collapse again. She could only hope that it didn't do so in the middle of the night while they were sound asleep.

When she returned to the stove, the water had all but boiled away. Luckily, there was an inch of water left, so the pan wasn't ruined. At this point, Salome was wondering what anyone saw in camping. What she wouldn't give for a nice hotel room, with someone else to cook dinner for them, and a soft bed to look forward to.

A few hours later, with bellies full of a surprisingly delicious can of stew and 'campfire biscuits', tinned biscuits steam-cooked on top of the simmering stew, the couple lay on top of their zipped-together sleeping bags, completely exhausted. The effort of setting up camp had tired them, as had the long day. But despite that it turned out you *could* make love in a tent. Roy would later tell her one of the most romantic things he'd ever said; that he was glad it worked because if it was not possible he would rather die in the doomsday calamity than be with her and not be able to do it.

Zipped snugly into her sleeping bag, her husband sprawled over both his side and part of hers, Salome woke with a feeling of fear. What was that noise? She lay quietly, holding her breath to hear the faint sounds coming from outside the tent. Roy's breathing was loud enough to obscure it, but Salome was certain there was someone, or something, outside the tent. Would the intruder, whatever it was, hear if she woke Roy? He'd probably make a startled sound. Would that make a bear attack them through the canvas that now seemed far too flimsy? What if it was one of the dozens of serial killers the FBI thought roamed rural areas, killing at random when a ready victim appeared?

An explosion of sound startled her into a muffled

scream, which woke Roy. Instead of making a noise as she'd expected, he rolled to her side and gathered her in. Whispering in her ear, he asked what was wrong.

"I heard a noise," she whispered.

"What did it sound like?" he asked, still whispering.

"Didn't you hear it? It was so loud."

"No, I didn't hear it. Just your scream. What did it sound like?" he repeated.

"I don't know, I can't describe it. Roy, what's out there?"

"Don't know, babe, but if it isn't in here with us, it's probably harmless. Go back to sleep."

Go back to sleep? Was he kidding? Evidently not, as he was already breathing steadily again, though he still had her wrapped in his arms. She wasn't going to sleep another wink that night. Someone needed to be alert, so when the attack came, they could fight back. She was as good a fighter as Roy. He had his gender and size to rely on; she had hand-to-hand combat from her time in the FBI. She could protect them.

When she woke again. Salome realized with a start that she'd fallen asleep after all. She knew immediately that whatever was outside the tent was still there, and probably wasn't human. At least, she assumed a human would have attacked them, if he was going to. It was probably a bear, which maybe didn't know what to make of the tent with its tasty human snack inside. As soon as they set foot outside, it would charge. And there was no question that she had to set foot outside. It was that or pee in the tent.

Carefully, she unzipped the sleeping bag enough to slip out. Thankful for her flannel PJs in the cool mountain morning air, she scooted around until her head was at the foot of the mattress and unzipped a few inches from the bottom of the tent. Cautiously, she craned her neck to peek out the tiny opening. What she saw startled a laugh out of her, waking poor Roy again.

"Hey, babe, what's going on?"

"You'll never guess what's out there," she said, speaking in a normal tone.

"Bigfoot?" he quipped.

"Nope. A whole herd of deer, love. Come look, they're so pretty."

Roy sat up. "That's what you were so scared of last night?" Salome scrambled to a sitting position, cross-legged beside him. She punched him lightly on the arm.

"Ow."

"Listen, Captain America. Next time I'm that scared, I expect you to defend me."

"Hey, I never claimed to be a hero. You're the former FBI agent, the chick with the gun. You should defend me."

"Well, I did, until I fell asleep. We're just lucky that's not a herd of bears out there."

"Babe, I don't think bears come in herds."

"You know what I mean. Now, help me scare these deer away so I can go potty."

"Aw, I was gonna take some pictures."

"Make it quick."

A few minutes later, she found Roy at the kerosene stove, trying to figure out how to light it so they could have some breakfast.

"Helps to read the directions, my genius," she said. Roy shrugged, pressed the red button and the stove lit in a civilized fashion, without attempting to set his hair on fire. From now on, she'd let him light it.

After breakfast, sitting on a folding chair with a cup of fragrant coffee in her hands, Salome had to admit that she could see the appeal of camping this morning. The air was delicious, crisp and fragrant with the smell of pine. Through the trunks of the trees, she could see a nearby tumble of granite boulders with the sun sparkling on the flecks of white in them. They looked like tiny diamonds. Waking up in a city, even one as small as Boulder, had never been like this. It occurred to her that she could be happy here especially now that they were such experienced campers.

"Roy it's nice to sit here and enjoy the quiet and beauty but we need to go cave hunting."

"Well there are some caves around here? Problem is they're all known. You want one that no one's mentioned online before, right?"

"That would be best, yes."

"Well, I can't guarantee that they don't link up somewhere deep underground, but there should be some in the hills around here. Limestone is a good medium for forming caves."

"I thought that was granite," she objected.

"Some of it is, but there are limestone outcroppings in these mountains, too. We just have to find them. Are you up for a hike?"

They set out soon after, Roy carrying what looked like a fishing vest with its pockets filled with odds and ends she didn't recognize. He'd brought backpacks for both of them that carried a couple of liters of water with a tube attached for drinking it. Those he loaded up with snack bars, fruit and small packages of mixed nuts. Then he tucked a small roll of tissue-thin paper in hers.

"What's that?" she asked.

"Biodegradable."

"Oh."

The hike was more strenuous than either of them were conditioned for, but Salome loved it, even when they returned to camp late that afternoon, dirty and bone-tired again. Roy had a surprise for her.

"Babe, did you know this whole region has hot springs?"

"No, how would I know that?"

"I don't know, it was just an expression. Anyway, it does, and there are several near here, I think."

"Really? What makes you think so?"

Roy pulled out a rolled-up printout of the satellite image that matched their location. "See this area, where it looks like white clouds, or maybe fog? I think that's steam from a bunch of them. If you're up for another quarter-mile or so, we can go take a look. With any luck, one will be the right temperature for a bath."

"Wow, that would be great! Wait, I didn't pack my suit."

"Who's gonna see? We'll skinny dip."

"You'd better hope there's no one around, buster."

"There's no one around, I promise."

Chapter Sixteen

IS THAT AN OPENING?

On Tuesday morning, Robert once again made the arduous climb to replenish their water supply, this time carrying JR's climbing filament, having left his own attached to the cliffside. He'd had an idea to rig a hammock of sorts to rest in as the water filled their Camelbaks. That task done, with JR of necessity standing by in case Robert had an emergency and therefore unable to continue the search, they once again began their painstaking examination of every square inch of the canyon floor.

"It's always in the last place you look," JR complained, as they passed the halfway mark.

"Of course it is," Robert said. "Why would you continue looking if you've already found it?"

This bit of practicality was too much for JR, who hadn't yet gotten back at Robert for an earlier joke. Besides, he needed to stand up straight. This creeping along, bent over to look at the ground, was not the ideal occupation for a man of his size. As he stood and leaned back to stretch his spine, his eye fell on something he couldn't quite make out, maybe just a bit of rock sticking out from the wall to make a darker shadow, on the opposite wall behind and above Robert's stooped form. Looking around to the entrance of the slot canyon, now behind them by quite a distance, he observed that whatever this was, it was at about the same level, maybe twenty feet above the canyon wall.

"Is that an opening?" he asked.

Robert looked up at him. "Sure it is," he said, as if he thought JR was having him on. Nevertheless, the curious tilt of JR's head held his attention, and he, too stood up straight and then turned to take a look.

"Not sure. We'd better check it out."

The pair hastened toward the opposite wall. When he'd gone far enough to get the slanted sunlight out of his eyes and see the wall more clearly, he whooped.

"It is! Robert, it's an opening, and damned if it doesn't look man-made!"

Robert's reply came in clumps as he ran. "Sure it's...not just...spalling?"

JR had no idea what spalling was, but he was staring at an arch-shaped opening in the wall that led deep into the side. Deep enough that he couldn't see the back wall. Robert arrived at his side at that moment.

"Crikey! That's definitely not spalling. You found it!"

Both men stared admiringly at the opening, inaccessible from their vantage point without going back to retrieve at least one of the climbing filaments. After a few moments, they reluctantly made their way back to their spare bivouac, where once again Robert made the climb to the water, this time to retrieve his cleverly-rigged hammock. While he was there, he topped off the water bladders, to avoid having to take the time for the climb first thing in the morning.

When Robert returned to the canyon floor, he remarked, "That climb's getting old, mate."

"I could do it. You want me to take a turn next time?" JR asked.

"Nope. I'm the better climber, and if you got in trouble, I'd be hard-pressed to help you out, you big lug. I'll do it. Unless our friends in the fancy building down there have running water. That would be ideal."

"It wouldn't surprise me. What would is if it's still working," JR answered.

"Same here, mate, same here. Are we going to tackle this today? We've got maybe an hour of usable light left. We could climb up, take a look around."

"Sure, why not? Nothing's on TV tonight anyway."

The end of that hour found the two standing in the archway, staring in awe-struck wonder at a pair of steel doors that were miraculously free of rust. Robert had arrived first, followed closely by JR, who was the less-experienced climber despite being the nominal expedition leader. The doors looked for all the world like a modern-day elevator.

"Is that what I think it is?" JR asked.

Robert had been examining it, wondering the same thing. "What do you think it is?"

"Is it...an elevator?" JR's tone conveyed incredulous delight.

Robert shrugged. "No call buttons." His laconic answer deflated JR. Chances were it wasn't an elevator anyway. What were the odds that two different civilizations, arising more than fifty-thousand years apart, would design a device with the same function in the same way? And what were the odds it would still be working after so long, if it was indeed an elevator?

The Skywalkers

The other possibility was that what they'd found wasn't the Eighth Cycle site they were looking for. What it might be otherwise gave JR pause. The real question was how to get the doors to open to find out. And the next one was what they'd do in any case. Trespass on a secret government installation? Trust their lives to a 50,000 year-old elevator? Neither seemed like the best option.

JR took matters into his own hands, pressing inward near the seam where the doors met in the middle. He'd have been flabbergasted if they opened, but of course they didn't. It couldn't be that easy, could it? Robert was feeling the wall on the left side of the doors, which were set into what looked like solid rock. His fingers found every protrusion and pushed, as well as poking into any depressions. JR took the hint and started doing the same thing on the right.

They didn't have long to complete their exploration. If night fell with them still in the alcove, they'd have to spend it there rather than descending to the canyon floor. And they'd have to spend it in a rather intimate space, as there'd barely be enough room sideways for them to stretch out, and the alcove wasn't all that deep, either.

Robert let his frustration lead him to a silly gesture. "There's one more thing we haven't tried."

"What's that?"

"The Ali Baba technique."

He placed his hands on either side of the seam, pressed in and spread his hands apart, as if showing the door what to do would affect the inanimate object, intoning "Open Sesame". To his surprise, they began to move under their own power, even after he sprang away in shock. "Holy dooley!

JR had tensed when the doors started moving as well, and was staring into the dark passage beyond. When the center of each door reached its own half-way point to the wall into which it was sliding, the passage was flooded with white light. JR's passing thought was to wonder if he looked as gob-smacked as Robert did. "Holy, shit, what now?"

Robert said, "I've been thinking about that. Like you said last night, it could be a government secret."

"In which case, we're about to be shot," JR deadpanned.

"Or, it could be an impossibly old installation…"

"With a faulty elevator," JR supplied. "In which case, we're about to be famous. Or dead. Or dead and famous."

"Only one way to find out," Robert said. And then, he dove in through the opening.

"No!" JR shouted, no doubt from watching too many Indiana Jones movies. He half expected the doors to slam shut, trapping Robert inside, or a deadfall trap, or a bunch of arrows flying out of the walls. However, nothing at all happened except the doors sliding home into the walls and remaining wide open. Robert was already at the back of the passageway, using the same gesture to open another pair of doors.

"Come on!"

JR needed no further invitation. His shaky legs carried him into the chamber where Robert was waiting, his hand hovering over a button inside. As soon as JR was in, Robert pressed the button, giving no thought at all to the notion that if this were truly an Eighth Cycle construct, the ancient machinery might not be in good repair. The doors slid closed.

Chapter Seventeen

I AM SURPRISED TO SEE YOU HERE

JR fought to reclaim his breath as the floor seemed to drop out from under them. Robert had uttered a startled string of incomprehensible Aussie curses and was now plastered to the back wall of the-whatever this was, his face white. They must have been going awfully fast, because JR could swear he was about to achieve a state of weightlessness. During this time, he could swear he could see the events of his life flashing before his eyes. *I'm dying. Rebecca, I'm sorry my love.*

After what seemed like an eternity, he could again feel the effects of gravity, and realized he was slowing. With a feeling of his entire weight settling after he came to a halt, he rebounded slightly. How peculiar. He could see the white light everyone described. He must have fallen to his death, but why wasn't there any pain? And when would St. Peter be here to guide him? Then he noticed Robert, still plastered at the side of the room, with a wide-eyed expression on his face.

"Oh, hi, Robert. I'm surprised you're here."

Robert turned a confused and still wide-eyed expression

on him, his cheeks still white as death. "Why the bloody hell would you be surprised? We were both in that Devil's contraption together. Where'd you expect me to go?"

JR, shocked at Robert's language before the Pearly Gates, shushed him. "I just thought you were an atheist. Sorry."

Robert replied with another string of curses, making JR wince. He said, "Listen, would you stop that? I don't know why you're here, but I want them to let *me* in. So don't be taking the Lord's name in vain while I'm standing right next to you."

"JR, what the hell is wrong with you? You want who to let you in?"

"St. Peter. I guess I should have said 'him'. I want him to let me in."

Robert's face changed. Where before he'd looked ready to punch some sense into JR, now he was howling with laughter. "You…you, hahahaha, you think we're dead? That's rich! We're not dead you dolt."

JR took stock. They'd stopped, and according to Robert, they were alive. He guessed that counted for something. "Robert, swear you will never tell anyone what happened just now."

"Oh, no, this is too good. I'll dine out on this one for a month."

"No you won't, because the first time I hear you've told it, I'll kill you." JR's tone was so matter-of-fact that he was certain Robert would understand he was serious. Since they were here, wherever here was, it was time to explore.

The doors they'd had such difficulty opening a few moments ago automatically slid back at that moment. JR hesitated. If they left the machine, would they be able to get back in? What if they became trapped down here, however far down they were? What if there were no other exit, no food, no water...no air? Robert, whose color was still slowly returning to normal, appeared to have no such misgivings. The minute the doors were fully open, he plunged out of their little cage as if being chased by demons.

For that matter, JR wasn't certain they hadn't descended to hell. They'd certainly been riding that express elevator long enough. As the doors started to slide shut again, he dashed out in Robert's wake. Wherever they were, he wasn't yet ready to be shot back to the surface like a rocket. Or to be trapped in the small room while Robert did all the exploring.

The room they found themselves in was featureless, except for another set of doors that looked exactly the same as the ones they'd just exited. In fact, if JR hadn't been sure he was facing away from the elevator that brought them here, he might have assumed they were the same doors. The walls were made of a smooth material that had a low sheen, like the old-fashioned brushed nickel fixtures in his parents' house in North Carolina. Metal, he assumed. Not a dimple or protrusion in sight. He and Robert looked at each other in an unspoken question. Should they open those other doors, assuming they opened in the same way?

With a shrug, Robert stepped forward. In for a penny, in for a pound, JR thought, echoing something he'd often heard his grandfather Nicholas say. He watched as Robert pressed his hands against the door and swung them to the side, triggering the powered slide of the doors. Beyond, it was dark. JR was a brave man, but a deep dread came over him as he looked into utter blackness. It was worse than just not knowing. Stepping into that inky void could mean a drop of unknown depth, or anything, really. It was literally impossible to see anything beyond the door. Even the soft light in the room in which they stood, which he only at that moment realized was coming from the walls in a glow with no discernible origin, couldn't pierce the gloom.

Robert's voice, after such a long silence, startled JR so much that he actually jumped.

"What d'you reckon is in there, mate?"

"No clue. Toss for who goes in first?"

"Nah," said Robert, as he stepped through the opening.

Nothing could have prepared JR for what happened. In a split second, bright white light exploded into existence, revealing a vast area with row after row of what looked like desks and chairs. Startled by the sudden light, JR looked for the source. Like the walls in the anteroom, these were glowing, along with the ceiling. But there didn't seem to be any fixtures or single point of light. It just emanated from the walls.

The room could have been any corporate cubicle farm in America in the Eleventh Cycle. To be sure, the chairs were shaped a bit differently, but they were clearly proportioned for humans, at least humans like Robert. All were too short for JR's comfort, at least as far as he could see. Then he realized what looked so wrong. The chairs were suspended in mid-air, with no visible means of support. Ever the reckless one, Robert sat down in one, then screamed like a woman as it yanked him six feet into the air, then gently lowered him to exactly the right height for his legs to touch the floor without strain.

When he picked himself off the floor from laughing at Robert, JR tried one. He expected the jerk, but it still disconcerted him until it lowered him as well, again at exactly the right height for his feet to rest comfortably on the floor. At the same time, the chair molded itself perfectly to his spine. "Hey, I need one of these back at the office. What do you suppose holds them up?"

Robert shrugged, now a couple of feet lower than JR because he'd stretched his legs out straight. "No clue. Magnets maybe?"

The desks were more like tables, with no walls under the desktop, and no legs, either. They floated at a height to match the chair that was paired with them, no matter what position the chair assumed. There wasn't a speck of dust or an object of any kind on any of them. Had they stumbled on some secret government installation? Maybe something from the cold war, in the previous century? But if so, why no dust? In fact, the air smelled fresh, not like JR would have expected after fifty-thousand years of being shut in a room with no windows.

Robert was counting a row. "Twenty to a row in each section. Five sections, that's one hundred. Times one, two, three..."

"Call it four thousand. Four thousand or more people in this room, doing what?"

Echoing JR's earlier idea, Robert said, "Could your government have built this for some reason? Are we going to be shot for spies, as soon as someone realizes we're here?"

"Nope. First they'll torture us for information. Don't worry about it." In truth, JR couldn't believe it was a government installation. There was too much here that hinted of superior technology. It had to be Eighth Cycle, but his brain wouldn't process it all at once.

Robert gave a nervous chuckle. "Let's see if there's more."

JR stood easily, but Robert had more of a struggle from his half-reclined position to get out of the chair. Once upright, the two men started forward down one of the wide aisles that separated section from section. JR felt slightly ridiculous in his dirty outdoor clothes, carrying gear for rough minimalist camping, when they'd clearly found something like an office building. The emptiness oppressed him, though. As modern and utilitarian as it appeared to be, the building gave him the creeps.

There were two possible explanations. Either this was a government facility from the Eleventh Cycle, his own, which he'd already dismissed. Or, it really was an Eighth Cycle construct, which meant the Eighth Cycle had achieved a greater level of civilization, or at least a more technologically advanced one, than the Eleventh.

In which case, the Eleventh was clearly on the wrong path--because this one was gone. The cataclysm that ended each cycle after 26,000 years if the people hadn't ended war hadn't been avoided, though it must have been a nonviolent event, since this place was intact. If this building was from the Eighth Cycle, then his sister-in-law Sarah was right, they were headed inexorably for doomsday.

Robert was out of his element in this place, and he suspected JR was, too. There was no need for a geologist in the man-made space. A metallurgist, maybe, to explain why the walls and ceiling glowed with white light that bathed everything in equal measure. There weren't even any shadows in here. Other experts, too, like engineers, architects, physicists to explain those crazy chairs, and some he couldn't even imagine. All he could do now was follow JR's lead and hope to be useful in some way.

The trouble was, JR seemed kind of clueless, too. After all, he was probably more at home at a dig where the civilization he was studying was barely out of the Stone Age. But, no matter what, they had to figure out what this was. Otherwise, they'd have to keep looking, and they hadn't really come prepared for much more than a five-day outing. That was if they could stretch their food that far. Can't carry much food, even dried stuff, in one backpack. The way Robert saw it, their first objective was to find some water down here. If they couldn't do that, they'd have to get back in that freaky elevator and go back where they came from. He shuddered. Didn't fancy riding back down again, either. That drop scared the shit out of him, and he'd never forget the effect it had had on JR.

They'd come to the back of the room, a distance of some three hundred feet, maybe. The room looked to be square... Crikey! He'd forgotten the instrument in his backpack.

"JR, I've been an idiot." He pulled out the instrument, showing it to JR. "This'll measure this room, and draw a three-dimensional map of it."

"Dude, it's just a big square, with, I'm gonna say a twenty-foot ceiling."

"I know, mate, but d'you realize how vast that is?" He did some quick mental arithmetic. "This room is around 90,000 square feet, under how many thousands of tons of rock, and there's not a support column in sight." He aimed the instrument at the opposite wall and set some dials, then pressed a button. As the camera lens moved around automatically, measuring all the distances and angles, he continued. "That tells us right there that this isn't construction from our cycle. I don't know of any engineering technology that could pull it off.

"I'm no expert in that, but you're probably right. So, we

need to find a way out of here and into somewhere that will give us a freaking clue what this is."

"All right, but give me a moment to get this measurement down. Then we'll go."

When the instrument was finished with its measurements, Robert brought the record up on the small screen. It showed a structure much as they had observed it, three-hundred and thirty-three feet long by the same width. The ceiling was higher than they'd thought, an optical illusion based on the sheer size of the room. It was thirty-three feet high.

"Someone liked the number three," Robert remarked.

There were two flaws in the perfect square, though. In the center of each of what Robert was thinking of as the side walls, a three-foot wide notch suggested a door. Either of them could lead to discovery of more of the building, and what was becoming increasingly urgent: water. Robert's preference was to stick together in this place, but there was no question that the more efficient idea would be for each of them to take one of the doors, and then meet back in the middle to compare what they'd found.

"We need to split up," he said, pointing at what he was only assuming were doors.

JR hated to split up, since he still had a tingle between his shoulder blades that was an awful lot like the one he always got just before a round whined past him in Afghanistan.

But, Robert was right. They'd find whatever there was to find more quickly if each of them took one of the doors.

"Is your watch working?" he asked.

Robert glanced at his wrist. "Yeah, I think so. It's been about half an hour since we got into the elevator."

Half an hour? Why did it seem like half the day? JR assumed the strangeness was messing with his sense of time. He checked his own watch. "Okay, it's twelve-fifteen. We meet back here, no, at the doors where we came in, in an hour." He pointed past Robert in the direction opposite. "I'll head out this way."

"What if one of us isn't back?" Robert asked.

"Then the other go to the door on the side wall and wait, let's say another hour. Then head back to the canyon, and trek out as soon as it's light in the morning. Someone needs to report back."

"In that case, leave the sat-phone at the door."

"Good idea."

JR felt a bit ridiculous, assuming deadly danger in such an innocuous-looking building. It was the emptiness that freaked him out. Where had they all gone, the four thousand or so people who'd presumably worked in this room? What had they been doing in here? In modern buildings there would have been a computer on each desk in front of each seat, but here was nothing.

He had the idea there should be some sort of formal leave-taking, just in case one of them didn't make it back. Turning toward Robert, he thrust out his hand. "Good luck, mate," he said.

Robert, using JR's slang in kind, shook JR's hand as he said, "Right back atcha, dude." The word sounded funny in his accent, as if there were more vowels in it. They grinned at each other, then turned and walked in opposite directions.

JR turned to peer across the enormous room at Robert, he had quite a way to go before reaching his. His friend looked small at that distance, about the length of a football field, from behind the goalpost to behind the other. He couldn't tell whether Robert was looking across at him or would see him, but he waved anyway. Not getting a responding wave, he took a breath and swiped the door open. Was it a good omen that he guessed the right direction the first time? Because this wasn't a double door like the others. *Never mind*, he muttered. *Quit procrastinating and get your butt in there.* The dark void in front of him would light up when he crossed the threshold, wouldn't it?

JR let out the breath he hadn't known he was holding when the light did indeed come on as he crossed into the next room. Except that it wasn't a room, more like a hallway, with doors at regular intervals on both sides as far down the hall as he could see. Once again, it seemed as if he'd never find anything useful. There was no choice but to start opening doors, since the hallway ran straight into the distance with no end that he could see.

With a mental shrug, he swiped at the first door, but it didn't open. Maybe he'd swiped the wrong way, though he could swear it was the same way he'd just opened the other door. He tried the opposite direction. Nothing. Pushing, swiping down and up, and an ill-tempered kick at the bottom did nothing to open the door, either. By now he was fully convinced there was no way this was a modern facility, though in some ways it was more modern than the city he'd left behind. He couldn't wrap his mind around it. As mind-boggling as finding a government facility hidden in the depths below the Grand Canyon, it was even more so to find a fifty-thousand year-old facility that was more modern than anything he'd ever seen before.

Frustrated, he gave up on that one and turned to the opposite side of the hall, where the next door in the staggered configuration waited. When that one also failed to open, he hurried along, trying each door in succession until he was out of time. He'd need to turn around and head back to meet Robert in time to keep him from making a fruitless trip to this side. He gave the door he was standing at one last kick, and to his surprise, it flew backward into the room, like a normal door instead of the slider he'd expected.

By now he was used to facing a black void whenever a door opened, but this time the light was already on. Must be a function of the door itself triggering what he'd decided were motion detectors that turned on the lights. As he stepped in, it was immediately apparent that this was a sleeping room. The whole hall must be a dormitory, and the other doors had been locked, though he hadn't seen any sort of mechanism that would require a lock. JR set aside that mystery for a moment, because for the first time since they'd dropped down the rabbit hole, the room he was in looked as if it had been inhabited.

A bed was pushed against the wall opposite the door, and there was even bedding on it. It looked similar to any bed he'd ever seen; a headboard, fabrics that he took to be sheets spread on it, even a pillow. It was narrow, meant for a single sleeper unless he missed his guest. The beds were like the chairs - no legs - hanging in the air. But no money on earth and not even Rebecca, not even Rebecca naked, would get JR in that moment to test one of those beds like Robert had done with the chairs. For all he knew, it would zoom him into the ceiling and lock him in for however long its last occupant had thought sufficient for sleep.

JR turned his head to take in the rest of the furnishings, which were spare. Another of the peculiar floating chairs a shelf built into an alcove. Hmmm, that wouldn't adjust, he figured. On the opposite side, shelves running from the floor to near the ceiling. Nothing was on any of them...no, wait. On closer inspection, a small box rested. Something the occupant had left behind by accident, when he--or she?--had left?

JR approached it with the caution he might have given an IED. Nudged it and jumped back, as if the action could have prevented an injury if the thing exploded. Feeling slightly foolish, he used both hands to pull it out of the shelf and turned it over in his hands, looking for some sign of what may be in it. Finally, he held it in one large hand and lifted the lid, a thin metal shape that showed a slight line around the edge, with his thumb. Inside there were a number of paper-thin metal leaves, quite a few it looked like. Not wanting to damage anything, he closed the lid again and tucked the box gingerly inside his backpack.

Now he'd really have to hurry to meet Robert, but at least he had something to show for his time. He wondered what, if anything, Robert had found.

Robert was pacing and looking at his wrist when JR got close enough to see him, about halfway there. He looked up when JR was a few yards away and visibly relaxed.

"Thought I was going to have to come after you, mate. What took you so long?"

"I'll show you."

JR had covered the remaining distance by that time, and was swinging his backpack off his shoulder. "What do you make of this?" He handed the box to Robert, who did exactly the same thing JR had, turning it over and around until he found the narrow seam that indicated a lid, and then opening that.

"No idea. Looks like microfiche maybe?"

"What the hell is that?"

"Before your time, nipper. They used to burn reduced-size copies of documents on film, like negatives, and you had to read them with special machines to magnify them."

JR regarded Robert with suspicion. "Are you having me on?"

Robert laughed. "No, mate. Ask your grandpa." He put the lid back on. "But one thing...that looked like metal, not film. Never mind. Put it back in your pack and let's get out of here, before it's pitch dark outside. Look what I discovered." He stepped up to the door, which opened with no other effort from him.

"Hmmm. So, you have to touch it to open it from outside, but from inside, it's automated."

"Right. Can't imagine why. And there's more. What I found on my side was all the infrastructure to take care of a large number of people. I'm assuming large, because, for example, the kitchen had these enormous cooktops and pans that were big enough they'd need a pulley system to move them in our time. But they floated when I nudged them, just like the chairs."

"It actually looked like stoves and pans, like we use today?"

"Sort of. Close enough I could deduce it, anyway. I looked inside one of the pans, and it was very thin, but probably held twenty gallons or more when it was full of food. Easy to figure out, really."

"All right. Just a kitchen then?"

"No. Another room with huge machines I couldn't figure a use for, until I started thinking about it on the way back here. Probably laundry facilities; but instead of washing clothes with water, it may have used some other technology, like microwaves or something."

"Let's go back and see."

"You're the leader, but let me point out to you that we've got a technical climb to get back down to the valley floor. And unless you found running water, we need to get back to our supply before too many more hours. But it's going to be too dark to climb today."

"Oh, right. Let's go."

Back in the elevator, JR reflected that this part would have already been over, if he and Robert had thought to save their conversation for later. He had just enough time to brace himself before Robert hit the button again, and they shot upward, leaving his stomach behind. Ruefully, he realized he'd be nervous about traveling in this thing for the rest of his time here. Not that he did not want to end up in heaven one day, but he certainly did not want to arrive there before his time.

In the alcove formed by the canyon walls, the two men stood shakily recovering from the long ride from the bottom at what seemed like two or three Gs. The sun was long gone from the canyon rim, so their descent on the climbing filament would need to be as quick as they could make it.

An hour later, the two stumbled back to the wall where the slot canyon opened twenty feet above them in near-total darkness. With most of their water gone, they decided to have energy bars for dinner rather than trying to reconstitute dried rations. Robert would go up to the seep the next morning at first light. Then they'd discuss whether to return to the strange construct below, or head back out to the river and try to get a call through to Daniel.

JR was already inclined to call the mission a success and

head back. It had been a remarkable feat to find the evidence in only four days, even though they had a map to it, more or less. He'd given up the idea that the facility was abandoned by any US government agency. If that had been the case, he reasoned, the place wouldn't have been picked as clean as it was. No doubt any facility that the government closed would be left in a state where it could be reopened and put immediately to use, or cleaned out but sold to recover the value of it. He'd have to run the theory past older and wiser heads, but for now, he was working under the assumption that it had been Eighth Cyclers who'd built it. What was the significance of the resemblance to modern office buildings, except with the addition of dormitory and living facilities? It came to him then that it resembled something else in that way...a military base.

JR went to sleep with the last idea circling in his mind. What if that had been an Eighth Cycle military facility, or more likely a military intelligence base? What would it mean if they'd required four thousand analysts working in a hive environment like that? The concept fueled dreams that wormed their way into his subconscious but left no remnant for his waking mind to find the next morning.

Chapter Eighteen

OPEN SESAME

Daniel left Nicholas' office with a heavy heart. It hurt to see the old man faltering, after being such a heroic figure all his life. He needed to make time to talk to Grandma, and see if she wouldn't help him ease Grandpa into retirement again. The story of that Grand Canyon trip was going to be a good one, though. Grandpa had been born in the mid-nineteen thirties, during the grip of the Great Depression.

What JR had explained to Daniel was unbelievable. What looked like a modern office building, deep underground, but made of some kind of metal that emitted light from the walls and ceilings, so it was even. It reminded Daniel of the light in Paradise Valley, but JR hadn't made the comparison. There was still some question in JR's mind, and Robert's as well, about what exactly they'd found. But, their instructions were not to talk about it until they got back to Boulder. The artifact they were bringing back, the only thing portable they'd found in the place, would either shed light on the subject or wouldn't.

In any case, a bigger expedition would have to go in.

This time, they'd be dropped in by helicopter, now that they knew the exact coordinates. He'd send some engineers, maybe even Roy. That seemed more practical than archaeologists. There'd be no digging to the site, if JR's impression of depth was accurate. Robert agreed. They hadn't thought to look at their watches as they went down in what they were calling the elevator, as good a word as any. But, coming out had taken about ten minutes, and both men reported the sensation of speed. JR had even said "G's", as if the speed had increased their perception of weight. Incredible.

Daniel was getting the itch to go and see for himself, actually. The picture of what looked just like elevator doors set into solid rock was unbelievable. If he hadn't known better, he'd have thought it was manipulated with digital photo software.

JR and Robert had spent the night in Page, driving there in their rental car and making arrangements to drop it there instead of back in Flagstaff. Then they'd found an old-fashioned motel and washed the dirt of six days off them before going to That Dam Bar for an excellent meal and some craft beer. Robert kept chuckling at the name of the place.

It would have been nice to get out on the blue waters of Lake Powell, but they were both exhausted. Six nights of sleeping on bare ground would do that to you. Not to mention the trek back to the canyon rim, dodging mules coming down. On Thursday night, all they wanted to do was sleep in a bed, even if it wasn't the most comfortable they'd ever known. JR in particular was wishing he'd kept looking for a place with a king-sized bed, but the town was packed for some reason. No room at any inn but this one, and that only because of a last-minute cancellation. They were lucky not to be sharing a room, for that matter, or staying in two different places.

They'd phoned Daniel on the sat-phone as soon as they found a signal, while still in the canyon, to tell him of their find. Here in Page, the cell phone worked, though there wasn't a strong signal anywhere. JR had learned that their private jet would be ready for them at around three p.m. on Friday. That gave them time to catch up on sleep, have a leisurely breakfast, and drive out to the dam to act like tourists.

Why the 8th Cyclers would have put their facility so far below ground, where the desert beauty was hidden from view, was one of the many unanswered questions in JR and Robert's minds. Unless what they'd found hadn't been an Eighth Cycle site at all. That possibility still remained, but JR was leaning toward another theory, one he would share only with Daniel and Sarah. Or maybe just Daniel. The implications were too ugly to throw out without regard for the feelings and psychological well-being of other people. He'd keep them to himself until he was able to share them with someone who might be able to help him sort them out.

Three-fifteen that afternoon found JR and Robert relaxing in the luxurious cabin of a Learjet on loan from one of the Foundation's generous supporters. JR didn't care who'd loaned it to them, but he was grateful as hell. The ability to stretch his long frame out in the relatively spacious cabin beat commercial flight by a long shot.

"I could get used to this," he remarked to Robert, as a pretty flight attendant handed him a frosty margarita.

"Same here," Robert responded, winking at the girl.

JR got a chuckle out of the blatant flirting going on. Suddenly, he missed Rebecca fiercely. She'd still be at her medical conference until tomorrow.

Daniel reflected that this was almost like old times. His most valuable friends, family and advisers were in the small conference room, its blinds drawn against anyone who wanted to snoop on this exciting meeting. Nicholas had returned to the building with Sinclair, Sarah was there, and Raj as well. The only new face was that of Stephen Matthews. JR and Robert were the center of attention. Even Luke was there, standing in for Salome, who would no doubt be unhappy to have missed this.

JR, with a fine sense of drama, had concealed his find in a small cardboard box, which he'd placed on the table, waiting for the last people to arrive. As soon as Sinclair had pulled out a chair for Nicholas and had taken one for himself, Daniel spoke.

"Friends, we could be on the verge of a discovery that could rival that of the original Tenth Cycle code. With certain caveats, JR and Robert believe what's in this box to be a relic from the Eighth Cycle. I'll turn the meeting over to JR to explain further."

If the others were impatient to see the artifact, they hid it well. But Nicholas, grown querulous in his old age, challenged. "What caveats? Quit hedging, boy, and tell us what you saw."

There'd been a time when such a demand would have

raised JR's temper. But, he loved the old man who made it as much as he loved anyone in the world, and was used to his ways.

"Well, Grandpa, what we found was so close to modern construction that we weren't certain we'd found the Eighth Cycle site at all. A few things lead us to believe we did. But, instead of a fabulous old city carved into the living rock, we found a buried office building, very much like this one. Or, more accurately, I think it was more of a military or intelligence headquarters. Along with a large room that was for all the world like a cubicle farm except for no walls, we also found what I think was a dormitory and Robert observed a kitchen and what was probably a laundry facility."

Underwhelmed, Nicholas sat back with a sour expression and a sound that could have been "Bah!"

JR ignored it. Grandpa would be interested again soon enough.

"We didn't have much time, because we were twenty feet above the canyon floor and it was already late afternoon when we went in. We wanted to be out again before dark, so we could climb back down. Robert and I split up, after finding a door on either side of what we'll call the desk farm." He flipped a switch, and the overhead lights lowered as the viewing screen lit up. "Here's a diagram of the room we found immediately after being deposited what we calculated to be several hundred feet underground, if not several thousand."

Nicholas sat forward again, his mouth open to object to that depth, but JR forestalled the remark by rushing on.

"You can see that this room is unsupported by interior columns, suggesting construction of enormous strength. That's the first thing that led me to believe this was in fact Eighth Cycle. To the best of my knowledge, we can't do this today, unless the ceiling is arched and therefore self-supporting. This ceiling, as you can see, is flat, not arched. I want you to understand, though, that these thoughts didn't come to us right away. A lot of what we concluded came from talking as we walked back out of the canyon. Frankly, we were too amazed to say much of anything while we were in the facility."

The diagram of the room had been replaced by pictures, which showed a rather depressing sameness to the vast space. The walls were a gray metal color, but they glowed as if they were a light source, which in fact they were. The ceiling was of the same material, and glowed in the same way. Nothing embellished the walls. It contained row after row of plain tables with what looked like ergonomic chairs, all made of the same metal. The only thing remarkable about them being, of course, the peculiar suspension system for both tables and chairs, and the way the chairs adjusted to the correct height for whoever sat in them. While describing that, JR couldn't help but smile, but a severe look from Robert with a significant glance above wiped the smile off his face in an instant. They had a mutual destruction situation. One word from either of them and the other would reveal their most embarrassing secret.

If it had been designed as a sensory deprivation chamber, the room would have been almost perfect, except that putting people in all those chairs and assuming they were talking, at least some of them, would have effectively created a rumble that would have been quite distracting. There was nothing on any of the table-desks that would indicate what the room had been used for.

"I don't understand," said Sarah. "This looks modern, sort of."

"That's what we thought," said JR. "We weren't sure we

hadn't stumbled onto an abandoned government facility of some sort. As you can imagine, we were reluctant to snoop much, in case that's what it really was."

"And yet, you entered closed doors and did explore," Sinclair put in. Luke nodded.

"We did. That's what we were there for, but it was creepy, let me tell you," JR said, for the first time sounding a little less than professional. "I'll let Robert describe what he found. What I found was a long hall, so long I couldn't see the end of it. With closed doors on both sides as far as I could see. I tried each door, with every technique I knew to try. None of them opened until I got impatient because it was time to head back and meet up with Robert. I kicked that one." JR had the grace to blush and look sheepish as he admitted that. Everyone but Sarah laughed. She was still skittish when JR exhibited anger, even after four years of no significant breakdowns.

"What happened then, boyo," Sinclair prompted.

"Well, – I used Robert's technique. I swiped at the door and said 'Open Sesame', and the door opened." This even more sheepish statement earned an even bigger laugh. "I still don't know if that's the way you're supposed to open them. After I went in and saw what there was to see, there was no more time. Robert would have already been at the rendezvous point."

Nicholas interrupted. "And in all your explorations, you didn't find any remains, or other signs of people?"

"No, Grandpa, we didn't. It looked like the place had been abandoned. I mean, there wasn't even a speck of dust, anywhere. I guess there could have been some kind of ventilation system. We didn't find it though."

"There'd almost have to have been, with that many people in a facility so far underground. But how it could have survived, still functioning after so long, is a big question. No sign of people or remains. Remarkable."

"Well, I did find a sign that someone had been there, in that dormitory room. It was in that room that I found this." JR pointed at the cardboard box. The mundane gesture did nothing to dispel the drama of the moment.

"Well, let's see it," Nicholas said.

JR opened the box and took out the object, another box, made of metal. He lifted the lid and picked up the box to tilt it and show it around the table. "May I?" said Nicholas, as if he hadn't been impatient about it for the last fifteen minutes. JR handed it to him.

Gingerly, the old man produced a pair of tweezers from somewhere in his clothing and grasped the edge of one of the leaves within, drawing it out and holding it up where everyone could see it. In contrast to the drab metal of everything else that JR had described, this was a wafer-thin sheet of what looked like metal foil that shone in every color of the rainbow, in a circular pattern that extended to the edges in the middle of the square sheet, but left the corners a single, coppery color.

No one uttered the obvious question, but it was surely on everyone's mind. What is it?

Raj supplied his theory in answer. "That looks like an electronic recording device."

His words broke the spell. Everyone started talking at once, but it was Sarah's voice that carried. "Do you mean like a memory foil?" The technology, consisting of depositing nano-metallic particles on a medium of silicon, had replaced the DVD technology in the first decade after Roy's discovery of how to do it. Instead of megabytes, a piece of material the size of the foil that Nicholas still held up would be large enough to store zettabytes of information; three orders of magnitude more than the terabytes that would have awed this group of people in 2014.

A soft noise was created by seven others letting out a held breath when Nicholas answered, "Exactly."

"Do you mean to say, Grandpa, that what's in this box could be as much information as the entire Tenth Cycle library?" Daniel demanded.

Nicholas shrugged. "I can't tell how many of these things are in the box. Could be, though. If this is what I think it is, it's got as much information in it as the entire Library of Congress did in my day." In fact, it would have been more, but that was the best analogy the old man could come up with at the time. He put the foil back into the box, careful not to crumple it, where it joined hundreds of others, as closely stacked as the pages of a book. "Trouble is, we have no idea how to read it."

Everyone looked at Raj, who paled under his brown complexion. "I...I'm afraid I'd destroy some of the information if I tried," he protested.

The material was indeed delicate, at least it looked delicate. The group sat, each silently raking his or her memory for anything they'd heard that could help. Then Robert perked up. "What about Roy?" he asked. "Couldn't he examine it under one of his non-destructive instruments and maybe get an idea? Say, where is Roy?"

"He and Salome took a well-deserved vacation. They should be back on Monday."

Chapter Nineteen

YOU'RE GONNA LOVE IT

By Friday morning, Salome despaired of finding the last thing they needed. The hot springs complex Roy had surmised was exactly where he thought it would be. Even more to their delight, it was a large field of "pots" as Roy called them, some large, some smaller, and of varying temperatures. Several had been the perfect temperature for bathing, but they confined their daily baths to one of the smaller ones, not knowing whether they would contaminate it with what they washed off. Already they planned to return if they could find fresh water and the cave system that Salome insisted would accompany the ideal spot. They had taken samples from the pot they chose for bathing before they got in. When they returned, they'd know whether the other pools were off limits or not, depending on how the water sample changed.

Roy insisted that fresh water wouldn't be a problem, and was proved correct well before the supply they'd brought with them was used. A spring in one of the limestone outcroppings flowed into a narrow crack that led to one of the nearby creeks. Though they couldn't use the water from the creek without filtering it, the spring water tested purer than city drinking water. It tasted wonderful, too. Salome had never thought about the taste of water before.

The only remaining problem was the cave system. They'd hiked for miles each day, always staying within reasonable distance of the hot springs area and the fresh water spring. They'd moved the camp closer to the latter, so they wouldn't have to waste time fetching water from half a mile away.

"Roy, we've covered every inch of the mountainside we'd be able to reach from here. It's a bust."

"No, it isn't. Look." Roy unrolled the last of the topographic maps they hadn't used yet. It was inconvenient, but they were in a spot that was covered by the contiguous corners of four different maps. Hard to see the contours of the land that way, without creasing the maps, which went against his compulsions. Last night, he'd done it anyway, and now he fitted the last map into the corners where the contour lines would line up with the others.

"We're right here," he said, pointing to a spot near the edge of one of the maps. We've been here." Now his finger moved, covering the areas they'd explored. "But not here." His finger rested on the last map, the one he'd just unrolled. The lines showed a steep upward slope, which he emphasized by pointing to the mountain that lay in that direction. "I've been hoping we'd find an entrance lower. But that's where we need to go before we give up."

"But Roy, if we have to run..." Salome objected.

"We may have to do a bit of covert engineering. But this spot has everything else we need. Let's see if it has a cave system, too."

Salome had to admit he was right. In the week they'd

been there, she hadn't even heard an aircraft overhead. No cars had come to interrupt their idyll. There was plenty of space for housing for a few dozen people, and natural resources that would help them provide the comforts of modern life. Roy had explained how he'd use the hot springs for geothermal energy to provide electricity. And for food, if they had to stay long enough to deplete the supply they'd bring with them, the herd of fat deer that had scared her so badly the first night seemed to have accepted their presence and only scattered when approached. Surely there was other game around, too, and the soil appeared to be fertile.

"We need to decide what we'll do if we don't find anything today," she said. "It's over eight hours from Billings to home, counting stops. And probably more than three from here to Billings. Do we want to make that drive in one day?"

"No, probably not. If we don't find anything today, we'd probably better head back no later than noon tomorrow. That won't give us much time to explore any more, though."

"No, because we have to break camp, and make sure we don't leave evidence we've been here. We'd better get started. Today's our last chance."

By now the routine was familiar. They shrugged on their packs, already replenished from yesterday's hike, and headed in the direction of the snow-capped mountain to the south. Salome let Roy break trail. Neither of them had been experienced hikers before this trip, though Roy had done a little with Robert and JR in the foothills north of Boulder. They'd pushed through the aches and pains on the first day, but the hot springs baths had soothed weary muscles. Salome had learned to use the alpine poles Roy brought, and appreciated the lift they gave her when a step was particularly steep. Today, they came in very handy. Roy had even brought his, though he'd foregone them in the past few days, claiming they were 'sissy'.

She couldn't help but observe that the route they were taking wouldn't make a great escape route. Even a fit adult wouldn't be able to run up this slope, not when poles were needed to balance on the rough terrain. And they couldn't very well build a path, since that would lead any attackers directly to them. When she mentioned it to Roy, he just said to let him worry about that if and when they found a cave.

Lunchtime came and went with no luck. They pushed their normal turnaround time, knowing that if they failed today, it could be a while before they could make another excuse to take several days of vacation. Maybe it was the long shadows of afternoon that did the trick. When they finally headed back by a different route down the mountainside, Roy noticed a shadow that shouldn't have been there, on the slope they were traversing, but above them.

"Look at that," he said. Salome, walking behind him, looked where he was pointing. "What's making that shadow?"

She scanned the slope, but couldn't see a protrusion that would have accounted for the shadow. "I don't know."

"Hurry," Roy said. "We have to get to the end of it and look back, before the light's gone." He lengthened his stride, soon leaving Salome behind by several yards. She was still struggling to catch up when he called out, "Eureka!" It startled a laugh out of Salome. Only Roy...

"What did you find?" she called back.

"You've got to see it," he replied, maddeningly she thought. A few minutes later, she was by his side, looking in awe at his discovery. A narrow ledge that had split away from the main bulk of the mountain made an entrance hall of sorts. Fifty yards back in the direction from which they'd come, a deeper shadow, overgrown with bushes and vines, indicated an opening into the mountain itself. Could it be what they were looking for? Or only a tease, too shallow or otherwise unusable. There was only one way to find out.

"Let's go see," she said.

"It's going to be dark soon."

"I know, but we won't have time to come back. We need to at least see if it's a possibility." She started for the cave entrance, but Roy soon caught up and passed her.

"I don't want you going in first," he said. "Stay back until I see whether it's safe."

Salome had been an FBI agent for several years when Roy met her, and was fully capable of taking care of herself, but she loved it when Roy went caveman. It was nice to be taken care of, now and then. She was close behind him when Roy reached the opening, which they now realized was bigger than it had looked from the entrance to what she thought of as the hallway.

It was more of a crack, she thought, than an entrance. About twenty feet high, maybe, and only ten or so wide, with jagged edges that hadn't yet been worn down by time. How long had it been here? Roy was stepping in, shining his little laser-bright flashlight...

His voice had an echo when he spoke. "I can't see the walls. It must be huge."

"That's good, I think," she said.

"It is as long as there aren't any critters in here."

"Critters?" Salome said.

"Bears, or mountain lions," he clarified, from the sound of his voice moving deeper into the cave.

"Roy, come back here right this minute!" she shrieked.

Bears! Mountain lions? Why hadn't she thought about that possibility? She couldn't hear him moving anymore, and now the light disappeared, too. "Roy!"

Thirty seconds later, which seemed like an eternity to Salome, with her heart hammering hard enough to jump out of her chest, the light reappeared. Thank heaven!

"You're gonna love it, Sal," Roy called.

"Love it why?" she called back.

"It's big enough. More than. We could hole up an army in here."

Chapter Twenty

FIVE IMPORTANT THINGS

Roy and Salome arrived at the Rossler Foundation headquarters building to localized pandemonium on Monday morning. Luke was on hand to greet Salome when she walked into her office, surprising her. They had left it that if nothing major happened while she was gone, Luke would simply leave her a memo.

His presence meant something major had happened, which concerned her but her concern was soon put to rest when she and Luke started talking.

"Salome don't worry you are not in any trouble at all, on the contrary. But before I brief you, tell me about your week in the wilderness? Did you find what you were looking for?"

Salome relaxed. To pay him back for scaring her, she decided to have some fun with him. "Well Luke, we discovered five important things." Holding up one finger, she said, "Roy and I knew nothing about camping before this week but discovered if you can read instructions you can be an experienced camper in a week." With each successive point, she added another finger. "Two, we discovered that an open air bath in a hot spring can be an exhilarating and soothing experience. Three, bears don't come in herds."

By now Luke was smiling. Salome had never shown him, or many other people, her playful side, but she was about to send him a zinger. She continued with a straight face, holding up her pinky finger. "Four, we discovered you CAN make love in a tent."

Now she laughed aloud as Luke blushed. Finally, holding her thumb up, she delivered the punch line. "Oh, and by the way, we discovered a cave system that could easily hold a hundred and fifty or more people. How's that for a productive week?"

Luke blew out a puff of air, and quipped, "I'm glad you didn't discover anything else. Not sure my heart could take it."

Salome laughed again. "You deserved that, for scaring me. Okay, what's been going on here?"

"Well, first I need to tell you that JR and Robert have returned from their trip, with an artifact Raj is certain is a data storage system. The three of them are probably accosting Roy in his lab right now, to see if he can shed any light on whether and how data is stored on what they found."

"How exciting! Tell me all about it."

"In a minute. Before we get into it, I need to tell you that I stole your thunder with Daniel. I'm sorry, but I didn't feel it could wait until you returned."

"Oh, Luke, I wish you hadn't done that. I wanted to explain to him, once I told him, why I hadn't brought it up earlier."

"Don't worry, I covered that. He was a bit shocked to begin with, as I'm sure you anticipated. But I smoothed it over; told him it wasn't a trust issue, but that you wanted to be sure first, and then have a solution. He's waiting for you to come and discuss it with him. You should be receiving a page any minute."

Right on schedule, the intercom chimed. It was Daniel. "I'd like you to attend an emergency meeting we're having in the small conference room," he said. "If Luke's with you, bring him along."

Roy, unaware of the goings-on, had gone straight to his lab, where he found JR Rossler, Robert Cartwright, Stephen Matthews, Nicholas Rossler and Sinclair O'Reilly waiting for him. He blinked rapidly, searching for what to ask first. Finally, he said, "What's going on?"

"Let's go, we're late," answered JR. This cryptic response bewildered Roy even further. Late for what? He hadn't forgotten a staff meeting had he? Even if he had, why would this crowd need to escort him there?

As soon as they arrived at the conference room door and he saw his wife inside, Roy's alarm grew even greater. Had they done something wrong?

Daniel stood as Roy walked in, and immediately drove all thought of possible wrongdoing out of their heads. "You two are never going to guess what happened while you were gone. We're sure glad to have you back."

Roy walked around the table and took the seat next to Salome.

"What's up, boss? All this drama..."

"It's big, Roy. And you're the key. Salome, I take it Luke has already briefed you on what's been happening here the past week, but let's discuss the Canyon expedition first and get that show on the road. And then, you and Luke and I can meet in my office to discuss other matters."

Roy was intrigued. He was the key? How so? He was about to ask, when Daniel produced a metal box from a locked case and placed it on the table.

"Roy, Salome, this is an artifact from the Grand Canyon site that JR and Robert reached while you were away. They got back on Friday afternoon, and we've been waiting with as much patience as we could for you two to get back."

"Why wait for us?" Salome asked.

"Because, we think Roy's the only person we've got that can examine it without potentially damaging it." He opened the box, and, with the greatest care, tweezed out the first sheet in the side nearest him. He held it up, where everyone could see the multi-colored swirl of colors in the circle. He'd known after Nicholas handled the foils to grasp it by a corner. The object shimmered in the light, almost as if it were alive. Everyone in the room but Roy and Salome had seen it the first time, but even they gasped in appreciation. For a mundane object like a square piece of metal, it held an otherworldly beauty in the rainbow of the circle.

Roy gazed at it curiously. "What is that?"

"We think it's for data storage. We've been calling these things foils." He tipped the box so that Roy could see the packed leaves inside it. "There are hundreds of them, near as we can tell. But we can't be sure until they're examined, and we don't know what might damage them if there is data. Do you have any instruments that you're fairly confident won't hurt them?"

Roy reached for the foil, but then drew his hand back.

Good idea Daniel had, to handle it with tweezers. As near as he could tell, if there were data, it would be in the circle, but the corners of the square were empty of color. "I can think of a couple I could try, if I knew what that material is. Any ideas?" Here, he looked at Robert. The stuff looked metallic. Maybe Robert knew what metal.

Robert shook his head. "No, mate, you need a chemist for that. And the tests are destructive. We can't risk it."

"What about a sliver of one of those corners? If there's any data on that thing, it's probably in the circles," Roy said. Others were nodding in agreement. Daniel looked dubious.

"I mean, I may be able to see something under a Tenth Cycle electron microscope, without damage. Definitely without damage. What I could possibly see is another question. I don't suppose that box came with a user manual," he joked.

Salome cracked the rest of them up when she retorted, "You wouldn't read it even if it had."

Roy's sheepish grin cut the tension. "Yeah, one of the things Salome and I learned this past week - when all else fails, read the manual."

Daniel smiled too, and handed the box over. "Don't hesitate to ask for anything you need. And Roy, this is top secret. We're not even supposed to have it, so don't talk about it to anyone other than those in this room right now, and even then, not any place you could be overheard."

Roy flushed. "I'll remember."

"Roy, that box is top priority. Okay, team let's get out and do it to them before they do it to us."

To Luke and Salome he said, "Let's go and grab ourselves a good cup of coffee in the canteen and take it with us to my office."

As they walked out Salome in the front, Luke with a big

smile on his face grabbed Daniel's arm and whispered something in his ear. Daniel blushed, looked away from Salome's retreating backside and cuffed Luke on the arm. "TMI"

Chapter Twenty-One

ENIGMA

By the time they'd obtained their coffee and made their way back to Daniel's office, Luke's revelation had stopped making Daniel uncomfortable, and he decided to have some fun with Salome.

In a mock-serious tone, he began, "So, Mrs. James before we get into it I am very interested in the five most important things you discovered this last week."

Salome's jaw dropped as she turned an accusing glare on Luke, who shrugged. *Luke Clarke I will get you for this.* Amusement got the better of her indignation that Luke had spoken out of turn, and she quickly regrouped. Her tone was clipped and professional as she shot back, "Mr. Rossler four of the five things have to be experienced in person to be fully understood, but the most important thing is that we found the ideal secluded site for a large number of people."

With that, Daniel knew the fun was over, and signaled Luke to summarize for everyone what each pair had discussed, so they'd all be on the same page. Salome confirmed for Daniel what Luke had conveyed, and also that they'd looked at the data this morning and she agreed with his analysis.

"Salome, I want you to know I appreciate your alertness and the work you've been doing on your own initiative. I wish, though that you'd have felt comfortable coming to me with your concerns. Please don't feel you're in any hot water, at all. I just want you to know that I've been thinking something's going seriously wrong with our society myself. Maybe I would have had something to contribute."

"I'm sorry, Daniel. I've been in a strictly hierarchical agency too long, I guess. In the FBI, you have to dot all your I's and cross your T's before you say a word."

"No apology necessary. I can tell you, though, that what Luke's been feeding me has me turned into a total insomniac. I don't think I've slept in three days."

"Would you like to see it for yourself, Daniel?" Salome asked. "Luke may have been able to glean some superficial information from it, in fact, apparently did. But I'm the virtuoso. I can show both of you things that will curl your toenails."

"Absolutely!" Daniel replied, thoughtfully considering his feet and hoping she wasn't being literal. He couldn't think of anything much more uncomfortable than curled toenails.

Half an hour later, he was convinced, not only that she was right, but that he agreed there wasn't much they could do to stop it. With the revelation that the president himself was the beneficiary of some of the schemes, there was no one to whom to report that they could be sure wasn't already compromised. Nothing the major players were doing was strictly speaking illegal, anyway. It was a nightmare.

"What I don't get is what they're after," he remarked.

"They have virtually everything they need to take over, literally the entire world. Why haven't they done so?"

"Probably because of the military, or whatever security forces each country has. They have no need to get involved in a war of resistance, when they've been so careful up until now. No doubt they're waiting to infiltrate, obtain power through political influence, or find a way to cripple the troops," Luke had given it some thought, and was ready with the answer almost before Daniel had asked it.

"Then, I assume we have some time to prepare," Daniel responded.

"I'm sure Luke is right," said Salome. "But, remember how much of the nanotech information got leaked during the Sword of Cyrus crisis. We could be looking at anything from individually-programmed nano-poisons to enough nano-sized anthrax spores to wipe out entire countries. We have to work as quickly as we can."

Luke spoke up. "So, you're thinking that the doomsday clock has advanced?"

"I'm thinking we were wrong when we estimated five minutes to twelve. It's probably more like one minute."

Daniel cleared his throat, gaining the attention of the other two, who were staring at each other in horror. "All right, here's what we're going to do. Luke, I'm afraid I have to draft you back into service. We need someone minding the store while our plans are developed and implemented. Work it out between you, but let's get a response drawn up. It will need to stay among the three of us for now. Luke, tell Sally whatever you need to, as long as she understands not to talk about it with anyone, not even Sarah's mom. Top secret, eyes only, and all that. No written communications, nothing on the phone or internet, as paranoid as Raj, Luke. Remember back in the day? Like that, only tighter."

"We should have a code name for it," Salome said. "So we can refer to it with others hearing, if necessary, but not understanding."

"Enigma," said Luke. "After the German encryption machine. If Turing hadn't already had his idea for a computing machine, it would never have been cracked."

"Let's hope this enigma goes un-cracked as well," said Daniel. "Enigma it is.

Luke lightened the mood with his final shot. "You won't need to prepare a place for me, because I'll be a dead man as soon as Sally figures out I'm back in the game."

Daniel and Salome laughed as if it would be their last chance for a long, long time. Finally, Daniel taunted him.

"Luke, I can't believe you're afraid of a woman half your size."

"Dynamite comes in small packages, Daniel. If you don't believe me, *you* go and tell her you drafted me.

Daniel quickly backpedalled. "Oh, no. That's up to you. Dismissed." He gave a mock salute, the signal for the others to leave and get to work.

Chapter Twenty-Two

ONLY ONE WAY TO TEST IT

While his wife was getting her thoughts in order to create the Enigma plan, Roy had been examining one of the foils from the box under a Tenth Cycle version of an electron microscope to determine whether the circles of color visible to the naked eye had a structure that could carry information, and what type of information it might be. Improvements made since the second Rossler expedition to Antarctica, when the same type of instrument had been used to help crack the viral code of the Ninth Cycle virus included a mechanism to translate electromagnetic data into sound.

Roy was certain that what was on the foils was data. What else could it be? However, there were many forms it could take. From grooves, like on an old-fashioned phonograph record, to binary data in the form of positive and negative ions, and anything in between. But attempting to 'play' the data with some of those methods could destroy it, if it were the wrong method.

His first task would be to determine how stable this

metal might be, and then attempt to determine how the data was recorded. For now, he was examining the outside corners, where the circle of color didn't extend, to attempt to see the molecular structure of the metal. But, he wasn't having much luck. He couldn't see any physical indication of what was making the colors. He needed quantitative chemical analysis. And that was destructive.

As Roy tried to reconcile the challenges he faced, he wondered if every foil in the box contained data. If he could find one that appeared blank, perhaps determine that there was no data to destroy, maybe Daniel would allow it to be analyzed as to alloy composition. One thing he was virtually certain of; unless this had been left by aliens of some sort, the metal had to be one of the ninety-one or so elements familiar to Earth. He suspected that at least one of the elements was one that produced a magnetic field, because handling the foils caused them to sway toward other metals.

Roy also suspected that he'd find blank foils, if any, at the other end of the box than the one he'd taken the first sample from. Carefully, he put the first one back in the correct end of the box, and selected the last one from the other end. As he held it up to the light, he was relieved to discover that the rainbow swirl effect seen in other samples was missing from this one. He selected the next in line. It, too was devoid of color.

Roy placed the second foil back into the box, and put the first under the microscope's lens. As he slowly moved the sample back and forth, nothing but a smooth surface, with no blemishes, pits, grooves, bumps or any other marks he could think of, met his eye. Just like the others, except there were no swirls of color. He'd found one that he was certain could be analyzed without losing any data. For the second time in a few days, he said, "Eureka!" He felt like Archimedes, discovering something previously unknown. At least, unknown since the Eighth cycle.

Considering the age and the fact the data and sometimes the materials they were working with was irreplaceable, careful thought had to go into what he did with it. In this case, Roy wasn't about to send the foil for chemical analysis without permission. Just having the foil off the premises for analysis would be an issue. Before they could even send it out, they'd have to vet the lab, and swear them to secrecy, then vet the scientists and ... It was a nightmare. Which he fully intended to drop into Daniel's lap.

"Daniel, I've found something, but before I go any further, I think I need your authorization."

Daniel looked up from his computer monitor, where he'd been preparing a proposal for the Board to fund a second expedition into the Grand Canyon and motioned Roy in.

"Shut the door, please," he directed.

Roy did as he was asked, and then got right to the point.

"Daniel, at least two of those foils have no data on them. We can take what we need off the corners, just to be sure." He stopped for Daniel to answer yes or no.

"Roy, I think you need to give me a bit more to go on. What are you asking me? And what is it you need?"

Roy blinked. It wasn't like Daniel to be so slow. "I'm asking you to give permission for me to have the blank foils quantitatively analyzed for chemical makeup. I need to know what the alloy is, before I can examine the structure of the metals. I'm almost positive these color changes we see are data written in the molecular structure. But I can't be sure, much less extract the data, without being certain what metals I'm working with."

"Oh. Why didn't you say so in the first place?"

Roy suspected that Daniel was having fun at his expense. He didn't know what he'd said that was funny, but Daniel seemed to be trying to suppress a chuckle. He waited again for a yes or no to his request.

"You can't do it yourself?"

"Well, I suppose I could. But I'd need more equipment, and even then, I'm inexpert in that field. I'd prefer someone qualified do it. Is there a problem?"

"No." Daniel sighed. "I need to run it past Salome. I'll let you know."

That was all Roy needed to hear. Without ceremony, he got up and left, forgetting to leave the door open after his exit.

"Salome, could I see you in my office for a quick chat?"

"Sure, Daniel. I'm free now. Anything you need me to bring with me?" she answered.

"I don't think so. Just your wits."

"You got it," she said. She arrived within a few minutes, looking as stressed as Daniel felt. Sadly, he noticed a few indications that she was working too hard. Her blond hair was not in its neat bun, as usual, but instead was in a ponytail, from which a few hairs had escaped and were floating around as she moved her head.

Salome had closed the door and now sat at his desk, waiting for him to speak. He got the easy question out of the way first.

"Do we have any trusted labs that could do some analytical chemical analysis for Roy? We need this to happen fast, but he was thinking ahead to know we can't let this out just yet. Who do you have on your discreet list?"

Salome thought for a minute, then named a lab she was sure could be trusted, from the collection of such useful information in her head. "I'm not sure they do what he needs, though. Let me take my contact there to lunch and find out. I'll have that for you by tomorrow afternoon."

"Okay, that'll have to do."

"Okay, next question. How am I going to fund the Enigma project without withdrawing a lot of cash from somewhere? And if I do that, will someone start watching what we're doing?"

"Hmmm, I don't know and probably. Let me get back to you on that one, okay?"

An hour later found her in the office of Dr. Greene, the president and CEO of a chemical analysis lab in Broomfield, a suburb of Denver slightly southeast of Boulder.

"Thank you for seeing me on short notice, Dr. Greene."

"No problem, Ms. James. Always happy to help the Foundation. We've benefited from some of the work over there. What can I do for you?"

"It's a matter of the utmost confidentiality. Would you mind if I did a sweep for bugs?"

"Bugs? Oh, bugs!" he responded, while looking both mystified and a little offended. "No, be my guest."

Salome assured herself that there were no listening devices either she or her detection instrument could identify, then sat down and prepared to reveal her errand.

"The Foundation has come into possession of some artifacts of great potential value. We'd like your company to do quantitative analysis on a sample, and prepare a complete report. Anyone working on it must have been thoroughly background checked, but time is of the essence. Can you assure me that your employees are trustworthy? Unimaginable harm could come from the slightest hint of this getting out."

Now completely spooked, the man stuttered a bit as he answered. "Of c-course. W-we do some government work, so all our employees have background checks and secret clearances. But I'll do better than that. I'll do it myself. Will that do?"

"Yes, it will have to. My husband, Roy James, will be here tomorrow with the material. Will you be able to get right to it? He'd like to watch the process if you don't mind."

"I'm afraid it's a bit tedious," he said.

"He'll be fascinated. Thank you, sir. May I make arrangements to pay for the service in cash?"

"That's most unusual," he said. "We're not really set up...tell you what. We'll do it without charge, if you can let us in on the secret someday. We've made good profit from some of the Foundation processes. Consider it our thanks."

Salome figured it was a good bet the secret would either be made public some day or something would happen to make the promise void anyway. "Done, and thank you."

Roy was all but certain that the swirls of color on all but a couple of the foils meant there was data written on them. In fact, he spoke to the others, when they discussed it, as if it were an absolute certainty. However, without determining how it was written and then devising a way of reading it, the data was useless. Daniel's approval to test the blank foils and Salome's help in finding a trustworthy company to do it may have been extraordinary to them, but as far as Roy was concerned, it was vital and therefore to be expected.

The following morning, he presented himself at the doors of the lab with the foils in a sealed, acid-free, non-reactive envelope, similar to those used to store ancient documents without harm. He was ushered into the offices of the CEO. Dr. Greene, very excited to get started and impressed by his famous guest, personally led him to the lab where the tests would be done.

"Thank you for allowing me to observe, Dr. Greene."

"I'm honored, Dr. James. Shall we get started?"

In the following hours, Greene shaved tiny slivers from the edges of the foil, close to the corners as instructed. The number of tests and purpose of each test made even Roy's head swim. After a full day, they weren't even close to solving the mystery of how the data might have been written, assuming his theory was correct. But they knew a bit more about the material.

"Preliminary results are that the main elements in the alloy are nickel and iridium," Green summarized. "Those are transition metals, which means..."

"I know what it means," Roy interrupted. Though metallurgy wasn't his field, he was of necessity familiar with the periodic table of elements, and he'd studied this as an undergraduate. During the day, his memory of the pertinent information had been dredged from the recesses of his mind and brought to the forefront. "Nickel is one that produces a magnetic field, if I'm correct?"

"Yes," replied Greene, who'd come to understand over a few hours' acquaintance that Roy's interruptions weren't meant to be rude. He simply didn't want to waste any time having someone explain what he already knew. Despite the man's lack of interpersonal skills, it was a pleasure to see his brilliance at work. "The interesting thing to me is these swirls of color you describe. If I could see one for myself, I may have a better idea of what it means, or how it's produced. Both nickel and iridium are white. No color. Something else must account for that."

Roy had severe misgivings about bringing a foil out of the Foundation premises to show him. If it were somehow lost or damaged, it could mean a gigantic hole in the data the box contained. He gave it some consideration. Salome had seen to it that this man was trustworthy, so taking him into Roy's office at headquarters would probably be all right.

"Why don't you come back to my office with me? I can show you there. What can you tell me about the tendency of this stuff to be soft enough to flutter when we wave it?"

"Nothing yet, unless it's just how thin the sheets are. The tests I plan to conduct tomorrow will throw more light on that. We have to identify the other elements in it, but they're present in such minute quantities that we need a more sophisticated instrument to catch them before they're destroyed in the tests."

Roy was getting worried that there could be data on these seemingly blank foils, too, and that the extent of destruction necessary to identify the alloy was potentially destroying the data, too. Nevertheless, it was his best guess that these had nothing on them. Almost as if someone had put them there for this purpose, so they could discover the way to read the others. If he had been the one to leave this record, he'd have left a reader for the foils as well. But, perhaps something had interfered.

The two men adjourned for the day at the chemistry

The Skywalkers

lab, but Greene was eager to see one of the other foils, and Roy didn't mind. After five p.m., they stepped into the building using Roy's key card and greeted the guard.

"This is Dr. Greene, who's assisting me with some tests," Roy said to the burly man at the entrance kiosk.

"That's fine, Dr. James. Let me know when you're ready to leave."

As they made their way to his office, Roy remarked that it was the Sword of Cyrus incident that necessitated these security measures now. Greene responded with a question about the last-minute save Roy had effected two years ago, and they continued through the building chatting amiably.

Greene turned out to be equally fascinated with the foil Roy showed him. They were still handling it with tweezers, by the corners. "I can see why you think this might be data. It certainly looks like an old-fashioned CD, only pliable."

"That's it."

"Well, you should know by the end of the week what the material is, at least. I can't imagine how they wrote data on it, though."

"That's my job to figure out," replied Roy.

When the alloy was finally fully analyzed, Greene explained to Roy that there was little chance he'd damage the underlying structure, though his theory about how the data was written made it possibly vulnerable. To destroy the foils themselves, you'd have to shred them or heat them to over one-thousand degrees Fahrenheit. Shredding them would do major damage to the shredder, he joked.

Roy agreed with the theory, and had formed it himself as soon as he reviewed the properties of transitional metals. This type of metal had valence electrons, that is, the electrons they used to combine with other elements, in more than one shell. Given the ability to manipulate them on the nano level, they'd exhibit the colors he could observe with the naked eye. With a full analysis of elements present in the alloy, he could analyze which were combined with which electrons, of which iridium had the most, to form which colors. He suspected that the nickel was included for its magnetic properties.

Each evening, Roy went home with some progress to report to Salome alone. As the work went on, she had to quell her excitement over each breakthrough because Roy refused to present his findings to Daniel until he had the final answer. Not only the answer to whether data was present, of which he had no doubt, but the answer to whether he'd be able to devise something to read it. When the solution to that problem came to him, he literally slapped himself on the forehead. As comical as it might have looked if anyone had been there to see it, Roy was genuinely disgusted with his own blindness to it. It had been there all along...magnetism. Could it be as simple as putting a foil under an electromagnetic field? There was inherent risk. If he was wrong, the process could forever destroy the data, which he believed to be contained in the variances between the electrical energy of the bonds formed by iridium and the other elements that produced the colors. There was only one way to test it, and that was to take the risk.

Chapter Twenty-Three

THE MORAL ISSUE

Salome busied herself with two major tasks; first studying the doings of the invisible financial world, learning everyday how to better interpret and read data and uncover who is who behind the big corporations. Second, she was meticulously outlining the Enigma plan.

She had disabled the internet connection on her personal tablet. Her to-do list and planning resided there, and it would never be out of her hands. Her first priority was establishing a method of communication that wasn't subject to snooping, and a way to deploy it.

She found Sinclair in his office, reading over some of the latest translations of their guest researcher, Dr. Matthews.

"Sinclair, can I pick your brain?"

"I'm afraid it's been picked clean, my dear, what's left there is probably stimulated only by Irish nectar and not of much use, but I'm glad to help if I can."

She explained to him that as part of her preemptive security measures and in the light of all the trouble the

Rossler Foundation had been going through in the past with compromised communications and infiltrators, she'd been thinking it necessary to get a secure method of communications. By that, she meant secure even if the bad guys could intercept it.

"I have the perfect solution," Sinclair said, as soon as she'd stopped talking.

Wow, that was even faster than she'd hoped. "What?"

"This will appeal to Nicholas," he said. "We need to recruit some Navajo code-talker re-enactors." He might as well have been speaking Greek, for all that Salome understood. She knew what Navajo code-talkers were. They'd been instrumental in keeping Allied plans secret from the Japanese enemy during World War II. It worked because the language wasn't related to any that the enemy would have expected. The men were able to talk among themselves in the clear, but in their own language, substituting clever everyday expressions for anything the language didn't have a word for, such as submarine, which became 'fish'. There had been a movie about them that her grandfather loved. She'd watched it more than once. As a child, she didn't really understand the significance of what they'd done, but she loved the name of the movie, The Windtalkers.

What she didn't understand now was the phrase *re-enactors*. Sinclair explained. When the last of the code-talkers died, there was an outcry both from elders of the Navajo nation and from folklorists and anthropologists, who mourned the near-death of the language. An extremely short-sighted effort to assimilate the Dine into white society had taken the children forcibly from their homes and forbidden them their language. It had taken an extraordinary effort to resurrect it, but now it was a matter of pride for the members of the Nation to be able to speak their language. And one of the ways in which they showed it was to stage re-enactments of critical battles where their forebears had used the language to prevail in the decades-past war. It was these young men Sinclair proposed to use as couriers. Because the language had no written form, they'd memorize messages and pass them on verbally after translation.

"How long have you been thinking about this?" Salome asked, when Sinclair had finished laying it out for her.

"Ever since the early days. Our communications were compromised then, too," he said. "I wanted to be prepared next time."

"I don't suppose you already know of candidates for the job," she said, believing the opposite to be true.

"Of course I do," he answered. Of course he did.

Salome would never know what Luke told Sally, only that he was in her office bright and early the next morning, and that they worked together quite well. After a quick reconnoiter of the Spiderweb each day, they each did a threat assessment for the day with regard to the Foundation's safety over the next seven days. Once assured they were still under the radar, they worked for the rest of the day on logistics for preparing the Rabbit Hole, as they referred to the cave system she and Roy had found.

They focused first on creating an environment where the group to be hidden could continue their work. Then on how to quickly move the most important assets, which they identified as the library databases, critical personnel, and finally family. Salome objected that their priorities were out of order, but Luke prevailed.

"Listen, I know what you mean. I'd normally agree, but would you agree, Salome, that sometimes a few have to be sacrificed for the greater good? After all, that's the philosophy behind a standing military. Some sacrifice their freedom of personal choice and maybe even their lives to become part of a protective team, so the rest can live in the security that no enemy gets past."

"You're right, Luke, but it speaks to the dilemma I've had all along. Just who are the critical personnel, and why the databases first? I think I know, but I want to hear you say it."

"All right. Let's say we're facing an annihilation event. A few of us scramble to the Rabbit Hole. We'll need a way to survive, and a way to rebuild, with the idea that we're going to be the ones who come out of the cataclysm alive. With the library, or I guess now it's plural – libraries - we preserve the technological advances that leaps us ahead of the first generations after all the previous Cycle's cataclysms.

"We go from a precarious existence to an advanced society within just a few years, instead of thousands. But, to do it, we need the people who can access the information in the libraries. That means Raj, for the computers, and the translators. Then we need people to act on the information. That means Roy, at a minimum. Other scientists as well, if we can recruit them. We need infrastructure to support these people, and they aren't going to be happy without their loved ones. So there you have it. The information, the people to extract and interpret it, and the people those people love.

"While we're at it, we need a diverse assortment of breeding pairs."

Salome, shocked, stared at Luke. He stared back. "What? You can't repopulate the earth with my generation. Roy and you, Raj and Sushma, you'll be there because of who you are. Rebecca, which means JR, Daniel and Sarah because they already have a kid. But we'd better pick the rest with an eye not only to what they can contribute to survival, but also to their fertility status."

Salome threw her hands in the air. "All right, I get it. Let's talk about something else." There'd be more discussion along these lines, because it touched on the moral dilemma. They had room for one hundred, maybe half again more. Who lived, and who died, in the event of a disaster? She wasn't willing to be the only one with a vote, even if Luke did seem to have an unarguable point.

However, there were more immediate concerns, not the least of which was the very real expectation that someone would be coming for their prized assets sooner or later. If Salome had to guess, she'd guess sooner. Her first order of business was to enlist Raj to plan for an extra off-site backup of the libraries, somehow without alerting him yet in light of Daniel's caveat to tell no one. Once they could bring Raj on board, his next task would be to plan for either quickly moving the hardware here at the Foundation, or destroying it so invaders couldn't get their hands on it. Luke made a note to take it up with Daniel at the next Enigma meeting. Raj had to be brought in immediately.

Clearly, they also needed to get started on turning the cave system in the Gallatin National Forest into a habitable ecosystem, with sustainable power, clean water and food, along with comfortable living quarters. And, it all had to be done in complete secrecy. If their activities were discovered, a huge PR problem for the Foundation was the least of their worries. It was true that the Foundation had an impeccable reputation with regard to the environment, so it would be bad. But neither of them knew what kind of penalties they'd face for defacing a national preserve.

This brought up the subject of equipment, supplies and laborers to put it all together. Salome began to think of it as Medusa, with a thousand details writhing around her head like dangerous snakes. Any one of them could strike at any instant, and then all the secrecy would be gone in an instant. And if that happened, they might as well have made no plans in the first place. Because if whoever and whatever was behind the creeping virus in the world economy caught wind of it, they were all as good as dead anyway.

"Luke, how many people can one doctor handle? Do we need to recruit someone to help Rebecca?"

"I don't know. We'll have to ask." He made another note for Daniel's approval: bring Rebecca into the Enigma circle. "This is nuts. We should just gather the old group and let them all in on this. The reason we've all survived so far is we all have different strengths."

"Well, you said that's what we'd need, when we started deciding on people. Let's make a list of the ones who have to be there, and why. So Raj, because he's the computer whiz, and Sushma and their kid, because you can't expect Raj to leave them behind. That's three."

"All right. Rebecca, obviously, which means JR. They're young, healthy, Rebecca's a doctor."

"Not that I'd leave him out, but what's JR good for, except getting things down from high cabinets?"

Luke guffawed. "Once upon a time, not much. But he's pretty versatile. Besides, Rebecca wouldn't go without him. Hey, I know. We're going to need security. JR was Special Forces. I'll bet he can recruit some old buddies."

"Good, write that down."

"We've got to have Sinclair. He's got a wealth of language skills, plus the translators are used to his leadership. So, Martha. Hmm, they're too old for the repopulation effort."

"Well, you can't leave Martha behind. It would be wrong, and besides, Sinclair would drink himself to death without her. I know! She's a gardener. I wonder if she knows anything about hydroponics?"

"We'll have to get her started learning." Luke hesitated to bring it up, because he didn't want to take the place of a young couple with the ability to help repopulate. But he couldn't help mentioning that Sally was skilled in animal husbandry. He'd want her to survive, even if he had no place in the Rabbit Hole.

And so the week went, with lists drawn up, estimates made, brainstorming about how to solve the logistics problems and more. Before they knew it, the next meeting was upon them.

No sooner had Daniel released Salome and Luke after telling them to go ahead with the immediate steps they'd outlined, than the phone on his desk rang.

"Daniel Rossler."

"Daniel, it's John Brideaux. I just wanted to know how that expedition is coming."

At first, Daniel didn't know how to answer, his head full of Enigma plans. He hesitated, then shook his head to reset his thinking. "Oh, yes, John. I have a meeting in just a few minutes with my expedition manager."

"That's your brother, am I correct?" Brideaux asked.

"Yes, JR. He's proven to be a valuable resource on an expedition."

"Yes, I remember some of his exploits. Well, I just want

you to know that I'm still ready, willing and able to get behind you on this, Daniel."

"John, I appreciate it. We're still doing some research with the artifacts, before we really know what all is involved. But, I'll be in touch as soon as I have the figures for your approval. And thank you, again, for all you've done for the Foundation."

Chapter Twenty-Four

EIGHT FOR AN OCTAVE

Roy was at a crossroads. Even if it worked, it might be a one-shot deal. Capture the data in that one shot or lose it forever. It was a decision he couldn't make alone. In the small conference room, with the same core group as the ones who'd first seen the box and its strange contents. Roy's first statement electrified the room.

"With the help of a lab Salome found, I've identified the material these are made of, and I'm 99% certain that the colors we can see represent a form of data."

Celebration broke out as Nicholas and Sinclair clapped each other on the back, JR and Daniel high-fived, and Salome hugged Roy. Raj was his usual conservative self, but he smiled. Roy's next statement quelled the enthusiasm.

"Unfortunately, I've only got one idea about how to read it, and that's possibly destructive. Maybe even probably."

Daniel stared at Roy in disbelief. "Do you mean to tell me that you can't capture the data without destroying the source?"

Roy shook his head. "I can't say for certain. But it's very

likely. That's why I haven't done it yet. Maybe there'll be scientific breakthroughs later that provide another way. I can't say. All I can say is that if you want this data now, you risk destroying the source, and you risk not capturing it as well. Basically, it involves forcing this material to give up its electrical charges and only then determining if they form any sort of pattern."

Daniel was aghast, and Nicholas nearly apoplectic. "You can't do that!"

Roy shrugged. What followed was pandemonium as the arguments pro and con. JR argued that destroying the data was no worse than not having access to it at all, while his grandfather and brother shouted him down that it wasn't fair to later generations, who might figure it out without the risk of destruction. Roy sat in the center of the storm with a slightly curious look on his face, as if all he had at stake was a bet on who'd win the argument.

Raj was the one who finally came up with something. "Roy, how many of the foils did you check for blank ones?"

"Just two. I only needed one."

"Go back and check the next two or three. See if there's a smaller area of color. Maybe this was all set up this way because whoever left this for us knew that the people who found it may not be sophisticated enough to have the means to read them, but could maybe figure it out."

"You mean, like test data? Some foils with just a little on them, so we wouldn't be afraid to destroy them?"

"It's worth a look, isn't it?"

Daniel agreed, but told the others to wait while Roy fetched the box.

Raj would never be able to say what caused him to have that hunch, but it proved correct. There were more than twenty foils with larger and larger circles of color in the center. Roy began with the one closest to what turned out to be ten blank foils, counting the one he'd used in the metallurgy lab. Its circle was barely larger than a nickel, Nicholas said. Roy had never seen one of the obsolete coins, so he had to take the old man's word for it. He thought it was ironic that nickel, the element, was one of the key components of the foil.

The first attempt did in fact destroy the data. Roy adjusted the strength of the electromagnet and tried again. By his third attempt, he was able to capture the charge variables, but the circle disappeared. He handed his results over to Raj, and tried again. By the sixth attempt, he was sweating the idea he'd never be able to get what Raj needed without destroying the source, but that was the day Raj came to him with outstanding news.

"It shows a pattern all right. It's binary. Once I was able to analyze what you got, it's all zeros and ones."

"You're kidding! What are the odds that an ancient civilization and ours would devise the same system?"

"I wouldn't have taken the bet, but I know what I see."

Together they took the news to Daniel.

"Roy, have you succeeded in doing any of this without destroying the source?"

"Not yet. I've got fourteen more sample foils."

"Work from the other end. Take the power down to as low as you can get it, and see if that destroys the source. If not, see if you get enough data to work with. Then take it back up if necessary. Let me know. I don't want to destroy the source if we don't have to."

Roy tried it a seventh time. To his delight, the underlying metallic structure was unchanged--the data was still there in its original form. However, the recording of the charge variables was depressingly blank. An eighth, a ninth and a tenth try had the same effect. Then, on the eleventh, a faint image of the variables came through. He called Raj.

"Hold your breath, buddy. This next test may be the one."

Raj was on hand as Roy tried for the twelfth time, adjusting the power only the tiniest bit. It was while the machine was running that he slapped his forehead again. Why hadn't he tried again on the foils that hadn't given up their data the first time? He had ten extra tries that way. But, as Raj shouted that he had data, Roy pulled the foil out and realized that it looked exactly the same as it had before it went in. They'd identified the correct level of power. Now all that remained was for Raj to determine what, if anything, the binary code produced.

At first, nothing Raj did to manipulate the code made sense. He tried at first dividing the ones and zeros into lengths of eight, like the bit strings he was used to. However, without a key to the language represented, the data meant nothing. Roy began working late into the night with Raj, throwing out more and more unlikely theories. Until the night he mentioned how funny it was that binary and music both used the number eight. Eight for a bit, eight for an octave. Raj decided to synthesize the data from the last test as sound instead of text. To his astonishment, though he should have been prepared for it, a very human-sounding voice came from the speakers, saying "ah, aa, eh, ee, oh, oo" and more.

"What the heck?" said Roy.

In the understatement of a decade, Raj answered, "I think we'd better get Sinclair."

As it turned out, Martha told them Sinclair was in no condition to help them that night, since he'd been celebrating the Galway club victory at football that evening. When asked what football teams were playing in July, she just said GAA. With the certain knowledge that neither of them would be able to sleep, Roy and Raj went home, Roy determined to find out what the heck GAA was and Raj determined to wipe from his mind the thought of a grown man getting that excited over a game with a ball.

The next morning, a fully-competent Sinclair arrived in Raj's office.

"What's all the fuss?"

"We're hoping you can tell us what this means, or what language it's in." Raj played the recording again and relished the look on Sinclair's face as his jaw dropped.

"Faith and ..."

"Yes, yes, yes, begorrah. What does this mean?" Raj demanded, well accustomed to Sinclair turning pure Gaelic when he was excited, and determined to forestall it so he could understand what Sinclair said next.

"Why, it sounds to me like someone reciting the vowels of their alphabet. Did this come from those data foils? Where's the rest?"

While Roy stabbed at the intercom to get Daniel there, Raj fed the rest of the code from the sample disk into the synthesizer. By the time Daniel got there, the speakers were going through the sounds as they'd come off a human tongue. "Buh, sss, duh, luh," and so on, including some that sounded like clicks, or someone choking on a 'k' sound. They all listened, fascinated, to the end of the data.

"Now, where are the text symbols that go with it?" Sinclair asked.

As it turned out, that was on the next foil. With the

assumption that each symbol produced by a bit of code corresponded to the sound on the previous foil and in the same order, Raj soon had a chart of sorts, though the symbols didn't correspond to any alphabet, syllabary or anything else Sinclair recognized. However, they could pronounce the grouped strings of symbols, more or less. The clicks and choking were more difficult to accomplish. Sinclair said they were fricatives, glottal stops and some other words neither Roy nor Raj were familiar with.

It was a start. What remained was to extract the data from each foil and translate it into the binary system. Roy and Raj would work as a team for that. When they had several gigs of data, Raj translated it into sound and symbols, turning the result over to the translation team. And there it got stuck.

Chapter Twenty-Five

GOOD EAR, NICHOLAS

The box of foils was priceless, as far as Sinclair was concerned. Not only did it have a complete account of the history of the Eighth Cycle, it had clearly been prepared to be found by later cycles. The first foil had provided a pronunciation guide to what he was terming the alphabet of the language, consisting of a number of symbols they later discovered 'written' on the other foils. Moreover, there was a dictionary of syllables, both spoken and in visual form that combined the symbols, or letters, into words. With that, the translators could read a group of letters on the data foils and pronounce them aloud. Sinclair, as an administrator, was curious about the Eighth Cycle material, but beyond the first hint he'd given Roy and Raj, couldn't be involved in the attempts to translate it. He still had important work to do on the library they could read, the Tenth Cycle library.

The translators likened it to teaching a child to read. First, they'd learn the sounds, a symbol or letter, represented, A, B, C and so on. Then, they'd learn how to pronounce groups of letters, then simple words, then more complex. What stymied them at first was discovering that the spoken words as read aloud from the data foils, weren't in any language familiar to any of the translators. After a recording of the first hundred words on the first full foil was circulated among them with no result, one of the group leads finally took it into his own hands to involve Sinclair, who didn't usually get involved in the actual translations anymore, unless one of his employees was having a hard time and his team or supervisor couldn't help.

Sinclair was delighted to be asked, if the truth were known. He missed the hands-on work. Becoming an administrator was an honor, of course. But, like many people who loved their work and discovered it to be a luxury once they became an administrator, he missed the work itself. The challenge of puzzling out what ancient symbols were meant to convey was still one that fascinated him. Especially now that he was older, and needed the mental exercise to stay sharp.

So, on the day when a group lead came to him and said, "None of us know this language," it was like having a holiday. He set aside the work he was doing.

"Let's see what you've got, then."

Instead of putting a piece of paper in front of him, his employee said, "Here, listen to this and see what you think."

Expecting to hear some form of Sumerian or another language from that region, Sinclair was astonished to hear something entirely different. When the recording had finished, he was still puzzled.

"It sounds vaguely familiar, but that's no language from the Tenth Cycle regions. I wonder if we've finally met one that bears no relationship to this cycle's ancient languages."

"What would that mean, if it were true?" his employee asked.

"It could mean we're screwed," Sinclair admitted. "Not really, but we'd have to build our understanding from the most basic of linguistic analysis tools. Could take a while. Can you leave this recording with me?"

"Sure. Let me get a copy made, and I'll bring the original back to you."

"That's fine," he agreed. He turned back to his paperwork, but was unable to concentrate with the mystery in his mind. Why did that language sound so familiar, yet be something he couldn't name? The answer came from an unlikely source.

Late in the afternoon, after the recording had been returned to him, Sinclair was listening to it when Nicholas dropped by.

"Got time for a drink with your old professor?" Nicholas asked.

"After five on any day, I've got time for a drink with anyone who suggests it," said Sinclair, laughing. To say the old Irishman was a hearty drinker was like saying a tidal wave was a big splash of water. Nicholas brandished a bottle of Jameson's and Sinclair waved him in.

As Sinclair produced two glasses from a desk drawer, Nicholas asked, "What was that you were listening to?"

"Preliminary language analysis. The first foil from that box your grandson brought back from the Grand Canyon had an alphabet and pronunciation guide in it. So someone got the bright idea of recording a few of the words on the next foil to see if we'd recognize the language and be able to translate from the spoken word."

"So," said Nicholas, "what is it?"

"That's the trouble. None of the translators recognizes it. It sounds familiar to me, but I don't know what it's saying, so it isn't a language I know or can name off the top of my head by the sound of it."

"Let's hear it," said Nicholas. Sinclair humored the older man by playing it again, though Nicholas didn't claim expertise in languages. His field was archaeology. Specifically the archaeology of the desert southwest of the United States.

"Hodeeyaadeh' Diyin yoh taahah eendah"

Sinclair stopped the recording after the first phrase. "I should get a copy of the alphabet and pronunciation guide. It sounds to me like there's something missing."

"It sounds to me like a white man trying to speak Navajo," Nicholas said.

"What? Why would you say that?" What a delicious irony, that the very language he'd suggested to Salome they use as a code could be the key to this discovery.

"I don't know. Just sounds similar to stuff I've heard on digs. Except they have all these clicks and shortened vowels, like their throats suddenly went dry. And it sounds more like singing," Nicholas said, before taking another sip of his drink.

"What do you mean, singing?"

"You know. The words go up and down." Nicholas gave a good imitation of the first word on the recording, varying his tone as if each syllable was written to a different note on the scale. It did sound a little bit like the only phrase Sinclair knew in Navajo, something Nicholas himself had taught him. "Yah-te-hey" which Nicholas had explained could mean anything from "Hi" to "How's it hangin'?"

"That's interesting. Navajo's a form of Athabaskan, but to the best of my knowledge, none of the Athabaskan languages ever had a written alphabet."

"To the best of your knowledge before my grandson

brought you his theory, there never was a civilization before ours. What if the written form was lost, and even the sophisticated vocabulary, but the language survived among some of the survivors of their cataclysm?" Sinclair had to admit that, despite his old professor's good-natured insult to his intelligence, he was right. What they'd worked out for the language that turned out to be the key to the Tenth Cycle library wasn't any less far-fetched. And yet, everything they'd been able to test so far proved they were right about it.

Sinclair began to get excited. What if a native Navajo speaker could make out the meaning, even if the recording didn't pronounce it quite right? Would that be possible? Would it be possible for such a person to work out how the written form corresponded to the modern language? It was worth a try. What they needed was a native speaker who was involved in translating English to Navajo, like the ones working on the Bible translation project. And he knew just the guy, a grandson of one of the original Navajo code-talkers from the Second World War. The man wasn't only trained in graceful translation; that is, getting the meaning of the text in proper context to his people's language, but also in linguistics. If anyone could confirm that the text recorded in the foils was a form of Athabaskan, Joseph Yazzie could.

After that, it would be Daniel's job to lure the man away from his work on the Bible project, and have him train a cadre of assistants. The work on the Tenth Cycle material wasn't even done. They'd have to hire more translators to work on the Eighth Cycle stuff, even if some of the existing employees knew Navajo. Which they didn't. Or, if they had, hadn't recognized it the way it was pronounced on that recording.

"Good ear, Nicholas," he said. "I think I know how we can confirm your hunch."

Sinclair's acquaintance, after being vetted by Salome, was intrigued by the question Sinclair put to him. Enough so that he was willing to take a week's leave from his job and come to see this strange artifact that Sinclair described. He'd heard of the Tenth Cycle library and the Rossler Foundation - who hadn't? The hint that another account of an even earlier civilization might be written in a form of his language was astounding.

Even more astounding was that Sinclair had come to him in person, rather than picking up the phone. The trip to Nation headquarters in Window Rock, Arizona wasn't easy by any other means than the private jet in which Sinclair had arrived. No less astounding that he was to travel with Sinclair in the same jet for the trip to Boulder. It all seemed rather cloak and dagger to him, but at the same time, exciting and maybe a lot of fun.

Joseph had grown up on stories of his grandfather's service to his country during World War II, and how the code-talkers had to use simple, unsophisticated words to stand in for the technology of the time. Navajo was a language that hadn't evolved by adopting words from other languages as much as some. Its form would be recognizable now to an ancestor from one hundred years ago, except for the different uses one might put the words to.

For example, his grandfather had used the word for bird to mean airplane, combined with other words to specify what kind of airplane. It was the fact the language had no written form that made it such a good code. The enemy never suspected the communications were being sent in the clear in a language unknown to them. In fact, it had nearly died in his parents' generation, because of the seemingly well-intended practice of fostering Dine children in white homes to assimilate them into mainstream American culture.

It was almost too late when tribal government and social anthropologists agreed it would be a shame to lose their native identity. All that was behind them now. The language was beginning to flourish again, and the rich culture was being preserved by people who appreciated its beauty. There were some who couldn't meld the old ways with modern life, and others who felt that they couldn't be Christian and remain true to their culture. Joseph wasn't one of them. Everything his people's version of history taught him could be taken as a parable, and that's the way he did it.

Like most of his people, Joseph Yazzie strove to walk the Beauty way. It meant being balanced in everything. He no longer had the strong passions of youth, other than his love for his family. But, he remained curious to learn everything he could about the world in which he found himself, and from which he would eventually pass into the next. This seemed like an excellent opportunity.

Yazzie and Sinclair arrived at Foundation headquarters just before noon on a Monday, and immediately put off the examination of the foils in favor of a good lunch of something both the Navajo and the Irishman loved: mutton stew. The seasonings were different at the Irish pub Sinclair took Joseph to, but it was good anyway. Joseph thanked Sinclair politely. He'd declined the beer that Sinclair ordered with his own food, but observed that Sinclair seemed to be able to keep his wits about him despite copious amounts of it.

Once Sinclair declared they'd celebrated their collaboration sufficiently, they returned to his office, where for the first time, Joseph heard the recording. Sinclair hadn't been able to take it with him because of Salome's paranoia, he told Joseph. The latter had no idea who Salome was or why she'd be paranoid, but decided perhaps it was the beer talking.

He listened carefully to the recording. If only... The language scholar in him took over then, and he asked to see the document that helped them decide how to pronounce the words in the text. When he'd done that, he substituted Latin text with some special characters the new way of writing Navajo used. Then he transliterated the text using his own substitutions, and read it himself, properly pronouncing the glottal stops and other phonology. After the first time, he spoke again, this time adding tonality to some syllables, based on both the pronunciation guide and his own mastery of his tongue.

It was a matter of only an hour or so, but the simple technique convinced him. "This is Athabaskan. Not quite my own form of it, but understandable." Pointing to the text, he continued. "These few words say, "In the beginning."

Sinclair almost dropped the glass of Jameson's he was handing to Nicholas at the time. The older man had wandered in and stopped to wait for Yazzie to finish so they could chat about some ruins Nicholas had excavated within the borders of the Navajo Nation. Sinclair wouldn't have dreamed of depriving him of his reminiscences. All thought of that now fled, though, as Yazzie dropped his bombshell.

"You mean, like Genesis? In the beginning God created...that beginning? Holy shit!"

Joseph smiled. "I haven't read far enough to say. I'm going to have to memorize this notation instead of transliterating it to Navajo text. But I'm confident I can. Now what?"

"Come on, we need to tell Daniel immediately!"

For a man now in his late seventies, Sinclair made it difficult for Nicholas to keep up as he practically ran through the halls of the building, Joseph in his wake. Nicholas knew the way, and Sinclair reasoned that he'd catch up soon enough, while he introduced Joseph to Daniel. Joseph was telling Daniel what he'd missed by never visiting Canyon de Chelle and other points of interest in the vast stretch of land that whites called the Navajo reservation when Nicholas arrived a little breathless and sent a glare in Sinclair's direction.

Ignoring it, Sinclair waited only until Daniel had said how much he'd like to see those places before interrupting.

"Daniel, we've got some tremendous news. As you know, Nicholas had a hunch that the language on the Eighth Cycle foils was similar to Navajo. Joseph here has just confirmed it. Daniel, he can read it!" Sinclair was all but doing an Irish jig around the office as what he said sunk in on Daniel.

"You mean..."

"YES!" shouted Sinclair, unable to contain his excitement long enough for Daniel to ask the question. "He can sit down and look at the text and read what it says, just like you or I read English!" Sinclair's enthusiasm was contagious. Nicholas stepped over to pump his old student's hand while Daniel stood with his mouth hanging open.

"Um, that isn't quite accurate," Joseph said, halting Sinclair's celebration and confusing Daniel enough that he sat down.

"Well, what is?" Daniel asked.

"I'll be able to say the text aloud as soon as I've memorized the unfamiliar orthography. It won't take long for me to do that, but I'd say the best methodology would be to develop a computer program that would take the orthography as it exists and transliterate it to Navajo orthography. Then any number of people would be able to read and translate it to English."

Sinclair began to dance again. "Just like Raj did for the Tenth Cycle code, Daniel. Only this is written in the clear. No skip sequences!"

Daniel got up and seized Joseph's hand, shaking it vigorously. "That's brilliant! We've got the right guy for the job. Please, have a seat. I'll get him here right away."

Daniel keyed the intercom for Raj and told him to get there as quickly as possible. Raj arrived within minutes, trailed by Salome, who'd been in Raj's office when the call came through.

"What's going on?" she asked.

Daniel explained, drawing Raj's intense focus immediately. This would be a piece of cake, they agreed. It didn't quite turn out to be that easy, but almost.

Chapter Twenty-Six

OUR HUMANITARIAN CAUSE

Each in their own private offices and connected by secure satellite link, the members of Eligo Rarus were discussing their latest acquisition. A new biotech company, GENT had developed a way to conduct a full human genetic test in a matter of minutes and provide a complete biological profile of a person, including any defects and susceptibility to diseases. The news hadn't gone public as yet. When it did, it was going to cause a bombshell in the markets.

They had been VERY interested in GENT for some time now. In fact they had invested seed capital into it through one of their hidden companies in the startup phase. That had proved wise when the new technology had been announced in-house. It would give them a head start when the run on shares commenced. They were already, collectively, in a controlling position. While others would take their profit in the run-up, the men and women in this group stood firm. They had plenty of money; what they required was control, and they already had it.

The discussion at hand was how best to exploit that

control. An interesting proposal was put forth. They'd never before looked into pathology labs as a worthy investment, because there was no money in them. But now, there was a tie-in between the new testing technology and the medicines and supplements controlled by their pharmaceuticals holdings. That tie-in was the pathology labs that were in the middle of the cycle: test, evaluate, prescribe.

Since there was no money in it anyway, it would also tie in with their humanitarian mission. If they controlled the pathology labs, they could use the results of the GENT genetics testing to determine what, besides the complaint that had brought the patient in to begin with, was wrong or could go wrong because of their DNA. A value-added service, if you will, one of them remarked.

Once they had hooked a person with all his genetic shortcomings and what ailments would befall him, they would be in a position to then sell the medicine and supplements (all of which they already owned) to him. That would be the biggest industry on earth, forget about energy, water, food or any of those. Every human being on earth would want to have the complete medical cycle in one convenient doctor visit.

Before the news about GENT broke, they needed to gain control of the pathology labs; and in this instance, they were after 100% of the industry.

Their financial business concluded, they reviewed the political pies they had a thumb in and learned with satisfaction that everything was going as planned.

Chapter Twenty-Seven

ANOTHER SHORT SECRET EXPEDITION

The program to transliterate the ancient alphabet, or orthography as Joseph called it, into the current Navajo, was very simple. Before returning to Window Rock to recruit some helpers, Joseph confirmed that the program accurately 'spelled' the sounds. The trouble was that some of the words weren't in Joseph's vocabulary. He suspected that if his grandfather had been aware of this text in his day, there would have been fewer birds and fish in the transmissions of the Code Talkers. They would just have to work those words out in context to the best of their ability.

Both Sinclair and Daniel expressed disappointment that it wasn't going to be as easy as they first thought. Nicholas was less surprised, though still disappointed. He had speculated, after all, that some of the language might have been lost in the cataclysm.

Joseph was brought fully into the confidence of the group after his revelation. Clearly, there was a need for as many translators as they could find and spirit quietly into the area. Salome asked Joseph to identify his candidates without speaking to them yet. She would travel to Window Rock and personally do background checks, having persuaded Raj to put her directly in touch with his hackers again. After all, they'd worked well together during the Sword of Cyrus crisis.

When all was in readiness, Salome and Joseph would return with as many as they could fly in the little jet with them, four besides themselves. After that, the others would make their way to Boulder by bus or car, avoiding any notice by people who undoubtedly had their eyes on airline records for any unusual travel activity.

Accordingly, Joseph also took the bus back to Window Rock. Too many visits from that plane would set his people's tongues wagging. Another two weeks passed while he gathered his team, and a third while they got them in place.

It was the first week in July when the project was ready to commence. Most of the Foundation employees were off on Friday, since Independence Day was on the Saturday. Only those who didn't care whether they had a holiday to substitute for the Saturday holiday were there. The Navajo translators had been at work for only the two previous days, and were too excited about their project to stop for a three-day weekend. Joseph, now supervising a dozen young men and women, was proud of his team. As always, he compared their situation to the time when America needed his grandfather's help to win a war. His war would have been Desert Storm, but he had been in college at the time, and it hadn't occurred to him to enlist. When he met young veterans of his people from later conflicts in the Middle East, he was deeply ashamed of not having been a veteran. Now, however, he had a chance to redeem himself, even if this wasn't, strictly speaking, a war.

He remembered well the near-disaster that his new

colleagues had forestalled two years ago, when leaked information from this very building resulted in an implacable enemy gaining access to an unimaginably destructive weapon. Joseph and Salome had impressed upon each and every one of his young charges that the same could conceivably happen again if they were careless. As a result, the kids were committed to speaking only Navajo when any were out together in public. And even then in only low tones. Boulder wasn't known as a place of heavy Navajo population, but it didn't hurt to be extra-careful.

So it was that, early in the afternoon of July 3rd, Chooli Begay, a daughter of Joseph's sister, made an important discovery. It was a description of the very facility where the box with the foils had been found, as she determined by the name they'd discovered in earlier translations for the Grand Canyon, Wide Crack in the World. The description proved JR and Robert had seen only a tiny portion of the facility. Chooli took it to her uncle immediately.

"Uncle, is this something Daniel would want to know today?"

The revelation changed Daniel's plans for the weekend.

Daniel worked on Saturday, and Sunday, too. The longer this discovery was drawn out, the more likely a leak would occur.

With the discovery there were more levels to the Eighth Cycle facility that JR and Robert hadn't noticed in their rush to get back to the Foundation with the box, Daniel's attention turned to getting another expedition into the entrance canyon, this time fully equipped to explore the facility more thoroughly. The first challenge was to assure

JR and Robert they'd done the right thing. Considering what they didn't know then, which was whether it really was an Eighth Cycle site or a top-secret government site with the potential for the two to be shot as trespassers or spies, it was the only thing they could have done.

Added to that, the new exploratory team would be able to do their jobs without destructive methods. The data on the foil with the schematic showing the different levels explained the methods for gaining entry to the doors JR and Robert hadn't been able to get through before. It also showed the location of several more elevators like the main access one, but designed to carry occupants from floor to floor within the building.

Daniel's preference would have been to send in an entire team of archaeologists, but the small canyon wouldn't support the number of people he'd prefer, and the method of getting them there had to be more covert. He couldn't see sending in any number of people to make the trek JR and Robert had, but a bevy of choppers seen flying over the Grand Canyon wouldn't do, either. Park Service would never stand for anything that drew attention to the activity. If other people saw it, there would be awkward questions at best, and demands for similar access at worst. Bottom line a smaller team, going in via a smaller helicopter. There would be plenty of time for a bigger operation if what they found justified it.

Daniel's solution was to pick up the phone and call John Brideaux.

"John! Daniel Rossler, I have a proposition for you."

"I'm all ears."

"Would you still be willing to fund an expedition? And if not, at least use your influence with the Park Service again?"

"Possibly. Is this about what Stephen Matthews found? The reference to the Eighth Cycle?"

"It is. The advance team I sent in has found something of potentially as much value as the Tenth Cycle library, or even more. But John, even if you fund the expedition, the knowledge we gain has to remain part of the Foundation's assets. Will that be a problem?"

"No, Daniel, not that I can see. As long as you give me access to it, as you have the Tenth Cycle material."

"That won't be a problem."

"Then, I'm happy to fund the expedition and do whatever I can to facilitate it. I'll even provide the satellite communications for you, if you need that."

"It's a deal," Daniel said, sealing it. He was relieved. Now there'd be no need to involve the board, since it would essentially be Brideaux's expedition. Anxious to get started, he called JR in right away.

Much to Robert's disappointment, he wouldn't be needed for this trip, though Daniel hinted he had something else in mind for Robert to do once this expedition was mounted. JR would go, of course, as lead field investigator. He'd take a couple of engineers, perhaps Rebecca in case of illness or injury, an architect trained in the use of the surveying tool and one of the translators who knew the language. JR requested a metallurgist as well. The architect would draw a schematic of the facility as it now existed, aided by the engineers to analyze the uses of any machinery or other unfamiliar items they found. Daniel assumed the facility was intact, his evidence being that the elevator was still operative. Nevertheless, it was the responsible thing to do, before sending in even more people, to determine the stability of the rest of it.

Robert had noted cooking facilities for a crowd, but

hadn't tested the stove. Accordingly, food for the first week would be only slightly better than Robert and JR had taken with them. The chopper couldn't carry six people and much in the way of water and other supplies. The temperature had been stable in the portion of the facility JR and Robert explored, a pleasant seventy degrees or so, and sleeping accommodations were available. It violated Nicholas's sense of propriety for an ancient site, but they'd make use of those rather than carry in bulky tents and sleeping gear.

It was a peculiar assortment of equipment they would take, then. Flashlights, thousands of feet of the light climbing filament, a small generator to recharge their electronics, MREs that could be heated to eat or eaten cold represented the type of equipment they'd take on a camping expedition. Small, sophisticated electronic measuring and mapping devices, tablet computers, and more clothing suitable for an indoor environment than outdoors betrayed the fact of an urban-type site. JB's private jet took them to Flagstaff, where a rented helicopter – supplied by John Brideaux - would take them the rest of the way to their destination and then return to drop more food and water in a week. The entire expedition was expected to take no more than two weeks, based on the schematic in the foils. However, there were contingency plans for a longer stay if they found anything unusual, such as parts of the facility collapsed, or other levels that hadn't been cleared of most artifacts as the first level they'd found had been.

Before they set out, Daniel called one more meeting in the conference room they'd been using. The expedition team would be there, along with the people who would interpret whatever they brought back. Daniel called the meeting to order rather formally, since the larger crowd

The Skywalkers

required more order to get through the meeting with any sense of organization.

After summarizing the objective, naming the team and explaining logistics, Daniel asked if there were any questions.

Nicholas was the first to ask. "We're certain we have no Orion Societies or Sword of Cyrus terrorists hanging about this time, eh?"

Daniel laughed. "I don't know how we'd ever be certain, but to the best of my knowledge, no one's out to get us this time. It wasn't the time or place to discuss Salome's findings, or project Enigma, even as he prevaricated.

No one else had questions, so Daniel adjourned the meeting. The group would leave the following morning.

Discovering the schematic for the Grand Canyon facility had sidetracked the Eighth Cycle translators while they found and translated everything around that subject. Once the expedition launched, they went back to translating the history and science of the cycle. Like the Tenth Cycle linguists, they had to have some better than basic knowledge of science to work those sections, and it was the focus of the Foundation, so more were working on that than on history and social sciences sections.

The history translators were naturally working from early to 'modern', that is, the last century or so before the Eighth Cycle cataclysm would be translated in sequence, after the ancient. Like the Tenth Cycle, the Eighth had discovered their own ancient history, beginning with a stone age, and progressing more or less in the same sequence as the current cycle's had. From the researcher's understanding of the Tenth Cycle description of the rise and fall of each cycle's civilization, it was a typical pattern. Even fewer researchers were reassigned to reading the Eighth Cycle translations than the handful who'd been redirected to the science.

No one thought to question whether the Foundation should be looking for the cause of the Eighth Cycle cataclysm. They already knew that war had collapsed the Tenth Cycle, from the warning written in the greeting. If they'd had the manpower to put more people on it, later events may have played out differently. As it was, however, the first hints the civilization they were just beginning to discover had collapsed not on war, but on a terrible secret, weren't discovered until it was much too late.

Meanwhile, by the end of the week after the expedition left, the science translators were discovering that what they had wasn't scientific research, but the history of Eighth Cycle science. When the team lead took his theory to Sinclair, the big question arose. If there were scientific advances, where were the records of that?

Chapter Twenty-Eight

HE'D MISS THE OLD COOT

Salome had continued to monitor several prominent and wealthy men and women after her initial consultation with Luke and later conversation with him and Daniel. For a while, there was no significant activity, and she'd begun to believe she was making more of her observations than she should. After all, wealthy individuals had always been attracted to gold and the hoarding thereof. So when she saw the price of gold go up radically, she assumed that someone was trading it aggressively and it was normal.

When the price of oil dropped steeply, she tracked the reason to several OPEC countries suddenly opening their reserves at the same time, though she only had a theory about why they'd do that. However, when it went up again, just as steeply and then some, she noted with interest that some of her persons of interest had purchased investments in shale oil, while at the same time, marketing campaigns about the safety of fracking were launched. She took it as a confirmation of her theory; that OPEC had decided to flood the market with oil to drive the price down until shale oil was no longer economically viable. That their plan had failed because someone put serious money into the industry was of extreme interest.

Other economic news, coupled with these items and all tied together in that sophisticated computer program she'd had Raj build for her, sent her mental alarms jangling again. In the interface Raj had built, she could see a visual image of how movement in any of her areas of interest affected other areas she'd connected to them. The image was of a field of green grass, flat and lush when everything was calm, but tossing like an ocean under a storm when shakeups in her indices were occurring. The field had been relatively flat for the past couple of weeks, so Salome had relaxed and helped with the security preparations for the Grand Canyon expedition.

This morning she was looking at the latest breakthrough news on the medical front. A small Silicon Valley company who IPO'd last year, GENT, had discovered a way to conduct a full human genetic test. Based on an individual's specific genetic shortcomings, a specific medicine, diet and supplements regimen could be worked out. Even more exciting, medicine specific to that individual could also be worked out. This would be true preventative medicine, the ideal medical scientists had been talking and dreaming about for decades. Although it had been possible to do it for a long time, it was cost-prohibitive, not to mention the time the tests took. Those tests were currently only available for the wealthy, high-ranking politicians, key government officials and top military personnel. The new technique would make it so cheap and quick it had now been placed within reach of any man on the street.

What concerned Salome was they'd just been bought by the biggest pharmaceuticals company in the world. They said they intended to bring this technology to everyone. Salome was torn. On the one hand, this could benefit mankind in significant ways, eradicating indigenous disease and relieving human suffering. On the other hand, a retrospective look at the company's stocks showed some big trading movement for two or three days a couple of weeks ago, and then nothing until the announcement. It looked very much like insider trading, or the work of her elusive prey.

This could be another company to put on the list for close tracking, and also to find out who really owned the company since the flurry of trading two weeks ago.

In doing her deep digging, one other thing Salome stumbled across is that the acquiring firm had become heavily involved in the manufacture and distribution of immunization medication and programs in third world countries over the past few months. It wasn't so much strange that they were involved in humanitarian work – after all, many big companies were and that is their way of giving back. But what was noteworthy was they had never done it in their thirty prior years of existence. Now all of a sudden, they are doing it and making a big splash about it in the press. Just as they were making a big splash about this acquisition and its importance to humankind.

Daniel had other issues to deal with; heavy on his mind was the obvious failing health of his Grandpa. He wanted to talk to Sinclair about it. Sinclair and Grandpa were as tight as they could be without living in each other's pockets and their almost daily Irish ritual at about 5 o'clock behind the closed doors of one of their offices was a well-known secret to Daniel and the others. Daniel wondered if that ritual were responsible for the lapses in Grandpa's memory lately. He'd also want to talk to Grandma, too, but not until he had a handle on it. He didn't want her to worry. Rather than call Sinclair to him, Daniel took a walk down the hall to the translation department.

The place was like being in a beehive since the Eighth Cycle team arrived. Since the spoken word was much easier to work with, and the program had been written to read it off, there was a low buzz of sound coming from a dozen headsets along with the translators themselves unconsciously reading along, some under their breath, some out loud. It was a wonder none of the old team had complained. There'd never been that much noise before, and Daniel wondered if it was a problem despite the lack of complaint.

That was his first question to Sinclair, when he'd been invited into the office and seated.

"No, I don't think so. It's at such a low volume that it's like white noise. No one has said anything," Sinclair answered.

"Even the Tenth Cycle crew?"

'Even them. Don't worry about it. I'll take care of it if an issue arises. Was that what you came for?"

"No, actually, it's about Grandpa." Daniel noticed the shift in Sinclair's body language immediately. The other man tilted his head to the left, chin raised, and narrowed his eyes.

"What about him?" he asked.

Sinclair was hiding something, no doubt about it. Daniel

paused, wondering what he could say that would break through Sinclair's reserve. He decided on a frontal assault.

Daniel laid his cards on the table. "He's getting more forgetful, and I guess that's normal for his age. What I need to know is whether coming in for work is helping or making it worse. I can't have him heading here and getting lost, or worse, getting into an accident and hurting himself or someone else. Sinclair, you have to tell me if you've noticed him having mental lapses."

Sinclair's eyes softened and the Irish brogue that often accompanied his most heartfelt utterances came out. "You can't put him out to pasture, lad. That would kill him, it would."

"So you have noticed..."

"Aye. Occasionally. It seems to come and go."

"Do you think he could be having mini-strokes?"

Sinclair considered the question. It hadn't occurred to him that something like that could be the reason Nicholas was lucid and as sharp as ever one minute and the next would forget he'd even asked a question. If it were true, his old friend needed to see a doctor. The next one might not be so mini.

"I suppose it's possible. What are you going to do about it?"

"Now that I know I'm not just imagining things, I'm going to talk to Grandma. Thank you for admitting it, Sinclair. I know you meant to be loyal to Grandpa, but you did the right thing. This could be serious. Let's deal with it before it gets worse."

Sinclair nodded, already wondering how Nicholas would take it if his old friend ever realized he'd been part of a conspiracy that ended up with him ousted from the work he loved. Sinclair sighed. He'd miss the old coot, if he weren't here to have a nip in the afternoons. But if it meant Nicholas had a few more years left, he'd gladly make the sacrifice. Maybe Martha wouldn't mind if he went by the elder Rosslers' house for a nip before coming home each day.

Chapter Twenty-Nine

DOWN THE RABBIT HOLE

Daniel had agreed with Luke and Salome it was time to let JR, Rebecca, Robert and Raj in on Enigma. While the others understood their roles immediately, Robert focused instead on the big picture, scaring the living daylights out of him and making him wonder if he shouldn't rather pull a Crocodile Dundee and disappear into the Australian outback with some of his Aborigine friends. However, his good nature set him straight after a minute and he asked what Daniel wanted of him.

He almost hit himself in the forehead when Daniel answered. It was so obvious! Not only a geologist, but an avid spelunker, he was to thoroughly explore the cave system, mapping it, surveying potential geothermal wells, everything. When Salome explained the full extent of the plan, Robert, never having even heard the word prepper before, became as avid a prepper as he was a spelunker. What could be more fun than hiding from the bad guys in a super tricked-out cave? Except possibly doing the same thing in the Aussie Outback. But then, his friends would be here and he'd never see them again. He returned his attention to the meeting, which had moved on without him, to learn that Raj would be going with him.

Raj already knew half of what was going on, through working with Salome on the software. In addition, he'd been a prepper since before he met Daniel. It was a natural outgrowth of his paranoia, and it had proved very handy when the group had been running from the Orion Society all those years ago. Prepping to go and survive doomsday in the wilderness was not exactly how Raj had envisioned it, but once he had all the information he was fully on board, and eager to get started.

So, it was settled. Robert and Raj would go, with the usual admonition against phones and contact. Raj was allowed to tell Sushma as much as he needed to, but they would not even be allowed to switch the cell phones on. Though there was no reason to believe they were under observation yet, they would behave as though they were. They were to go, do the job and get back without anyone knowing where they were going or what they were doing. Not even that they were together. And more important than anything else, under no circumstances could anyone see them there at the Rabbit Hole.

Salome gave them all the details she and Roy had collected before - coordinates, maps, photos and all. With a twinkle in her eye, she warned them about the "herds" of bears and the mountain lions, freaking Raj out. Robert wasn't really an expert on the fauna of the region, but he obviously knew better than to believe in herds of bears. Seeing Raj's reaction set off his big, hearty Aussie laugh.

In the same spirit, Raj made plans to get him back. A good, old-fashioned snipe hunt, for example. Something he'd been sent on while attending a private prep school in upstate New York as a teenager away from his native India and on his own for the first time. Although the two knew each other from their mutual work at the Foundation, it was a small surprise to both of them how well they got along, and how enjoyable the planning for the trip was.

Taking the latest of Roy's toys and all other necessary equipment that they could get into backpacks, they set out. They planned on leaving the car several miles from their final destination and walking the rest of the way to avoid anyone's notice of their whereabouts. Since they were in the car together for several hours and then more during their hike, inevitably they ran out of things to say about prepping for disaster. After a period of silence while both of them tried to think of another mutually interesting topic of conversation, Raj tentatively brought up the subject of aliens.

Raj was well-used to ridicule from anyone he tried to talk to about his convictions that aliens had visited and were still visiting earth, and the resulting government cover-ups. It didn't matter to him. He knew what he knew. To his astonishment and pleasure, Robert allowed that it was possible. After all, the Universe is a big place, and they'd already discovered wonders no one had ever dreamed of. Why not aliens?

At last, after trekking nearly ten miles from where they left the car parked in an almost-empty camping spot parking lot, they arrived at their final destination. Robert, fit and used to such expeditions, set to work, measuring, taking pictures and a few samples. Raj rested, and then set up their rough camp inside the cave. For the next few days, they worked together to collect soil samples and rock samples and explore the entire cave system, which proved to have several exits. Serendipitously, they also found two large fresh-water pools that tested safe for drinking, in addition to some hot spots that Robert felt certain would turn out to be geothermal wells waiting to be tapped.

By the time four days had passed, they had discovered that the cave system was actually several miles in both length and width, though some passages were too narrow to be of any use except getting from room to room. Most interesting, though, was the discovery of other levels both above where the main entrance was found and below. So far, they hadn't found exterior exits from other levels. It might have been better if they had, or if they could make one, so if the Rabbit Hole were ever discovered, there'd be a back way out for the residents to escape. But for now, the cave system was more than adequate to house up to one hundred and fifty people.

"This reminds me of Carlsbad Caverns," Raj remarked to Robert.

"Really? I've wanted to see it, but haven't gotten 'round to it," Robert replied.

"Yeah. I went the first time I checked out Area 51," Raj answered. "It's close to there."

Robert ducked, looking up wildly at the cave's ceiling. "You don't suppose there are any aliens around here, do you?" He chuckled, to show Raj he was just kidding.

"You never know," Raj said, an evil twinkle in his eye. He'd just had another idea to get Robert back for the bear herd embarrassment.

When they were done, both were satisfied that Salome and Roy had found the perfect place. So remote as to be unknown, yet with sufficient space for the group to live there for many years, assuming the population stayed stable. They'd be out of sight, and after a few years, out of mind.

Of course, there would be challenges. How to feed a group that size without attracting notice from passers-by in the forest, or nosy small-town grocers, not to mention satellite photos that would easily show crops. How to heat a cavern that size in the winter. Although the temperature inside the caves was the average of the year-round temperature of the surrounding outdoors, that wasn't very warm around here.

Geothermal energy would solve that problem, but not all of them. It was time to turn the logistics over to people with special knowledge, including other preppers. Armed with a mountain of data and photos to support it, the two made their way back to Boulder. Raj never did find the time to send Robert on a snipe hunt or arrange for a visit from 'aliens.'

Chapter Thirty

IT WASN'T UTOPIA AT ALL!

JR was satisfied that no expedition he'd led before had gone quite as smoothly as this one. He liked the skeleton team, no extras to slow them down. He'd picked one of the translators as much for his size and physical fitness as for his translation abilities. Discovering the young man was an ex-Marine was a happy bonus. The engineers and architect were as fit as could be expected. One advantage of having their headquarters in Boulder was the culture of fitness in general. These men hiked, skied, and kayaked for fun, so they could be counted on to carry their own weight in any physical activity.

JR made the initial climb, since he'd done it before. This time, he had harnesses and slings, so once one of the engineers had followed him up the rope, the two of them were able to haul the rest up, along with their supplies, with the translator, Tahoma Chee, belaying them and then scrambling up under his own power. On the flight from Boulder, Tahoma had explained that no, he wasn't named for the vehicle. Rather, his name meant 'Waters' Edge' in his language. The others had quickly nicknamed him Homey.

JR had waited until everyone and everything was staged in the small alcove before opening the first set of doors. As Homey made his ascent, the others were milling about in the small space and gawping at the metal doors, remarking on their similarity to the doors in the Rossler Foundation building and joking that someone was playing a monumental joke on them. When the translator was safely up and had made his own jokes about the door, JR told them again how he wanted them to proceed.

As soon as these doors opened, they'd pick up their assigned packs of supplies and enter the antechamber, waiting for him to open the second set of doors. He warned them that the sensation of dropping would startle them, and assured them they'd slow down before coming to a halt. Once they were assembled outside the room where he and Robert had first seen the Eighth Cycle office, for lack of a better word, they would go in single file to each of the spaces where they'd drop their supplies before going immediately to the next level up to document what they found.

Single file, because he wanted to protect Rebecca in particular from anything they didn't expect, whether it was an animal that had somehow found its way inside or a gaping hole in the floor. The order of the procession would be himself, the engineers, Rebecca, the architect, the surveyor and then Homey, bringing up the rear. With a seasoned fighting man on both ends, and Rebecca right in the middle, it was as safe as he could make it for everyone but himself and Homey, but they could take care of themselves.

They'd carry snacks and water with them, but hoped to

find working restroom facilities along the way. In the evening, they'd return to the kitchen area to determine if it was operative and could be adapted for such a small group. JR was optimistic about both the restrooms and the kitchen. It would be a real pain to have to return to the canyon floor to camp each night, though they were prepared to do so if necessary.

His main concern was that, in the unvarying light, they'd get disoriented as to day and night on the outside and miss the chopper's supply run. It was almost like Paradise Valley in that regard, with the light on at all times. With plans to sleep in the dormitory, or what he'd taken to be sleeping rooms, he hoped there was a way to turn the light off in there. Sleeping under full light was possible, but not ideal.

Their plans outlined one last time for review, JR opened the elevator doors and the party descended. His knees were shaking as he remembered all too well the last time he went down with this thing. He was hoping no one could see how scared he was - he was holding Rebecca tight and she felt him shaking – she said nothing but decided to ask him later what was happening.

Several days later, the team lead for the Eighth Cycle research team followed Nicholas into his office during what had become a rare visit. Nicholas was distracted. Bess was hounding him to see a doctor, and he suspected it was because his meddling grandson had told her he was forgetting things. Nonsense. Of course he forgot things. After all, he was eighty-nine years old. Everyone forgot things, but he never forgot anything important.

The Skywalkers

As soon as he noticed his employee standing inside the door like a fool, he took out his pique on the man.

"What is it? I'm busy."

"Oh, er, I thought..."

"Spit it out, man, I don't have all day!"

"Yes, sir. Uh, one of my team is pestering me to bring something to your attention," he said. He looked as if he might bolt at any minute. Nicholas forgot he was annoyed, and tilted his head.

"Well, what is it?"

"I'd better let her tell you. I don't, I mean, it doesn't seem to be that big a deal, but she insists."

Nicholas trusted the opinion, but his curiosity had been aroused. Obviously the girl had made enough of an impression on the team lead to persuade him to mention it. "Well, send her in."

A few moments later, a pretty little thing that looked like she might still be in high school arrived. When had they started recruiting high school students?

"Good morning, Dr. Rossler," she said. What a sweet little thing! She'd be perfect for one of his grandsons. He'd forgotten where they were, but they were about this age, weren't they?

"Good morning, dear. What can I do for you?"

"I wanted to bring a passage from the Eighth Cycle material to your attention. Do you remember Brave New World, sir?"

"Of course I do. Excellent movie, excellent. Starred Gregory Peck, didn't it? Where's it playing? Maybe I'll take my wife for date night. It's a love story, right? She likes a good love story." Nicholas winked at the bewildered girl.

"Er. I'm sorry, sir, I don't understand you. It's a dystopia, sir. Are you all right?"

Nicholas had tried to smile at her and lost his balance, sitting hard into his chair. His next words were slurred. "I dun fee sssssoooo guh."

"Dr. Rossler? Oh, my God!" She ran out of the office, calling "Help! I think Dr. Rossler's having a stroke!"

If the translation room had seemed like a beehive, the research department more closely resembled a hornet's nest that had been knocked out of its tree. Half a dozen researchers ran into the office, while several more all tried to dial nine-one-one at the same time. The frightened girl sat numbly on the floor, watching as a man she'd admired for as long as she could remember became the center of a storm of activity.

Someone had thought to call Daniel, who came at a run and cleared everyone out but one of the researchers who insisted he was a volunteer EMT.

"Grandpa, you're going to be all right. We'll get you to the hospital as soon as the ambulance gets here."

The young intern's information wouldn't be heard for another couple of days, until Daniel finally was able to leave his grandfather's hospital room and ask what had happened.

On the Monday when the expedition was due to return, Daniel was back in his office and asked who'd been with his grandfather when he had his stroke. Someone had told him a girl in the department had run out of the old man's office yelling for help. He wanted to thank her for her quick action, since the doctors had told him there was every chance Grandpa would almost fully recover, though he'd have to retire for sure now.

A shaking girl was led into his office by Sarah, who'd

tracked her down in Daniel's absence and was just waiting for his return to add her thanks to his. When they'd assured the girl she was in no trouble and she'd calmed down, Daniel asked, "Did he seem to be ill when you went in?"

"No, sir. My team lead went in and told him I wanted to talk to him, and then I went in. He said good morning and what could he do for me. I wanted to tell him about a passage I read in the Eighth Cycle material that reminded me of this book." Here, she hesitated. The last time she'd named the book, it apparently gave Dr. Rossler a stroke. She didn't want that to happen again.

Sarah said, "Go on, dear. What book?"

"Uh, it was a book I studied in high school, called Brave New World. Do you know it?"

Daniel nodded, still intent on hearing how Nicholas came to have his stroke. Sarah frowned.

"Well, this passage about the height of the Eighth Cycle, it sounded like that. I mean, everyone was all happy and well fed and stuff. But they had forced birth control. Like Nazis or something. Anyway, I asked Dr. Rossler about it and he started talking crazy, like, he thought it was a movie, with Greg Pickler or someone, and he thought it was a love story. Then he made this horrible face and fell down in his chair, and his face went weird and I couldn't understand what he was saying." By now, the girl was in tears and shaking again. Daniel had turned white.

Sarah put her arm around the girl to calm her, but she was frowning even harder. "Daniel, do you think it was the shock?"

"The shock of what?" he asked, still focused on the awful story.

"Daniel!" Sarah spoke sharply, to bring him back to the present.

He gave a brief shudder and looked at her more closely. "What?"

"Do you understand what she just said? The Eighth Cycle wasn't what we thought. It wasn't Utopia at all! It was a police state. How did they bring the whole world under that? Something's dreadfully wrong with this."

Chapter Thirty-One

SOMETHING WRONG WITH EIGHTH CYCLE

During the second expedition, the engineers and architect had explored six of the nine spokes of corridors fanning out from what they thought of as the back of the administrative building, since entrance was always gained from the elevators at the 'front'. Although they found many rooms and surmised the purpose from the size and fittings, the rooms had been cleared of anything they could carry. The last three corridors proved difficult to get into, as the entry doors at the admin building end were resistant to being opened. However, in the meanwhile, the translation team had found records concerning these corridors, and the method of entry was included.

The second expedition found five more metal boxes in a room in the third level, which they carefully secured and packed and took back with them. Now they knew that there were medical and communications facilities on the second and third levels, from records found in the earlier scientific reports. The most exciting thing to come out of the whole site so far was casual references everywhere to a healthy lifespan of up to one-hundred and fifty years. Their most important target for this expedition was the medical data.

Roy, in particular, was ecstatic. The Eighth Cycle had been highly knowledgeable about nano-technology, his primary field. The five metal boxes JR brought back, each filled with foils, turned up some very exciting information for him. On a number of the foils he found the symbols he'd come to recognize as the word for nanotech. The Navajo translated it as 'tiny magic', áłííł yázhí a phrase they'd had to make up because their own language had no such concept. Only when Sinclair had looked at the context had they even come close to understanding what it meant, and that was when they'd made up the phrase.

All Roy could think of was digging in and building everything he could, for testing purposes. He'd need a whole team of assistants, but that didn't faze him. Daniel had assured him there'd be money for all of it, as licensees vied for access to the technology. All this he constantly babbled to Salome, who sometimes wished for the days when he was more taciturn.

Salome's part in the celebration was short-lived, though. Sarah came to her about a week after Nicholas Rossler's stroke, with a concern brought up by one of the young research interns. Salome didn't blame her for being spooked by it. After all, she had her own concerns.

She stopped by a bookstore on her way home the night after Sarah told her about the girl, and picked up a copy of

Brave New World. It had been published originally in 1932, eighty-eight years ago. Considering Nicholas had only been a baby of one year old when it came out, Salome had her private doubts about the theory being the reason for his stroke. She would find the girl and reassure her tomorrow. Rumor had it that the poor kid was afraid to say anything to anyone now, having been in the room and talking to Nicholas when he collapsed.

Sinclair took a personal interest in the foils from the metal box JR had brought back in May. Now that several of the foils had been translated and indexed, he had an idea that what the box contained was a fraction of the history of the cycle. Wondering about the selection, he began haunting the cubicles of the Navajo translators, asking them to give him an idea of what they were translating at the moment. The records seemed to cover mostly the height of the civilization, very little about the rise from the ashes of the Seventh Cycle.

The plan had been to translate each foil in order, though the dozen or so translators were working on them in batches. Now Sinclair began pestering Raj to do all the computer work for each one, so he could have one translator dip into them from the back to the front. He had a hunch they weren't working fast enough, going the other direction. Something was bothering him, though he didn't know what.

Sinclair visited Nicholas in the rehabilitation facility religiously. What he really wanted to do was bring in a wee nip of Jameson's and see if that didn't help Nicholas as much as all the fol-de-rol medicines they gave him. Daniel had threatened to have him banned from the hospital if he did, so, grumbling that the doctors didn't know good medicine when they saw it, he agreed.

One day, when Nicholas brought up the work himself, Sinclair decided it was safe to talk about it. There'd been some speculation that something one of the researchers said had contributed to his stroke, so no one talked to Nicholas about work. Until now. He seemed ready. Sinclair had learned to understand the slurred speech, so he had no trouble with Nicholas's words when he asked the question. The trouble was with the meaning.

"Does that girl still think something's wrong with the Eighth Cycle?" he asked.

"What girl?"

"One of my researchers," Nicholas said. His eyes flashed with frustration. It had to be difficult to make himself clear, Sinclair thought. Patiently, he tried again.

"I'm not sure who you're talking about, old friend. Do you have any notes about it in your office?"

Nicholas shook his head, sighed, and tried again. "She said, that day. Something wrong with Eighth Cycle."

Now Sinclair was a bit worried. Was Nicholas talking about the day of his stroke? He didn't want to bring it up. But Nicholas was insistent on getting an answer. "That day," he repeated.

"Do you mean the day you had your spell?" Sinclair asked, hesitating to name the stroke for what it was, in case it upset Nicholas. However, the old man was made of tougher stuff.

"Yes, day of stroke," he answered. "Girl, telling me something wrong with Eighth Cycle."

There it was, confirmation that something a researcher

said contributed. Sinclair didn't want to pursue it. Another stroke might kill his old friend.

"It's okay. We're learning all about it. They had it good at the end. Nothing was wrong."

"Why ca-cly?" Nicholas demanded. Cackle? What did he mean? Sinclair shook his head, indicating he hadn't understood.

"Crash! Why crash, cycle?"

Oh, Sinclair realized. Why did they have their cataclysm, if everything was so wonderful? Good question, and one no one had thought to ask, as far as Sinclair knew.

"I'm not sure. We haven't gotten that far in the records." Unable to resist, Sinclair asked a dangerous question. "What did the girl say?"

"Brave New World. Good movie," Nicholas answered.

Sinclair remembered a movie being made, but didn't think it had high ratings. "Do you mean it was a good book?" he asked.

"Yes, yes, good book. Bad society."

That was true. Sinclair gave a shudder. Big brother watching you, and all that. People had been saying that about the internet for a few years now. Then it clicked.

"The researcher told you the Eighth Cycle reminded her of that book?"

"Yes. True?" Nicholas looked worried, so Sinclair hastened to reassure him.

"Oh, I'm sure that wasn't true. But I'll look into it. Will that make you feel better?"

"Feel just fine. Let's have a drink," Nicholas said, grinning.

"Next time I come, I'll try to sneak in a flask, old friend. You be good and don't harass these young nurses, okay?

They aren't good for your blood pressure anyway. Now, I need to get back to work."

As soon as he left Nicholas, Sinclair went straight to Daniel.

"I need to know which of the researchers was with your granddad when he had his stroke. He's just told me what she said. If it's true, it may give us a hint of what JR should be looking for."

Surprised, Daniel gave him the name. "What did she say?"

"She may have hit on the key to their Utopia," Sinclair answered. Privately, he thought, 'or dystopia.' He wasn't ready to reveal his hunch. It sounded too pessimistic, especially when everyone was marveling at the perfect society. With the hint of extra longevity, many speculated that it was a natural extension of age and therefore longer productivity, even wisdom, might be the answer to the perfection. But, what if the perfection was the result of some kind of social engineering?

Sinclair went from Daniel's office to the research department and found the girl. After assuring her that she wasn't in any trouble, Sinclair insisted she follow him to the canteen, where he bought her a soda and asked what she'd said to Nicholas the day of his stroke.

Tears rolled down her cheeks as she remembered the old man's reaction. "I'm afraid to tell you," she whispered.

"Don't be afraid. I'm prepared, and I think I know anyway. Besides, I'm perfectly healthy. It's not going to shock me into a stroke."

With fresh tears at the implication that she'd caused Nicholas to have a stroke, she barely managed to stutter out the words. "I t-t-told h-him they sounded l-like." She took another deep breath as Sinclair waited for her to finish her sentence. "L-like B-Brave New World," she finally finished.

Sinclair sat back. "You mean that a central government was controlling everything? That's what the Eighth Cycle material reminded you of?"

She nodded. "I didn't mean to upset him."

"Don't worry lass. Nicholas was sick before you said that. It was only a matter of time before something happened, and at least this way you were there to get him some help immediately. He's going to be fine."

"I'm so glad. I really like Dr. Rossler."

"I need to ask you why you told him you thought the Eighth Cycle was like Brave New World."

"He thought it was a movie," she said, twisting her hands together.

"Yes, but his brain was a little mixed up. I'm more interested in what you thought. And whether you still think so."

"I do! I mean, not everything was alike, but they like, controlled all the information. It's all in the records. You don't even have to read between the lines. This guy, I guess the one that left the foils, left a letter that said it." She'd become very earnest, now that someone was listening to her.

"A what? A letter, you say?" Sinclair couldn't believe his ears. How had this been missed?

"Yes, sir. A letter that was a warning for whoever was left, he said. That's what I was trying to tell Dr. Rossler, when..."

"Yes, of course. And did you bring it to anyone else's attention?"

"I tried. My lead said to move on to something more

concrete. And of course, Dr. Rossler hasn't been here." She frowned. "Should I have tried harder?"

Sinclair thought maybe she should have, but he wouldn't put that guilt on her. She'd been through enough trauma when she witnessed the stroke, and it was really the team lead who'd dropped the ball.

"No, lass, you did fine. I'm glad I've asked, though. Do you think you could find the letter for me?"

"Yes, sir. I kept a copy in my cubie. Do you want it?"

"Aye that I do. Shall we go and get it?"

Chapter Thirty-Two

WE GAVE AWAY OUR BLOOD

The young researcher, whose name Sinclair now learned, was Aubra Dennis, eagerly led the way to her cubicle. On the desk space were a workstation monitor, wireless keyboard and some knickknacks that revealed her interest in Ancient Egypt and cats. Sinclair couldn't understand why everyone was so enamored of cats these days. Pesky beasts wouldn't follow commands and weren't good for protection; what good were they, anyway? He suppressed his opinion, though, as Aubra picked one of her figurines up and handed him the pages underneath. Without conscious thought, he took the rolling chair in the cubicle and sat down to read. Aubra found an unoccupied chair in a nearby spot and pulled it near to wait.

The translation read:

Person of the Future,

I have very little time. I beg you to read this letter entirely, I beg you to heed the warnings in this letter and to take all action to stop this evil from happening ever again. I beg you to not ignore this – we have met our end because we did not pay attention, we gave away our freedom, we gave away our blood. We became slaves because of our unwillingness to give up our decadent life of luxury and carelessness for our fellow humans.

The end is near and I do not know whether I will be able to complete my task. With this letter, I leave a brief history of the end times of our cycle, so that in the event someone from a distant future, or a distant world, may find our remains and wonder, they shall be warned. You will find our history locked up in The Room of Knowledge on the 4th floor of this place of all evil. I beg you to find it and to read it and to learn about us.

Our world has developed out of the ashes of the cycle before us, after their destruction by fire from the sky. Our world has long been stable, it was perfect, with no dissent, no war, no disease and no poverty such as in the old days. We should be happy, but we are not. We have no freedom, we are oppressed, we are controlled because they have our blood. I beg you again read and be warned! The Council of Selected provides us with all our bodily needs but they own our spirits and our thoughts. Our happiness, our being belongs to them. We are their servants, because they own our blood.

Within my lifetime, a movement has arisen to throw off the yoke of thought control imposed by The Council of The Selected. At first, known dissenters were taken away and re-educated, to return and recant their subversive opinions. As more dissenters appeared, a mysterious illness began to befall them and many died. A fearsome beast was released against all citizens. We learned to guard our words carefully, lest we be among the victims, yet growing displeasure with our way of life made more and more speak out as more and more died.

That was where the translation ended. Sinclair glanced at Aubra, his brows raised. "I see what you mean about Brave New World. But where is the rest of the letter?"

Aubra responded, "It is here on this disk. After what happened to Dr. Rossler, I was too afraid to continue with the translation. Look at what happened to him!"

"My dear please don't blame yourself," Sinclair said. He continued, "Dr. Rossler did not have his stroke because of what you showed him that day. The doctors have confirmed that he has been having mini-strokes for a long time, but on that day he had a major one. You had absolutely nothing to do with it. It has been building up for a long time. Please stop beating yourself up about it."

Sinclair had a bad feeling about all of this. Daniel needed to hear it, in detail, along with the partial translation of the letter. He took the disk from Aubra, thanked her for her excellent work and reassured her again that she had nothing to do with Nicholas' condition. And then, he headed for Daniel's office.

Sinclair had seen many ancient texts warning of global disaster, including the ones in the Tenth Cycle library. Where once he might have found such a letter the product of a paranoid mind, he had no such feeling about this one. How unfortunate that it had gone unrecognized since the girl, Aubra, found it, because of Nicholas's stroke and her fear of repercussions. However, what was done was done.

If this letter was what it purported to be, they had no time to waste, they had to get the rest of it translated immediately.

Daniel was immersed in something he would later have no memory of when Sinclair reached his office. As he looked up at his visitor, the look on Sinclair's craggy features alarmed him.

"Sinclair, you look like you've seen a ghost."

"Aye, and I may have. The ghost of the Eighth Cycle," Sinclair answered, with a grimace Daniel took to be an attempt at a grin.

"Sit down and tell me what you're talking about, old man. You're scaring me."

Sinclair sat heavily. "You recall I went to talk to the girl who was there with your granddad when he fell ill?"

"Of course."

"Did you talk to her, afterward?"

"I did, yes. And Sarah, too. Why do you ask?"

"Did she not tell you, lad, she'd found some disturbing material about the Eighth Cycle?"

"Yes, she said it reminded her of Brave New World. That bothered Sarah, as I recall."

"As well it should. Did she show you the letter?"

Daniel's interest sharpened. "What letter?"

"Another letter from the man who left us these records, I suppose. In any case, it was a dire warning. Here, here's a transcript." Sinclair handed the paper to Daniel, who read it quickly.

"What's all this about blood?" he asked. "And where's the rest?"

"The wee lass was frightened to continue, after what happened to Nicholas. You agree it is important?"

"Hell, yes, it's important! We need the rest of the translation right away. But, Sinclair."

Sinclair had already risen from his chair and was

preparing to leave and handle the emergency right now. "Yes?"

"Let's keep this under wraps. I don't want anyone going off half-cocked. Could you fill Joseph in and have him do it himself? Make him understand it's eyes-only, okay?"

"Sure, Daniel."

Sinclair was privy to almost everything going on, but he hadn't seen the latest news from Salome. Something about what she'd most recently reported to him was bothering him. He wanted to know what it was before a wider alarm was spread.

"And, one more thing, Sinclair. Get with Raj and make sure there are no other copies of that, either translated or untranslated, on anyone else's desk or workstation, okay?"

"You've got it. Anything else?"

"No, I'll fill in Salome myself; see if she has anything to say about it. Thanks for bringing it to my attention, Sinclair."

The older man saluted Daniel like a military man and hurried away. Daniel gathered his thoughts before getting up and walking to Salome's office.

Sinclair took his mission as urgent and called both Joseph and Raj to the small conference room to show them a copy of the letter and convey Daniel's directions.

Raj, seemed to take it in stride, and left immediately to carry out Daniel's wishes. He wouldn't be able to vouch for anything they had printed out on paper — that would be Salome's job. But Sinclair was satisfied that he'd make damn sure not a shred or particle of it would remain anywhere but where it was supposed to be; on the servers or on Joseph Yazzie's personal workstation. And the former would be encrypted so no one else could accidentally access it.

When Raj had left, Sinclair turned his attention to Yazzie, whose expression was troubled.

"What are you thinking, my friend?"

"This is very disturbing, Sinclair. Once I translate it, I may need a ceremony to restore my spiritual balance."

Sinclair looked at Joseph in surprise. "I thought you were a Christian, Joseph."

"I am, but nothing in the Christian faith requires me to abandon those of my people's beliefs that go hand in hand with Christianity. An Enemy Way ceremony helps remove negative emotions caused by war or other trauma, and restores balance. Just as Catholic confession offers absolution for sin, our ceremonies return us to a state of harmony with the Creator."

Sinclair hadn't been to Mass in years, but the words resonated, even though he suspected the Church wouldn't necessarily agree with Yazzie regarding heathen ceremonies. He let it go, but asked, "What makes you think you'll be that damaged by translating the rest of this letter?"

"Revelation 13:16-18 And he causeth all, both small and great, rich and poor, free and bond, to receive a mark in their right hand, or in their foreheads:

And that no man might buy or sell, save he that had the mark, or the name of the beast, or the number of his name.

Here is wisdom. Let him that hath understanding count the number of the beast: for it is the number of a man; and his number is Six hundred threescore and six."

A shiver passed through Sinclair as Joseph's voice fell away. If anything in the Bible could have reminded him of the police state found in the novel Brave New World, this was it. Some kind of mark imposed on everyone who would enter commerce and provide for their families summed up nicely the understanding that Biblical times peoples would have had of a police state. Could the well-ordered society described in the Eighth Cycle material that had so far been translated have been bought at the cost of personal freedom? It was a chilling thought.

While Raj was getting started on his practical chore and Joseph was scaring the daylights out of Sinclair, Daniel had made haste to Salome's office, where he handed her his copy of the letter. His sense was that, while important, the letter didn't change anything that would pose an immediate threat to the Foundation, or indeed to society in general.

Nevertheless, he wanted Salome's take on it, and to see if she could identify the cause of his strange feeling about it. While his rational mind told him there was no threat, his subconscious insisted there was something he was missing. If it were a security threat, Salome would be able to identify it, he had no doubt.

"What do you make of this, Salome," he said, holding the paper with the translation out for her to take. "It's a translation of a letter from the Eighth Cycle materials."

Salome took it and read it quickly, then frowned and read it again. She looked up at Daniel with troubled eyes.

"What's all this about giving away their blood? The writer repeats it several times, so it must be important. But what does it mean? Where's the rest?"

"The girl who translated this took it to Grandpa on the day he had his stroke. In fact, she was in his office at the time. She was so afraid of what had happened that she buried this and didn't want to translate the rest of the passage."

Salome's eyes grew round. "So… she thought this was what caused the stroke?"

"Yes, apparently. We've assured her it wasn't this, but in any case, it just came to my attention. What is it that bothers you?"

"Something about all these references to blood. I almost think… But, no, I'm just being paranoid. It's nothing."

"I have the same feeling, that there's something I'm missing. I can't quite grasp it."

"So, what are you thinking, Daniel. What do you want me to do about this?"

"I don't know. Maybe nothing. But, I can't help thinking that it's relevant to now, and to your study of what's going on in the financial and industrial worlds. Somehow, it's all tied in with stuff I've been mulling over for a while now."

"What kind of stuff?"

"How dependent we are on being connected to electronic networks."

Salome encouraged him with a gesture, and he began to tell her of the thoughts he'd been having even before she brought the behind-the-scenes wheeling and dealing in financial markets to his attention.

The seeds were sewn early in the century. A computer on every desktop was the goal. Thanks to advancing technology and the tendency toward smaller and smaller devices, it took only a decade to reach the goal in every modernized country. By then, a teenager could easily afford a device the size of an old-fashioned matchbox or smaller that would store recordings of every song they ever bought, far more than their fathers and mothers had ever owned on the bulkier vinyl recordings, tapes, even CDs.

By then, every busy adult and many teens had cell phones as well. They were constantly connected to each other by messages that seemed to have taken a step back, technologically speaking. Text messaging was the realm of the young, until their elders recognized the only way to speak to their kids was to learn how to type on a tiny keyboard - with their thumbs. The dominant cell phone company soon heard the cries of men with bulky fingers and developed a voice recognition application, so the message could be heard, converted to text and sent to the recipient, all if the speaker could make the application understand his or her peculiar accent or speech habits.

Not to be outdone, the next biggest cell service provider developed a better one. Only five years ago, it wasn't uncommon for every person in a family, from a two-year-old to the very elderly, to be connected to mass communications by no fewer than three devices--their cell phones, portable computers in either laptop or tablet configurations, and usually still a desktop, though those were beginning to be relegated to stuffy offices.

Daniel had lived through that era, boy and man. Only now was he able to articulate his concerns about it to Salome.

"People have stopped talking to each other in person, Salome. Instead, we sit across from each other at the dinner table with cell phones in hand, texting, surfing the internet, or playing video games."

Salome smiled. She was a couple of years younger than Daniel. None of this was new to her, nor very alarming. "Go on."

"You know, even though I'm not of the generation when children played outside all day, my parents made us go outside. Everyone then was concerned because children were joining the obesity epidemic. Kids who hadn't seen the latest viral YouTube video were made fun of — it even happened to my brothers and me. No one was speaking out about it. Even those who occasionally thought it was an issue weren't willing to give up their own electronic tethers. It set us up for what's happening now."

"What do you mean?" she asked.

"You've been telling me there may be some insidious force behind these trends. We may be the only people on Earth who have any idea that a handful of the wealthiest men in the world are quietly destabilizing every long-held value in their respective countries."

Daniel was referring to the media undermining Great Britain's royal family by printing stories about the future heir romping in bed with someone other than his wife. Of course, it had long been tradition in the media to undermine American confidence in their elected leaders by, among other things, spreading rumors on the internet that the President hadn't been born in the US as required, or the Secretary of State was a lesbian. The insidiousness was compounded by the same media then printing articles assuring the public that those things weren't true, prompting cries of cover-up, which further undermined confidence.

The truth or lack thereof wasn't the point. The point was that no one could believe anything they saw in print or even in a photo anymore, but everyone believed anything they were told often enough, with or without facts to back it up. What could have been the greatest boon to mankind, an archive of every bit of human knowledge, free for the asking, had become the greatest disinformation machine in the history of mankind.

"Salome, don't you agree that this environment is ripe for enslaving the minds of ninety percent of the earth's inhabitants by those who would exploit it for their own ends?"

"I do. It's happened so slowly, compared to the growth of technology that almost no one noticed."

"No one but you, Salome."

Daniel resumed his rant. "It's dangerous, having everyone think the same way."

They agreed: It was an election year in the US. All year, the news had been full of campaign rhetoric, accusations, mudslinging and more and more bitter recriminations by candidates who were behind in the polls. They accused the dominant party of lies, but the more they did so, the more their approval ratings sank.

After exhausting the subject, which was easy to do since there was no argument - each agreed with the other's assessment, they also agreed that there was still no immediate threat they could identify. But both of them were even more worried now about the upcoming election.

Chapter Thirty-Three

I PRAY YOU FIND IT

Four hours after he had returned to his own office, two people who could very well have been ghosts, walked into Daniel's office without knocking.

Sinclair said without preamble, "Daniel, we have a serious problem, have a look at this." He handed Daniel the piece of paper containing the full translation.

Daniel read:

Person of the Future,

I have very little time. I beg you to read this letter entirely, I beg you to heed the warnings in this letter and to take all action to stop this evil from happening ever again. I beg you to not ignore this – we have met our end because we did not pay attention, we gave away our freedom, we gave away our blood. We became slaves because of our unwillingness to give up our decadent life of luxury and carelessness for our fellow humans.

The end is near and I do not know whether I will be able to complete my task. With this letter, I leave a brief history of the end times of our cycle, so that in the event someone from a distant future, *or a distant world, may find our remains and wonder, they shall be warned. You will find our history locked up in The Room of Knowledge on the 4th floor of this place of all evil. I beg you to find it and to read it and to learn about us.*

Our world has developed out of the ashes of the cycle before us, after their destruction by fire from the sky. Our world has long been stable, it was perfect, with no dissent, no war, no disease and no poverty such as in the old days. We should be happy, but we are not. We have no freedom, we are oppressed, we are controlled because they have our blood. I beg you again read and be warned! The Council of Selected provides us with all our bodily needs but they own our spirits and our thoughts. Our happiness, our being belongs to them. We are their servants, because they own our blood.

Within my lifetime, a movement has arisen to throw off the yoke of thought control imposed by The Council of The Selected. At first, known dissenters were taken away and re-educated, to return and recant their subversive opinions. As more dissenters appeared, a mysterious illness began to befall them and many died. A fearsome beast was released against all citizens. We learned to guard our words carefully, lest we be among the victims, yet growing displeasure with our way of life made more and more speak out as more and more died.

I am among the few left who dissent and I will be dead soon. The Council of Selected has lost control of the beast; no one will survive. All I have left to do is to leave you this sad and dark message. I hope you will learn from our mistakes and build a better future for your children than we did.

In The Room of Darkness on the 5th floor of this place of all evil will you find the beast. You MUST destroy it; you MUST destroy everything that mentions it. But you must be careful — you must handle it with great care – others have tried to destroy it and were killed by it. In the room with the beast you will find the book that tells you how it works and in The Room of Knowledge on the

4th floor of this place of all evil you will find more about it. Don't touch the beast until you have learned how it works, otherwise you will surely die.

My time is here. The beast knows my blood, it knows my name, and the invisible messenger of my death from the sky is on its way now. I have but a few breaths left.

It is not to be I cannot get to the beast before my death, we are all doomed.

Reaching the last paragraph, barely able to hold the piece of paper in his visibly shaking hand Daniel read the rest of it aloud.

Heed me, person of the future. You must seek the beast in this place of evil and you MUST destroy it. I pray you find it.

The blood drained from Daniel's face, "Oh my God!"

During several speechless moments, Daniel was released from his psychological paralysis when Sarah walked in and saw the three of them looking like death.

"Daniel! Darling, what in the world is the matter?" she cried. Daniel wordlessly handed her the letter. Sarah read it, her face turning whiter as her eyes traveled down the page. When she'd finished, she sunk into a chair. "Dear God what now?"

Despite his shock, Daniel was the first to recover his composure. "We need the whole team in here now, to address this new danger at the site. Matthews, too. We need all the brains we can get."

Even though everyone looked up to Daniel as their leader, the Rossler Foundation and in fact the inner circle even before the formal group was founded, had always operated more by consensus than by fiat. The inner circle had grown since the beginning, and sadly, one was missing; Nicholas. Yet, Daniel was comforted by the knowledge that he had the best minds he'd been able to gather around him in the past eight years to help him decide on the best course of action.

10 minutes after Daniel sent for his team, they were all in the conference room and had heard Daniel read the letter aloud with varying degrees of shock.

JR broke the silence first. "Well, what is this beast?"

"That's just it," Daniel replied. "It doesn't really say. Although I tend to think it isn't really a beast in the literal sense."

"Whatever it is, we need to track it down and destroy it," JR said, full of the conviction of youth, and the fire of a Marine. Once a Marine, always a Marine, he was fond of saying. "Send me in with a few buddies I can call up. We'll handle it."

"Now wait. I get the impression it isn't going to be as easy as kicking down the door and shooting the shit out of it," Daniel objected. JR smiled at Daniel's uncharacteristic vernacular.

Daniel went on.

"This letter has cautioned us not to tamper with the thing unless we know how it works. I suggest we don't go off half-cocked. Let's get all the information we can get and then plan in detail what we're going to do and how we're going to do it. That is, if we are even the ones to do it."

JR looked around the room. Everyone was avidly following the conversation between the brothers, and no one looked as if he or she might have a contribution just yet. He answered, "Yes, you're right about that not going in there half-cocked but let me tell you one thing, we *will* be the ones doing it. In the past we were always the ones doing it. Yes, we had help from others but we were always part of it. You'll see — this is going to be no different."

Daniel nodded in acknowledgement. "Good, I'm glad we agree on the most important part for the moment. Now, let's start by looking at what we know and what we don't. We know how the 8th Cycle ended but we don't know what this beast is that apparently ended it for them.

We know where the beast is located and we know where to find its instruction manual - The Room of Darkness, whatever that is, on the 5th floor. No one, and I repeat, JR, no one, is going to attempt to destroy anything until we have translated and read that instruction manual. "

Daniel glanced sternly around the room, noting the nods of approval before continuing. He hoped someone would have something to contribute soon, or he might as well have made all these decisions by himself. "All right. Does anyone have any ideas about this Room of Knowledge on the 4th floor where we're supposed to find more information about the beast? Why do you suppose they have the user manual and the 'more information', whatever that is, in two different places?

Salome raised her hand. Daniel acknowledged her, "Salome, we don't stand on ceremony in these brainstorming sessions. Jump in."

She smiled. "Okay, well, we can't know for sure until we find out what the other information is, but sometimes highly sensitive intel is kept in different places so that no one person knows everything about it. Like a security measure."

"Oh, okay. Good! That gives us an idea to work with, and it sounds plausible here. If this beast is so dangerous it could bring down an entire cycle, no wonder they wouldn't have wanted all the knowledge placed in the hands of one person, or even a small group of people. Now, what else?"

"The place of all evil," Sarah said. A buzz of whispered conversations among two here and two there had broken out, making Sarah's soft voice all but indistinguishable from the background noise. Attuned to her voice, however, Daniel heard that she'd said something.

"Please, everyone. Let's stay focused here. Sarah, what did you say?"

"*the place of all evil,*" she quoted. "I guess that's the Canyon site?"

Hearing no dissent, Daniel stood. "All right, throw those ideas out for discussion, people. And remember the only stupid idea is the one you did not tell us about. Anything is welcome," Nodding at Raj, he continued, "Even alien theories. Nothing is out of order."

Salome turned to Rebecca, "Rebecca what do you make of those two references to blood? What had the author been trying to tell us?"

Rebecca shrugged. "Who knows? Maybe it's just a figure of speech. Do we know enough about their language to know colloquialisms?" Sinclair shook his head.

Robert looked at Roy and then at Raj. "What do you guys think the writer meant by '*invisible messenger of my death from the sky*'? Some sort of death ray? An alien weapon? A satellite weapon? Invisible? Could it mean some sort of nano technology somehow?"

Raj put his palms up in protest. "Slow down, my friend! One question at a time."

"Yes, it could be nano technology. We know from the Sword of Cyrus situation it's possible to send nano-poisons and nano-bots." Roy said, oblivious to the looks of consternation that appeared as soon as he mentioned the last evil group they'd been up against. Roy got up and strolled to the whiteboard, in lecture mode. "Those things are invisible to the naked eye, and could easily kill people or make them sick enough to wish they were dead."

Not to be outdone, Raj hurried to put his two cents' worth in. "But it could also be things like invisible rays in the electromagnetic spectrum, alien technology that could kill you."

The room erupted in protest then, with JR's voice winning the escalating volume contest. "If aliens were killing people fifty-thousand years ago, why aren't they still here, killing people now?" He and Raj were glaring at each other in what at any other time would have been comical - the six-foot-ten ex-Marine looming over a slight, five-foot ten computer nerd. Daniel decided it was time to rein it in.

"All right, I think we're agreed that there are a quite a few options, but we can only think as far as our current technology understands. There could very well be something we have no knowledge of yet, with our current understanding of science.

"Are we agreed that our first move is to locate this user manual for the beast as well as the Room of Knowledge? And is there any value in continuing to translate the material we already have?"

"Aye, there is value in that." Sinclair had something to say at last. "We know what the word for the beast sounds like and looks like in the text. Why not have Raj input the rest of the foils immediately and search for that word? Then all the translators could focus on translating every bit of information we have on it, if any, while someone retrieves the user's manual and the information from the Room of Knowledge, which I take to be a library."

The others looked at him in astonishment. His affected Irish accent, which he'd started with as he began to speak, had disappeared entirely in the longest speech anyone remembered him making recently.

Daniel took the ensuing silence as an opportunity. "Okay, I think that's a great plan. JR, you and Robert will go through the drawings of the facility we have so far from the architects. Use the information we have collected about the structure and try to find the 4th and 5th floors to see if the entire floor has been mapped and all rooms accounted for. Let's narrow down the rooms you'll have to open and go through when you go to retrieve the items Sinclair has suggested."

He paused only to take a deep breath, then continued, "Raj, you'll throw every bit of computing power you have or can acquire in a hurry at the disks we have now. You know what to do next to create those sound files and store them in a database you can query to find anything that sounds remotely like the words for 'The Beast'. Then hand that off to Sinclair's team."

Raj had been nodding since Daniel had said 'you know what to do next'. He was practically jumping out of his skin to get started, and waited only until Daniel finished out of politeness, before bolting from the room to get started, with Sinclair right behind him. After all, someone needed to show Raj the text for the word and create a sample sound file with which to compare the data on the disks.

Daniel was speaking only to Matthews at this point, but continued his thought for the benefit of the others. "Sinclair, Joseph and Stephen will work out a system with the translators to translate and transcribe that information at the best possible speed."

Salome took over at this point. "I'll fill Luke in on everything we have so far and if he thinks it necessary, we'll revisit the entire Foundation's security setup. This information needs to be protected and secured at all cost." She didn't state the obvious, that from this moment on, their lives were in danger, more so than on any other occasion before. Because, whatever the beast was, someone with monomaniacal aspirations would stop at nothing to get it if the facts were known.

Daniel took it on himself to inform John Brideaux. Since he'd been sponsoring this investigation from the beginning when Matthews discovered it, he needed to be brought up to speed. Daniel would also give him a chance to say if he was willing to continue to fund what came next — a new expedition to go and find The Beast and destroy it.

Matthews kept his own counsel. He, too, owed John Brideaux a report, but evidently everyone here had forgotten it. And if he knew John Brideaux, he would bet a goodly amount that destruction wasn't what Brideaux would want for this artifact. No, Brideaux would more than likely want to own it, just as he wanted to own every other unique and arcane artifact he'd ever heard of. But, could he safeguard what was apparently a very dangerous artifact? It wasn't Matthews' place to ask, only to do as Brideaux directed him.

Chapter Thirty-Four

OUR TIME HAS COME

Daniel located John Brideaux via his cell number. Rather than in his office, Brideaux was fortuitously in Salt Lake City. As soon as Daniel told him there was an important matter to discuss, but not over the phone, Brideaux agreed to fly to Boulder by private helicopter. It would take about two hours, during which time Daniel prepared copies of all the evidence they'd obtained.

Brideaux could barely contain his true reactions to the letter Daniel handed him. Now and then, he glanced at Rossler and shook his head, or raised his eyebrows. Could this be true? Why hadn't Matthews yet reported it? If this letter wasn't a hoax, he and his compatriots were on the verge of world dominion and a chance at peace for all human beings. It was an extraordinary opportunity.

Brideaux finished the letter, looked at Daniel and smiled. "Daniel what the hell is this? I'd hate to think you summoned me here on the double over some sort of hoax"

"No, John, not at all. This came from the files we found in the artifact our team brought back from the Grand

Canyon site. We've had it checked by our best translators. It's as real as the nose on your face.

"I'm a busy man, Daniel. I can't run around after fairytales."

"I'm telling you, it is not a hoax. Or, if it is, then the entire site is, and a multi-billion dollar one at that. But there's technology there we don't understand yet. I'd bet my life we're looking at an Eighth Cycle site with a huge problem in it," Daniel replied.

"I agree. If this is all true, and I am still trying to believe it is true, we have some goddamn serious fuckin' shit on our hands." Brideaux noted with satisfaction that his language had thrown Daniel for a loop. Off-balance, Rossler wouldn't question his own reactions. He continued, "We need to get that fuckin' beast and destroy it, like yesterday. It must not be allowed to leave that canyon, ever."

Visibly relieved, Daniel said, "That's why I asked for the face to face meeting. I believe it should be top priority, and we have already thrown all the manpower we have at it. Can we count on you to keep on funding this?"

Brideaux answered without hesitation. "Yes of course! I never do a job halfway. What do you need from me? Name it, and I'll get it or fund your acquisition.

Daniel gave him an overview of the steps they had taken, to Brideaux's approval. "It looks like you've got things under control. I have nothing to add except that you must stay in touch and let me know your progress and if there is anything else I can do. Whatever you need, you've got it."

Salome walked by just as Daniel was walking someone she hadn't met before out of his office. Daniel stopped her and introduced her to John Brideaux, who he said was a great friend to the Foundation and a great supporter.

"It's nice to meet you, Ms. James. I must say, you're by far the sexiest head of security I've ever met."

Salome felt her eyes grow as big as saucers as she shot Daniel a look that plainly said 'what the hell is this?' She'd automatically held out her hand to shake Brideaux's but the time had come and gone for him to let go, and yet he still held her hand. He was going on about having heard of her heroics during the Sword of Cyrus crisis. She tugged on her hand a bit, but he held it fast.

Salome had met his type before; filthy rich and most probably could buy as many women as he wanted. She despised men like that, especially men who acted this way. She tugged her hand again, this time successfully extricating it from his. If he ever tries to get funny with her, she thought, I'll get Roy to shove a nano nuke up his ass and detonate it.

When he and Daniel moved on, Salome went to the bathroom and washed her hands to get the sticky feeling of Brideaux's touch off them. While she chafed her hands under the dryer, she decided to check him out as soon as she can get a free moment. For now, she had her hands full, with the security audit of the Foundation she and Luke were running.

John Brideaux felt what had to be the ultimate feeling of satisfaction as the secure satellite link showed him his group's faces one by one. Though there was a babble of questions, he intended to wait until everyone was here. Out of the background noise, he heard, 'John why did you call us?' 'What's going on?' and 'What is so urgent?'

When the noise had grown to an almost unbearable level and all were in attendance, Brideaux took a sip from the cognac in the crystal glass in front of him and started with the words, "Gentlemen, our time is here. We must start to prepare ourselves at once. I have called this urgent special meeting of Eligo Rarus due to very important information I gathered from the Rossler Foundation today."

It was not for his wealth alone that John Brideaux was president of Eligo Rarus. He'd made a connection that hadn't yet occurred to even the geniuses of the Rossler Foundation. As he recounted to his compatriots what he'd learned about the latest discovery, he quoted the letter almost verbatim. Expressions of shock followed his presentation, yet he smiled throughout, until even the most vocal fell silent. Finally, someone thought to ask why he seemed so pleased, and he revealed to them the connection he'd made. The beast was some sort of device that was programmed with the "blood" of the citizens and that was how the Eighth Cycle government got control and kept control over everyone. "We now have the opportunity to do the same, as soon as the Rossler Foundation locates this 'beast' for us. Rest assured, we will be on hand to take control of it."

Next, he laid out the simple plan to exploit the beast. "We must buy up all pathology labs at once. From now on each and every blood test will be used to create a genetic profile using GENTS. Within a few years, the genetics of almost the entire world population will be in our hands.

"Furthermore, we must activate all our contacts in government security agencies and extract the medical files, DNA sequences and genetic profiles of all high-ranking politicians and security force officers. Everyone's files that are kept in government hands must be collected at once."

It needed no further discussion. Each had long been prepared with their assignments in case something like this fell into their hands. Within 24 hours they were fully operational. They had activated sleeper agents and other contacts with generous sums of money and benefits, or bribed and threatened others. In some cases their network of hackers had broken into the servers of government security agencies and downloaded what they wanted, carefully taking all precautions to wipe out their tracks after the hacks to make sure no one would know they had been there.

Within three weeks they had everything they wanted from the entire senior officer corps of every security agency of almost all of the Western countries, as well as those of Russia and China. What's more they had all the required information for each and every political leader and other high ranking politicians and government officials for all of those countries as well.

All they wanted now was The Beast, so they could deploy it at the right time. With no news from the Rossler Foundation in this time, Brideaux assured the group that if they couldn't get their hands on it they will develop their own beast and take over the world. But, why wait for that to be developed when they can have it delivered to them on a silver platter in the next few weeks?

All this activity was managed without a single alarm being raised in any security agency. Their well-placed contacts and carefully-laid plans made sure of that. When it was done, they raised a gleeful toast to John Brideaux, their leader, for his foresight.

Raj hadn't wasted time in writing a program that could search the sound files for the words relating to the beast. He not only threw all the computing power he could at doing the work, he bought more servers and put them to work as well. Though he had it all done within a few days, now the translating team was swamped with work. As usual, the human component was the bottleneck. Raj trusted his computers far more. He suggested the expedition not wait for them to finish. Instead, he recommended they get to that Room of Knowledge on the 4th floor described in the letter, so they could find the rest of the information pertaining to the beast and produce the sound files and search them.

Daniel agreed with Raj. At one of what were becoming interminable meetings, he proposed to the rest of the team that they go sooner rather than later. Everyone agreed it was a good idea, as long as they stayed away from the room of the beast. JR and Robert were the first to volunteer to go and get it. With Brideaux's earlier assurance that he would be more than happy to fund their trip, Daniel made arrangements to fly them out by private jet and helicopter as with previous expeditions.

This trip was becoming like a commute to JR and Robert, though they were happy for the helicopter ride as opposed to the original trek by mule and foot, through the slot canyon and around to the entrance of the site. Apart from the unnerving elevator ride, it was a walk in the park, so to speak.

It was the work of less than an hour to locate the room. JR and Robert had assumed it would be quick, and had the helicopter pilot wait. It took rather longer to move out what they found: 100 metal boxes, each containing 10 smaller metal boxes like that first one and the other 5 they found before. 1,000 small metal boxes in total. They could imagine it being the entire history of the Eighth Cycle - or would it only be the part of the history that the Council of The Selected decided should be recorded? They were about to find out.

Once JR reported by sat link how many boxes were on the way, Raj got permission from John Brideaux via Daniel to get whatever computer power he needed. Two days later, JR and Robert were back at headquarters with the boxes and Raj went to work. With his new server setup Raj was in the seventh heaven. The only thing that could have given him more pleasure would have been if Sushma had told him he was going to be the father of twins. Within two hours after JR and Robert's arrival, he had five parallel streams of computers running, producing sound files while churning through about fifty of the small metal boxes per hour. At this rate they would have all the sound files ready in less than twenty-four hours. And they did.

All the files were now in an enormous database and again Raj did his magic, split the database into five segments and started all five server clusters in parallel search functions. When the entire search had been completed in the next 12 hours, about 100 references to the beast had been found.

Those Raj handed off to Sinclair and the translation team, with Stephen Matthews helping where he could. After flying through the preliminaries with the computers, it was a slow and tedious process for the translators to do what they were tasked with – like watching grass grow. It would take a few weeks to get through the translations.

Chapter Thirty-Five

IT'S 30 SECONDS TO 12

Meanwhile, Salome and Luke continued with their security audit. There wasn't much more they could do to make things more secure around the Rossler Foundation, nor to protect everyone. But they kept an eye on the Spiderweb, and periodically updated the Enigma timeline.

When they estimated the doomsday clock had moved to 30 seconds to 12, it was time to brief the inner circle, those who didn't yet know, about their findings and what the Foundation was going to do about it.

Thus it was that the old team and those of the newer group who'd proved themselves part of the family found themselves once again in the large conference room, hearing all about something called Enigma. Raj, Robert, Roy, Salome, Luke and now JR, Rebecca and Sinclair were about to be brought fully up to speed on what had been a closely-held secret before.

Since Salome had been the one to initiate these plans, Daniel asked her to bring everyone up to speed and then hand out individual assignments. Sinclair had been through something like this back in the original search for the Pyramid code, so he wasn't surprised. JR and Rebecca were more so, but they took it in stride. No one there was a stranger to crisis.

Each member of what they now decided to call the Enigma "group" naturally had an assignment according to their specialties.

With no further questions or discussion for the moment, Daniel adjourned the meeting. He had a feeling the final decisions on who went with them would rest on his shoulders. He could only hope he was strong enough to know when to say 'no'. If only he could save everyone.

Chapter Thirty-Six

FIND THE INSTRUCTION MANUAL

Although the progress was slow, over the course of the next few weeks the translation team found the information they were looking for about the beast. It came in bits and pieces and slowly but surely they build the picture. Adding to some confusion, the translators had to substitute words they had for sophisticated concepts, just as the Code-talkers had done decades before. But, at last, the picture emerged.

The beast was a machine, probably a computer, which somehow communicated with "birds" in the sky.

"Planes?" Sinclair questioned. "Joseph told me the Code-talkers used the same word for planes."

"I doubt it," Roy said. "I suspect those would be something similar to what we would today call a satellite."

The "birds" in the sky had the blood data of every person on earth at the time, and strangely, were somehow aware of the whereabouts of each person in its database at all times. While Sinclair declared it mindboggling and demanded to know how such a thing were possible, Salome pointed out that since GPS was built into cell phones, today's communications companies were able to track and pinpoint anyone who had one in a similar way in seconds. And who these days didn't have one? It had been going on for years; how else had Special Forces tracked terrorists in the early part of the century but with GPS and satellite photography so sensitive it could identify a face from outer space. So maybe they had something implanted in their citizens to track them?

However, the mechanism for control wasn't so clear. The records mentioned something the translators called an invisible ray of death or pain that came from these "birds" in the sky. Some accounts even stated that no one had ever seen it, but millions upon millions had been killed by it or extreme pain inflicted on them. Invisible ray? Raj thought of alien ray guns, but Roy had a more plausible suggestion. Maybe nano robots or the type of nano-poison or disease the Sword of Cyrus tested in Africa, he suggested.

Daniel thought it was like building a puzzle with some of the pieces missing and no picture to look at.

Despite, or perhaps because of, the concern everyone felt about the mysterious 'beast' references and the need to hurry to secure and destroy it, Enigma was moving along with good pace. This was largely because Daniel had now thrown his full support behind the idea, for which Salome was grateful. She had a feeling of looming disaster that had less to do with the increasingly disturbing data from the Spiderweb than it did a gut feeling.

That Daniel now had it too was both encouraging,

because his authority lent hers wings, and alarming. Because all the time she'd known Daniel, even in the midst of the Sword of Cyrus crisis, he'd been an optimist. Raj was a different matter. Even before Salome had met him, by all reports Raj was paranoid.

He always said something strange, that he attributed to a habit Daniel used to have of twisting aphorisms. "Just because you're not paranoid, doesn't mean someone isn't out to get you." Or something like that. She'd never been able to sort out the cancelling negatives. And besides, Raj *was* paranoid, so it made no sense.

Raj designed a mirroring system among his servers so that at any given time, one set was within ten minutes of powering down while the others took the load. This way, he could reliably shut them all down, with the one that had gone through the proper sequence most recently serving as backup in case an emergency shut-down corrupted files in the others. Then he performed drills to make sure it all worked.

Rebecca would have a complete medical setup, including a small surgery room, ready and waiting at the Rabbit Hole, so that she would be free to help Sarah with her family. For now, Emma and Sally were packing everything they could think of to take with them, as if they were pioneers setting out across the land for a new way of life. In a way, they were.

Taking a leaf from Rebecca's book, Roy had a duplicate lab designed to be included in the Rabbit Hole engineering plans. Of course, he'd still have to pack up and take his current projects. As Salome had warned him, he couldn't leave anything behind for the use of whoever or whatever invaded the building after they were gone. She encouraged him to practice the bug-out, to try to cut his time down from half an hour to ten minutes, like Raj.

Going into Daniel's office one day, Salome found him staring at nothing and wondered if he were sleeping with his eyes open. She wouldn't have blamed him; he'd been stretched thin over the past few weeks.

"Daniel, am I disturbing you?"

"What? Oh, no, Salome. I was just thinking. Do you remember the zombie apocalypse craze that was popular eight or nine years ago?"

"Yes," she said, smiling. What was on his fertile mind now?

"I was just thinking, we're acting like a zombie apocalypse is coming. Are we over-reacting to things?"

Salome took a minute to consider her answer. "No, I don't think so. I have a bad feeling about what I see on the Spiderweb, and an even worse one about this beast in the canyon site. It may not be zombies, but if we fail to destroy it and it falls into the wrong hands, it could be just as bad."

"You're right," he said. "Fortunately, I think we're just about ready to go after it. Did you need something? If not, I need to give John Brideaux a call and get final funding to get the expedition on its way."

"No, what I have can wait. Send for me when you're ready."

"Okay, thanks Salome."

Her next stop was at JR's office, where she found him and Robert with their heads together, planning something.

"What are you two up to?" she said.

"About 6'10"," JR deadpanned. Robert chuckled.

"Very funny. Bend down here so I can smack you," she joked. "But seriously..."

JR relented, knowing he couldn't get away with much when it came to Salome's sense of humor, which wasn't as silly as his. "Robert's come up with an idea. He's thinking of going to some of these prepper groups and telling them he's going home to get himself ready for whatever it is they're worried about. Maybe they'll give him some pointers we can use."

"They probably could, but I think you two are going to be busy. Daniel's talking to John Brideaux about funding your expedition at last."

"That's great news!" JR exclaimed.

Salome's final visit was to her husband in his lab. She noted with approval that instead of the usual chaos, he had everything neatly packed away except for what he was working on at the moment.

"I have another list of requests from Sarah and the other women, my love. Can you get to these right away?"

"My lord, when will they dry up for ideas?" he asked. "They've got me so busy I can hardly get my real work done. What is it with women? You can't ever satisfy them."

Salome smiled at him and moved into his arms, forcing him to put down his tools and hold her. "You satisfy me, lover."

Roy immediately turned bright red, and said, "But you're not a woman."

She raised her eyebrows at him.

"I mean, not like those women. Oh, heck, I don't know what I mean."

"I'm glad to see I can still get you riled up," she said, still smiling.

"Every minute of every day," he sighed, surrendering to the kisses she gave him until he relaxed.

Patting him on the back, she said, "Remember, get those done right away, in case they have more."

As she left his office, Salome suppressed a giggle when she heard him say, "Women!"

Raj gave the translation team the final sound files, and over the next three weeks they got to the last translations.

In the meanwhile, Daniel kept Brideaux informed of progress on a regular basis through a satellite phone Brideaux had supplied. He assured Daniel the special phone was absolutely, 100%, safe and secure – no one would be able to track or eavesdrop on their conversations. Since Salome had warned him about that months ago, Daniel was glad to have it.

The two men agreed that Matthews could now be released from his contract - they had other things to focus on now than looking for ancient flying machines. Brideaux would pay him the agreed amount for helping tremendously with the Eighth Cycle work, but he would no longer be required for now. If and when things settle down, Daniel assured Brideaux that Matthews was welcome to come back and continue his research on flying machines.

When the translators had finally worked through all of the information about how the beast worked – that is, excluding the instruction manual, Daniel, JR, Robert and Roy convened to assess what they now knew. The problem was, the material was mostly vague. But, at least it confirmed a few things the unknown correspondent said in the letter. The instruction manual would be located in the same room as the beast. The warning to be careful, and accounts of others who tried to disable or destroy it being killed on the spot.

Something new, but not entirely useful was that only members of The Council of The Selected knew what the beast looked like. There was some description, but the translation was weird – the best Joseph's team could come up with was that there were three "eyes" on the beast. Two sitting next to each other and a long square one below the two. JR remarked it sounded almost like a face; two eyes with a mouth below. Other words they thought might refer to measurements or what they think could be measurements since there were no words like them in the Athabaskan tongue and measurements made sense in context. But, no one had any idea how the Eighth Cyclers measured things, so it was impossible to say how big this thing was. Another strange description mentioned the "eyes" were like water with a light shining out of it. JR and Roy reckoned with a bit of imagination that sounded like a computer screen. It also mentioned a table with "sticks" on it, which they imagine could be some sort of control device, something like a keyboard or joysticks of sorts. The conclusion was the beast could look much like the desktop portion of a modern computer – maybe.

Finally they found an article with very sobering contents explaining in much detail how the Eighth Cycle system worked. Each human being was implanted with a "thing" (the translators' word for an untranslatable word) in his or her right hand at birth. That "thing" kept them in touch with each other at all times. Roy's immediate thought was a nano-computer or chip, something similar to the ID chips placed in pets, but much more sophisticated.

Now the group had to pause for a break while Raj was sent for and brought up to speed on the discussion. Roy reminded him about a discussion they'd had about building a nano-computer the size of the head of a match stick. Now Raj excitedly jumped in.

"Yes! We talked about that. You were saying it could be more powerful than any computer we have today!"

When the group reconvened with Raj now in attendance, they learned Roy was on the right track. The "thing" in their hands not only kept them in touch, but it directed the lives of Eighth Cycle citizens. They would just swipe their hands past an "eye" at the "storehouses" where they would get their food and supplies. A device not only registered but controlled what they obtained. It also reminded them when to go in to see a doctor, which Joseph had mentioned to Sinclair was designated by the Athabaskan word for shaman. Within this part of the information was a great deal of detail about medicines, ceremonies and other archaic notions of medicine. Sinclair suspected the Athabaskan words concealed something sinister with regard to the constant monitoring of every citizen's health.

It became very clear from what they read as they continued that there were no financial concepts such as we have today for money or payments in the Eighth Cycle. It appeared from what the translators had so far given them that it had been a moneyless society. The "thing" will allow them to only get the food and medication that was prescribed to them based on their "blood", although no mention of other necessities such as housing and clothing were mentioned in any of the translated articles. Sinclair speculated it was probably the same; however, he pointed out, they had only translated portions Raj had identified as having to do with the beast. Apparently the beast was concerned with the health of the citizens, which didn't make sense given what they also knew about it – it killed.

At this point, JR said, "You know, the more we read, the more I think we should have included everyone from the beginning. We need Rebecca for this part."

Daniel agreed. "Let's break for lunch and I'll gather up the rest of the inner circle. We've got to know everything we can, and as JR pointed out, we're missing some key people. Be back here in an hour and we'll continue."

As it happened, the entire group convened in the canteen, but they kept the discussion of what they were doing in the conference room out of their lunch conversation. By now, with the secret of the Enigma project and the sensitive nature of the Eighth Cycle project, there was little to talk about except subjects long considered taboo in large gatherings. Like politics.

Salome asked if anyone else had noticed the proliferation of political chatter on social media. Most of the group turned blank faces to her. Who had time for that drivel? Daniel, however, spoke up immediately.

"I have. You know I keep up with the old Times crowd, right?"

A few of the others nodded, Raj shrugged and Roy swiveled his head back and forth between his wife and Daniel with a curious expression, as if he'd never heard of social media.

"So," Daniel continued. "We used to pride ourselves on balanced reporting. When I worked there, I mean. But now, the editors seem to have hand-picked a Presidential candidate and all the stories are about how great he is and how lame all the others are. What's that all about? It's like they're trying to brainwash the public. And it's not just the news site itself. A lot of the reporters have Facebook pages, and that's all they post, too."

Salome was nodding. "I've observed the same. Let me guess. The hand-picked candidate is the incumbent, yes?"

"Yeah," Daniel answered. "You've read the Times, too?"

"No," she said. "But it's everywhere. I've never seen anything like it. It can't help but sway the election. The average person doesn't think for himself any more. He does what the media suggests."

"Sounds just like the Eighth Cycle," Sinclair muttered. He'd had more opportunity to read other bits of translation, before they started focusing on the beast. His young team member was right. It sounded exactly like Brave New World.

They were soon back at work, now with everyone present and filled in on what they'd already discussed. They were ready to keep reading and discussing. The "thing" in the hand was also connected to the beast it seemed, and it didn't seem to matter how near or far the physical location was. If a citizen tried to tamper with the tracker (as the group were now calling it) or remove it that citizen would be dead very quickly. If someone did not eat the food or take the medicine at the time he was supposed to, he would get severe pains, something like the shocks from a dog's bark collar, Robert suggested. The others stared at him in horror. Who used those these days? He quickly went back to the reading. If a citizen kept on ignoring the prompts, the pain would get more severe and in the end would just be killed if he didn't "listen".

It also seemed that the "thing" would be "looking" at their "blood" and decide who should be married to whom and how many children they could have. The article stated that part was only introduced recently and many people were very unhappy. Some tried to remove the "thing" and died, some "protested" and died. After a period of upheaval, they just had to accept it. They were told it was better for them because the "new" people (babies that were born after this rule was enforced) were healthier than before. They should be happy, because it looked like their children would live to 200 and beyond!

Rebecca had been quiet until now. Whatever this device was that the group was calling the tracker, no one needed her help to understand its function. It obviously both analyzed and monitored the citizens. Now she did have something to contribute.

"This is almost certainly a reference to genetics. In fact this looks very much like genetic engineering."

The others picked it up immediately. Coupled that with what they knew about the potential of nano medicine and Roy telling them about nano-bots and poison and nano computers, it could very well be what was going on in the Eighth Cycle – a deadly nano-bot, virus or poison linked to the DNA of the people, each individually programmed. They'd been controlled by a nano-bot implanted into them and any dissidents were punished or killed by the beast. But, how was it done, specifically?

Except for poison, nothing the group could think of would kill quickly, much less instantly as the letter had hinted. And how could poison be delivered precisely and individually? Could it have been introduced into the prescribed food or medications? Wouldn't the citizenry have rebelled if that were the case? And what mechanism would strike a person dead for attempting to tamper with it? It was all very puzzling.

By the time the group had made it through only a tiny fraction of the translated material, they were all exhausted. Yet, more research was needed and they had to get through the rest of it. With all they were doing for the Enigma project and now this, progress was painfully slow.

But, after a few weeks, they all knew what would have to be done. Every one of them feared it and no one wanted to talk about it before now, but even Sarah and Rebecca accepted it. They would have to go back again – this time to find the beast and its instruction manual.

There was no time to waste. They would still have to translate it very carefully; there could be no misunderstanding – that warning was all too clear. Once they knew how the beast operated and could be shutdown, they'd have to do it. Based on the fact that the rest of the facility was still operational – the elevators, the still-undiscovered ventilation system that simply had to be there – it had to be assumed the beast was also still operational. And even though there were no trackers implanted in their hands, how could they be certain its defense mechanisms couldn't still kill or gravely injure them? They couldn't.

They still had no certainty how exactly the beast was killing people that got close to it in the past and then also how exactly it was connected to the "birds" in the sky and how that was used to kill people. Was it poison, a gas? Could it be a nano robot or nano poison, even an invisible death ray? They hadn't discovered how, but they did now know with certainty that death was very quick once the beast was activated – the victim would be dead in less than a minute.

They were speculating, but no one doubted their only option was to go and find that manual now.

Daniel had duly reported to John Brideaux as their

deliberations continued. Now he had to report they would have to go back again, if only just to get that manual and get it translated. As always, Brideaux was helpful and supportive, still willing to fund anything Daniel required. As he told Daniel, now the beast had been discovered again, it was imperative they get to it and destroy it before news of it leaked and it fell into the wrong hands.

Chapter Thirty-Seven

I AM GOING

After weeks of learning everything they could, the Rossler Foundation inner circle knew it was time to start planning for the expedition. They had some serious issues to work through, and every one of them had a stake in it. Daniel, Sarah, JR and Rebecca, Roy and Salome, Raj, Sinclair, Robert, Luke and of course Joseph convened for a pre-planning meeting, to lay out the problems. Daniel had a presentation ready.

First they had to be able to identify the correct room. They couldn't go and open every door on that floor and look inside, because it could trigger the beast. If they did somehow identify the correct room in advance, the question was if the door could be booby trapped. Would it set the beast in motion when the door was opened or broken down?

Would the door open like the other doors in the facility or would this one have a different mechanism and if so, what could it be and what will happen if the door is not opened in the correct way?

Before Daniel went on with the next problem, Roy offered a potential solution to the first one.

"We can get past this without bothering to open any doors or risking setting off the beast. We can use a remote control robot equipped with one or more of my laser cutters." Roy was referring to the extremely powerful handheld laser cutters he developed and used during the Sword of Cyrus crisis. Daniel and the others no doubt remembered very well the demo Roy gave them then, when he cut through a six foot granite block in a few seconds with a little handheld laser – the evidence was still very visible outside in the Rossler Foundation garden.

Roy was still explaining his thinking. "We can cut a tiny hole in the wall of each room and send in a nano-robot with a camera to check it out. Once we have the right room, we can cut a bigger hole and send in a bigger robot to retrieve the manual."

"What's this 'we' business," Salome muttered, but everyone else was attending Roy's discourse, so no one heard her.

"We'll have to scan the walls before we cut, of course," Roy was saying, "to make sure we don't disturb anything that might trigger the beast." He further explained that they'd use tools similar to what electricians use to determine if there are electrical wires behind a wall before drilling into it. Doing it with the robots would give them a chance to see what the beast looked like and the layout of the room, not to mention what may be going on in that room without putting themselves into too much danger. It was entirely possible that a robot might even be able to disable or destroy the beast. They couldn't know for sure until they get there and could get a robot into the room.

With that solution agreed upon, Daniel presented the

next. How quickly and easily could the manual be translated? Should they get the manual and come back to the Rossler Foundation, get it done here and then go back and destroy the beast? Daniel had a concern about that, and relayed what Brideaux had said to him. The longer they delayed, the higher chance the beast could fall into the wrong hands and be used with disastrous consequences.

After some discussion and argument, the group finally agreed it would be best to try to translate the manual while they were there. If it proved easy enough with the manpower and tools they had available, they would destroy the beast then.

But again, they could only decide once they'd located the beast. This translation would have to be done with precision; they couldn't guess or assume or have any maybes – it has to be 100% accurate and they would take as long as necessary to get that done correctly. Raj pointed out that the only way to do it would be to take his specifically modified computer equipment to run the records through, assuming they were in the same format as the other information they'd found; that is, the foils. Once again, they could only determine if it would work once they were there. This was becoming a pattern.

Daniel had yet another issue to discuss that looked to have the same outcome. What exactly could happen if they make a mistake when trying to shut the beast down or destroy it? Would it explode, send out poisonous gas, nanobots, or some sort of death ray? Could this thing somehow be connected to trigger a nuclear explosion? The Eighth cycle demonstrably had advanced nanotech users. The beast could very well be rigged to explode and destroy the whole facility or worse the Canyon or even worse than that.

And again they had to agree they wouldn't know until

they got the manual. Until that time they would have the risk that whatever they did might trigger the beast. But that is a risk they would have to take, because they had no way to put this genie back in its bottle. It was even more risky to leave it there and hope no one with evil intent found it.

This brought up Daniel's next prepared point. Why not just go in and seal the whole facility off? Pump it full of concrete, put a fence around it and guard it so no one could ever get into it again? But they come to the conclusion we would never be safe; everyone would forever want to get in and get their hands on it. Every bad guy and every government would want that thing. Even our own government wouldn't leave it like that. No, it had to be destroyed – there was no other way.

Sarah brought up the next point, the beast couldn't be connected any longer to the "birds" in the sky. If it relied on those to kill, maybe it wasn't even a problem. Surely by now, after more than 50,000 years, any satellite would have burned out and dropped back to earth or disappeared into space.

Raj had a different opinion. "Haven't you guys ever heard of the Black Knight?" he asked. Incredulous when no one admitted to having heard of it, he went on. "That could easily be one of those "birds" that survived from the Eighth Cycle." He went on, explaining that there was an object of some sort orbiting the earth that no government had claimed or could identify. It was something to consider possible even if the chances were remote - it could be a survivor of Eighth Cycle times.

In the face of skepticism from the others, Raj stood his ground. He was used to the ridicule that sometimes accompanied his obsession with the unexplained.

When the others stated with certainty that it couldn't

still be operational after all this time, he retorted. "If it doesn't work now, it doesn't mean it can't be reactivated by whomever owns it. And why wouldn't it work now? The elevators and ventilation system do. So, even if it can't kill the world population, it might very well still be able to kill whomever walks into that room and tampers with it."

In the end, Raj prevailed. They had to assume the beast could potentially trigger some unknown device (perhaps the Black Knight) in the sky that had survived for more than 50,000 years and start wiping out people again as it did the last time it was operational. However remote a chance that might happen. So it became problem number five. Daniel still had a couple more for discussion.

Why not take this to the government and let them deal with it?

Raj was the first to object. "How would we know they have destroyed it and have not kept it for the exact same purposes as the Council of The Selected have? Do you trust the government with that? Can you imagine what power they will have in their hands if they find out about this? They can control the world – get rid of anyone, terrorists, bad guys, good guys, everyone. No, don't trust the government."

Of course, his distrust of the government and paranoia were well-known to the group, and might not have carried much weight, if Salome hadn't seconded his opinion. As before, they concluded JR had been right when he said at the beginning, "You'll see, we will have to do it." No one else can be trusted.

And that brought them full circle, as if the intervening weeks had never happened. Finally the question everyone had been avoiding had to be posed. Who will go and do it?

Daniel never expected the havoc he caused when he put the question on the table, though.

JR answered right away. "I am going. I have to go. I've led all expeditions since Antarctica, and this thing will not get done without me."

Daniel shot up from the table. "Absolutely not! You are not going anywhere near that place again. We've already risked your life too many times. Let someone else do it."

JR balled his fists. "You've got to be kidding! You would have me stay safely at home while someone else does my job? Over my dead body."

Daniel was the older brother, but JR had him by six inches and a wealth of combat training. Even so, it would have descended into a brawl if Rebecca and Sarah hadn't cried out and Sinclair and Robert hadn't each grabbed a would-be combatant from behind.

"All right," Daniel backed down, breathing heavily. "If you insist on going, then I'm going, too. You're my responsibility."

He hadn't counted on the women joining the fray. Sarah said, with outward calm, that she might as well kill Daniel right now on the spot and save him the trouble of going to the canyon to die there. At least she would then be with him when he died. Her certainty of doom made Rebecca lose her composure and burst into tears. Through her sobs, she threatened to inject JR with some paralyzing poison or give him a good dose of laxative to make sure he couldn't leave their home.

By the time Sinclair had managed to restore calm, Roy had thought it over. "I obviously will be going as well. None of you know how to operate my equipment." Salome, caught by surprise, pulled out her gun and threatened to shoot him in the leg so he couldn't go either. This dramatic announcement was met by derisive laughter from Luke, who advised her to put the gun away before she shot the wrong person by accident.

"He's right. And by the same token, I am going as well," said Raj. No one can operate my computer equipment either, and even if they could, I wouldn't allow it. You will need the sound file extracted before anyone can translate it, so I have to be there." To defuse the tense situation, he added, "If I am not at work tomorrow morning then know that Sushma has crippled or killed me – but if I am still alive and here tomorrow morning then I am going."

Even Sarah, Rebecca and Salome had to laugh at that, and at their hysterical responses to the decisions their men had come to. Of course, they were right. It was up to them, as JR said, and they wouldn't be the men they were if they sent someone else to do a dangerous job.

After the laughter subsided, Joseph chimed in. "Luckily my wife is not here to try and cripple or kill me. I will go to do the translation. Better me than my young relatives, and no one else can do the translation."

As one of the few who hadn't yet spoken, Sinclair opened his mouth and got a few words out to the effect that *he had to go with these youngsters to keep a watch over them because it was obvious they couldn't behave.* Before he finished, everyone else in the room, as if they had practiced it, said at the same time in one voice, "No Sinclair, you stay!" Sinclair tried to argue, but the rest of them made it clear he was not going and that was the end of it. If he had any further arguments they threatened to get Martha and bring her in to sort it out. Sinclair knew better than to take his chances with the lovely Martha.

Luke didn't even try. He knew it was a young man's job, and though he would have taken the burden on himself before risking these 'kids' who'd become his extended family, the greater good required those with the best chance of succeeding to go instead.

This left only Robert. After all the chaos, he cleared his throat and said, "I have been trying to say something now for the last fifteen minutes. I am just letting you all know I am going as well. I have been on each and every expedition the Rossler Foundation has launched and I have been there at the Canyon site from the very beginning. I don't know how I'll help, but I'm going." With a significant look at the women present, he continued, "I have no wife or girlfriend to threaten me, so I am going." To no one's surprise, no objection was raised.

The final straw, though, was Rebecca. Once she got over her tears and thought about it, she announced, "Listen up boys. I am going as well. If JR goes, I go. Besides, if there is any chance anyone might get injured or sick or poisoned or whatever the beast can inflict on you, you will have a better chance to survive if there is a doctor at hand."

At first, JR was stunned. By the time he realized what she was saying, he had his argument ready. "No you aren't. This is the most dangerous thing we've ever done, and we can't predict the outcome."

Rebecca lifted her chin to stare her husband in the eye, even if she had to climb on a chair to do it. "Yes. I. Am."

With that, JR jumped up and walked over to Salome demanding to have her gun. "Just for one second. I want to shoot my wife in the leg as well, so she can't go! Your gun and just one bullet please! And if you don't give me that gun I will go and get a knife and stab her in the leg."

The old, combative JR would have taken on the whole room when they began laughing. However, he had to see the humor in his ridiculous statement. But, his argument was reinforced when everyone teamed up against Rebecca and "persuaded" her not to go. Still, to say the least she was not a happy doctor.

With everyone exhausted from the commotion, Daniel adjourned the meeting for the day and called Brideaux with a report about their decisions. Everyone else had assignments and were even now making preparations to leave in five days.

To Daniel's surprise, Brideaux began to suggest potential travel arrangements, but kept referring to "us". After several such references, Daniel had to clarify. "John, you keep saying 'us'. Surely you are not thinking of going?"

"You were not seriously thinking to leave me behind were you?" Brideaux replied. "Of course I am going. I have been funding this and the buck stops with me. Through my researcher's discovery, I am responsible and I need to clean it up."

Daniel couldn't take any more of these *"I am going"* arguments and the threats that followed them. He just quietly accepted that Brideaux would be going with them.

Brideaux also very kindly suggested that Daniel leave behind at the Foundation headquarters the secure satellite phone he gave him earlier. He would give them another handset when he meets them in Flagstaff. This was so they could have the ability to talk to their people on a secure connection while they were on site.

Chapter Thirty-Eight

GOODBYE MY FRIENDS

The next morning, a new crisis took Daniel's attention when he had to rush to the hospital. Bess called and told him Nicholas had taken a turn for the worse early that morning, and this time it looked bad.

Sarah met him there. Daniel kissed Sarah, smiled at little Nick, and told Sarah she'd better keep him out until he knew Grandpa's condition. Then he rushed to the room, anxious to be there for Grandma if the news was as bad as it sounded. He found her peering into the window of an ICU room. Grandpa was inside; at least Daniel assumed it was Grandpa. It was hard to tell, since the bed was surrounded by monitoring equipment and several people.

"Doctors?" he asked, after kissing Grandma on the cheek.

"I'm not sure. One of those alarms went off and they all hustled in and pushed me out," she said.

"Was he sleeping, before, or what?"

"It was strange, Daniel. He was asleep, and then he woke up. His eyes went big, and then the alarm went off."

Oh no, Daniel thought. His chest tightened and tears threatened. With all his heart, he wanted to barge in and sweep the doctors away, just so he could give the old man a hug. Instead, he put his arm around Grandma and pulled her to his side. "He'll be okay, Grandma. He has to be."

Bess put her arm around his waist. "I know. I can't imagine life without him. Do you think we ought to call your dad?"

"Yeah, Grandma. He'd be upset if we didn't. We told him not to come the first time, but I think he'll want to now that it's happened again."

"You're right. It looks like they're going to be a while in there. I'll go outside and call now." For the first time, Daniel noticed all the "No Cell Phones" signs.

"I'll go with you and update Sarah. She's downstairs with Nick."

"Oh, Daniel, you should send her home. This is no place for kids, and they won't let them into the ICU."

"Okay. She'll want to see him though. I'll wait with Nick while she comes up. She loves him too, you know."

"I do know, and he loves her, too. I'll see you back here in half an hour?"

"Okay. Love you, Grandma."

Daniel sent Sarah to look in on Grandpa, while he took little Nick on his knee and explained that Grandpa was too sick to play and that's why he couldn't go. Sarah came to them, her face drawn with grief. "I don't know if he'll come back from this one, Daniel."

"He will. He's too tough to go, you watch." Daniel would never admit that he, too, was worried. More worried than the first time.

It was several hours before Daniel and Bess had any news from the doctors, but by then Ben, Nancy and Aaron were on their way. To their astonishment, when the doctor did come to speak with them, he said he'd never seen anything like this. Nicholas had suffered a stroke so massive it should have killed him. But miraculously, Nicholas had rallied and was asking to see Bess and Daniel. Grandmother and grandson looked at each other in shock. Could this be possible, or were they having a shared dream?

The doctor continued, "Don't stress him or say anything to make him uncomfortable. I don't know how he survived that stroke, but I believe it's only a small reprieve. Given the medical history, another one is almost certain. It's unlikely he will survive another, even a small one. You should prepare yourselves."

Bess stifled a sob and made a visible effort to pull herself together. With Daniel's arm around her for support, she gave the doctor her word that Nicholas wouldn't know of her distress. He nodded and admitted the two of them to the ICU room.

At their entrance, Nicholas opened his eyes. When his glance fell on his beloved Bess, he smiled and said in a thready voice, "You thought I would leave without saying goodbye?"

Bess gave her sturdy answer. "No, my love. I knew you wouldn't do that to me." She couldn't say more; there was no hope to give him and she wouldn't lie. Neither would she betray the doctor's trust. It didn't matter. Nicholas knew.

He smiled again, before saying in surprisingly clear words, "I know I don't have much time. I have made a deal with God that I will be happy to go as soon as I can say goodbye to you all."

The doctor had come in quietly and heard Nicholas's

wishes as he said he wanted his son Ben and daughter-in-law Nancy, along with his grandchildren Daniel and Sarah, JR and Rebecca and Aaron to come to him. Also his great grandson who carries his name, his best friend Sinclair and Sinclair's wife Martha. Finally, though they weren't family, he wanted Raj, Luke and also Roy and Salome to all come to him. So many, and people who weren't family it was against hospital policy, but the doctor was inclined to grant this final wish.

Nicholas continued, "So what are you two waiting for? Go get them all. I am not going anywhere, but I can't wait forever. I have an appointment to keep!"

The doctor and nurse standing there at his bed with them were shaking their heads in wonder. They had never seen anything like this. As Bess and Daniel scurried from the room to carry out his orders, it was really as if God was giving him time to say goodbye – there was no other explanation. He shouldn't even be able to talk after that stroke. How on earth he could be so clear and strong defied all medical logic and experience. It's just not humanly possible as far as they were concerned. With his family gone for the moment, the doctor decided to keep vigil with the old man. He'd be surprised if they made it back with half the people Nicholas had requested before he suffered his final stroke.

By the time they returned, four hours had passed, and the old man had grown weaker. Somehow Ben, Nancy and Aaron had made it there, though Aaron had to take a separate flight since all were nearly full and none had three seats. Sarah had picked them up in Denver and then raced back to Boulder, certain they'd be too late.

Daniel had called in Raj, Luke, Roy and Salome, while Bess went in person to Sinclair and Martha and returned with them in their car. It was too large a crowd in the small room, and by now Nicholas was too weak to make himself heard. Bess leaned over him with her ear to his mouth and relayed the messages he had for them. One by one, she called in each couple or individual that he requested. To each, Bess conveyed his thanks for their friendship and loyalty to his family, especially his grandchildren. He wished them lives as long and happy as his had been with Bess, and whispered a goodbye. Each touched him briefly through his blankets, and each left with tears in their eyes. It was the end of an era, and with everything else going on, it felt like the end of the world.

Sinclair and Martha were the last who weren't family. Martha had Bess let her give Nicholas a hug, and then she gave one to Bess as well. The two old friends had one more laugh about the time they got so drunk when they discovered that time travel thing and agreed they will always have good memories of their time together. Sinclair promised to come looking for Nicholas in Heaven when it was his turn to arrive, and to bring a bottle of their favorite Irish whiskey with him.

His doctor was hovering, and showing the strain of the long day as he urged the family to take their turn before it was too late. But against all odds, Nicholas seemed to be actually getting stronger. He now summoned the entire family into the room at one time, crowding together in an attempt not to jostle the medical equipment.

Nicholas had a speech ready for his family, including little Nick, who was behaving very well in spite of the heavy tension among the adults.

"Son, and grandsons, you have always made Bess and me so very proud, haven't they, Bess? We've been blessed by God to have a family like this.

"Sarah and Rebecca, my granddaughters that I never

thought to have. You have more than filled that void in Bess's and my lives. Thank you for loving and caring for my grandsons, and thank you especially, Sarah, for my great-grandson. Nick, I love you."

His voice grew weaker again as he thanked them all for their years of love and care and asked them to take care of Bess and then gestured for them to come and hug him one by one. When it was Daniel's turn, he whispered, "I know what no one has told me, boy. You are facing another crisis at the moment. Don't give up. Things are going to look very bleak and as if all will be lost."

Daniel tried to reassure him, but he gripped his grandson's arm with surprising strength. "No, don't talk, I don't have much time to say this. You and the others must be strong and bold as you have been on all previous occasions. You must never give up. Rosslers never give up and they always come out on top. Remember that."

All of the family was gathered around with most touching Nicholas somewhere; all but Sarah, who took out little Nick as he finally realized something very bad was happening and began to cry. All heard his final words, "Don't grieve for me, I had a full and happy life, God has blessed me richly with the best wife in the world and the best family and friends anyone could ever hope to have. I am ready to meet Him now. The God who has blessed and protected me for more than ninety years will also bless and protect each and every one of you in the same way."

He lifted his hand a fraction of an inch and made a tiny gesture to wave goodbye to them. At last, he closed his eyes and with a smile on his face the old patriarch was gone. A man amongst men, he died like he'd lived – an honorable man.

Grandma's face crumpled, and Daniel put his arm around her.

"Ben, Daniel, I'm very tired. Would you take me home, please? There'll be arrangements to make."

They marveled at her strength. They were jelly, no strength in their limbs at all, and she, after almost seventy years of marriage, was already thinking of others and their expectations. No wonder Grandpa had been the tower of strength everyone always thought. He had a woman of steel propping him up.

The memorial service was a few days later. A small private affair attended by the family, the Foundation staff, Sarah and Rebecca's family as well as ex-president Nigel Harper and his wife, Esther. Sam Lewis and also John Brideaux attended in support of the Rossler family. Although it was sad it was also a celebration of the life of a great man.

They all remembered his last words, "Don't grieve for me" and so the family, Sinclair and some of the employees had them crying instead with laughter at times, as they recalled the antics of the old man.

When it was ready, the epitaph on his headstone would read:

We only live once, but once is enough if we do it right. Live your life with class, dignity, and style so that an exclamation, rather than a question mark signifies it!
Gary Ryan Blair

Chapter Thirty-Nine

THE END GAMES

A day or so before the expedition left Salome and Rebecca were having a drink in the cafeteria and started talking about the article which told them in so much detail how the people were controlled by that "thing" in their hands – how bad must it have been to live in that society? Salome reminded Rebecca that our society today was not too far off, with the universal demand for constant connection. Coupled with all the information the government, and worse, private companies, were collecting, current times were not many steps behind the Eighth Cycle.

Rebecca shuddered. "At least we don't have something that can kill us with no warning, constantly monitoring us."

"Yet," Salome answered, with dark prophecy.

"You know, Salome," Rebecca began. "I've been wondering about something since JR and Robert returned from their first expedition. What happened to the remains of the humans in that place?"

"Wasn't it just abandoned?" Salome asked.

"No, I don't think so. According to that letter people

have died in that place. The person who wrote the letter died there. But none of the expeditions so far have found any remains whatsoever."

"Why is it bothering you?" Salome asked.

Rebecca remembered then that both Salome and her husband Roy were newcomers since the Antarctica expeditions. "I'm just remembering all too well what happened on the second expedition to Antarctica when we dug up the hospital site and unleashed that dreadful virus. You have to remember, that killed half of the population of the Middle East, and almost brought the world to an end then. And surely you remember it was revenge for it that caused the Sword of Cyrus crisis."

Salome felt a cold shiver running down her spine. Of course she remembered. She'd lived through it, even if she hadn't been in the middle of it during the Ninth Cycle virus. "We'd better make sure the boys remember to be careful of opening another Pandora's Box like that. Should they be wearing biohazard suits from now on while onsite?"

"That's not a bad idea," Salome replied. "I should have thought of it."

On the day before he was to leave to meet the Rossler expedition in Flagstaff, Brideaux convened a special meeting of Eligo Rarus to give them an update and explain his mission.

"Daniel Rossler has given me a comprehensive report, and I'm satisfied that this is the time we'll be able to seize the device they're calling the beast, along with its full operating instructions.

In answer to a question from the group, he explained

that he'd have men waiting on standby for his signal. He'd be going with the expedition to determine the ideal moment. "Are there any questions about what you are all to do while I'm gone?"

The discussion centered for a while on stepping up their efforts to obtain control of all the pathology labs. Those that were stubborn about selling must be "persuaded" by other means. The rule of the day was 'just get it done'.

The next order of business was the upcoming G20 meeting in three weeks. Now that they had a hope of backing it up with real teeth in the form of the beast, it would be the ideal time to make their move. All the world would be watching and many world leaders would be there. General Whitehoff, an Eligo Rarus member, was tasked with planning and preparing for the takeover. If they had the beast in their hands by then, his plan would be executed.

"And if we don't?" the general asked.

"Then we'll call it off and wait for the next opportunity. Keep your plan flexible," Brideaux snapped. If only all the members had superior intellect. Then he wouldn't have to always make the important decisions on his own. After all, that's why he'd formed the group. To get help with his ultimate plan.

Daniel kissed Sarah goodbye, then lifted Nick into his arms and gave him important instructions. "You're the man of the house while I'm gone, buddy. You mind your mom, and take care of her, okay?"

Around them on the tarmac, similar scenes were occurring between JR and Rebecca, Raj and Sushma and Roy and Salome.

Raj comforted Sushma and the little one, who was also crying because mom was. "I'll be all right. Daniel, JR and Robert will all protect me. We'll be back before you know it. Do your best to help Sarah and the others."

As the helicopter took off, chosen for its ability to carry their equipment rather than speed, the women smiled through their tears and waved. When it was out of sight, Sarah invited them all to her home for a meal and a planning session. They were in charge of the Foundation on their own until the others got back. She wanted to solicit the help of the others in concealing the fact that the heart of the Foundation was away on assignment.

In Flagstaff, Brideaux awaited the Rossler group, but sent his elite security force ahead to dig in and remain concealed until they were needed. Once the Rosslers landed, they'd continue on the last leg of the trip with Brideaux joining them in their helicopter. Among his equipment were a few items the Rossler group never suspected.

After attending Sarah's luncheon and agreeing with her plan to act as if the Foundation were conducting business as usual, Salome joined Luke at headquarters to catch up with her research. It had to some extent taken a back seat to the more urgent events of the past few weeks - the translations, the security audit, Enigma, Nicholas' death and the funeral.

"Luke," she said, alarmed at what she immediately discovered, "have you seen this?"

At his own desk, which had been jammed into Salome's office so they could interact without having to interrupt their thoughts by walking back and forth between separate offices, Luke looked up and asked, "What?"

"Look here. There have been major movements in the pathology lab sectors over the last few weeks." What do you make of it?"

Both were on alert immediately. Why were those two big pharma companies buying up labs? There was no money in pathology labs.

Luke said, "I can't see why, but we'd better find out. Something's up, that's for sure."

Salome agreed. There was a snake in the grass somewhere, and if they didn't locate it immediately, there could be hell to pay.

Chapter Forty

LOOKS JUST LIKE A FACE

Day 1 - the Canyon

The Canyon site looked far different within a few hours of the group arriving there. In the huge room that JR and Robert had first encountered, they set up an impressive array of equipment, including Raj's computer lab in one corner and Roy's workshop in another. The room was more suited for the former than the latter, and Daniel knew they were in trouble when he saw Raj zooming up and down and back and forth in his Eighth Cycle floating chair. Raj would never be satisfied with an ordinary Earth-bound desk chair again.

Roy, though, fretted that his equipment was out in the open for anyone to see. In spite of the fact that it was only them and their benefactor in the place, he felt exposed and vulnerable. However, it couldn't be helped.

Since the power source wasn't obvious and in any case may not have been compatible, they had set up solar panel chargers outside the building to charge the batteries for all their equipment. Some of it made such a draw on the batteries that they would have to go out at least three times a day, every four hours or so, to get recharged batteries. However, it wasn't a total waste of time, since they would also use that same time to make contact with their families back home.

Joseph was set up with a smaller array of equipment in a third corner, and desks for the explorers were located in the fourth. It left an enormous space in the center with nothing but the floating tables and chairs. Some of the group would have preferred to bivouac here, with others around for a feeling of security. But, no matter what they did to push the furnishings out of the way, they snapped back into place as soon as someone stopped pushing them. Defeated, they each chose a room in the dormitory wing and spread out their sleeping bags on the floating beds. As Raj remarked, no one wanted to sleep on linens that someone might have died on, despite the fact they hadn't found any evidence of that yet.

Per Salome's suggestion and Rebecca's second of the motion, the explorers, Daniel, JR and Robert with John Brideaux tagging along, put on biohazard suits for their reconnaissance of the floor where the beast was supposed to be. It was an ordinary site floor, consisting of a hub where the elevators let them out, with five spokes leading off it. Each spoke had four doors leading from the hallway down its center into the walls on both sides, just as the rest of the floors other than the community floor had.

The community floor was their designation for the main area, where the large room, the kitchen and laundry facilities spokes and the three dormitory spokes were located.

Satisfied the only way to locate the beast after the quick recon, they had Roy set up their remote control robots to start scanning the walls of the rooms on that floor. None of the doors had any signs on them and certainly none of them had a warning sign on them saying 'danger don't enter' with a skull and cross bones. Neither did any of them have a sign that said Room of Darkness or looked darker than any of the others. The latter was Roy's observation, but no one saw his look of confusion when the others laughed, due to his biohazard suit obscuring his face.

Roy had brought equipment to scan the walls of the place before risking damage or worse by drilling into them. As the others stood around or paced, he carefully used every gadget in his arsenal to determine the composition of the strange, light-emitting metal. Nothing he had reported anything at all about the metal. As he remarked to Robert, he'd hoped it was related in some way to the lighting from Paradise Valley in the Antarctic, but that didn't seem to be the case.

While he worked, Brideaux grew bored and left, asking Daniel to send for him if anything developed while he was gone. However, with the afternoon wearing long and no discoveries yet, everyone but Roy and Robert eventually abandoned the vigil as well. Roy worked on until he had scanned every wall in every way he could, with Robert loyally keeping him company.

When he was finished, Roy suggested they stop for the day and join the others. He had a suggestion, but didn't want to make a unilateral decision. It should be discussed with the group.

Day 2 - the Canyon

Roy had outlined his plan while everyone enjoyed their evening meal, even John Brideaux to his surprise.

They needed to test all the walls, and it was going to involve some risk since Roy's scans hadn't penetrated the strange metal. They needed to find out if there were anything like electric cables or some other sort of energy conductors or electromagnetic fields. The light had to be coming from some kind of power, and before they burned peepholes for a mini robot to enter, it would be better not to fry the robot or the person controlling it by shorting out an essentially alien power source with it. As soon as Roy said 'alien', Raj's eyes went round, but Roy settled him down. "I mean, not like ours. Not little green men."

It was rather disappointing, since everyone had envisioned waltzing into each room, locating the beast and unplugging it. Clearly, that wasn't going to happen. Roy suggested that since he was the only one who could operate his other equipment and he'd need only one assistant to record measurements, maybe it would be a good time for Daniel, JR and Brideaux to explore some of the other floors.

By early morning, Roy and Robert were set up, and if the others were exploring the other floors between visits to the fourth to learn of his progress, they didn't talk much about what they were finding, if anything.

He had determined that there were indeed electromagnetic fields and some sort of electric conductors in the walls, but as far as he could tell, only around the doors. After carefully mapping it all, they would try to burn holes in the places where there was no electrical activity. But first, Roy, who was almost compulsive about being thorough, wanted to map all the doors and the walls in between before attempting to burn through any of them.

After breaking for lunch, they found one door that had more of what Roy was now thinking of as protection around it. He had also found a way to measure the approximate thickness of the doors, if his instruments were telling him what he thought they were. Compared to the other doors, this one was about four times thicker.

Roy paused in his work while Robert went to locate the others and report they might have found the room they were looking for. When Daniel and the others returned with Robert, they decided to take a chance and work on that room first. But, by now it was late and everyone was tired from the long day. Rather than risk a mistake, they reluctantly stopped for the night.

Day 3 - the Canyon

Everyone from Daniel to Joseph was on edge the next day. Joseph had been brooding ever since he'd first laid eyes on the doors in the canyon wall. Legends of his people had filled his thoughts with foreboding, and he regretted getting involved with these men who were meddling with something they knew little about.

The others were simply anxious to get started. They'd each come here for a purpose, and the first phase of that purpose was about to be fulfilled. Yet, no one had anything to do about it until Roy had done his part. It made for some tension-related strife among them until Daniel called their attention to what they were doing and the necessity for teamwork. Then apologies all around settled them down as Roy got to work.

With his nano-enhanced laser, he cut a small hole through the outside wall and sent in the mini robot. Everyone watched the monitor showing the room through the robot's onboard camera, most of them holding their breath. A sigh of disappointment escaped several at the same time as the screen was pitch black. There was no light in the room, not even the light that emanated from every wall they'd seen so far. Had Roy damaged the light source when he cut the wall?

Before anyone had time to ask, the movement of the robot advancing was apparently caught by a motion sensor. In the midst of the gloom, three lights had come on. Before the camera adjusted to the light, everyone had the impression of the lights forming a jack-o-lantern face, with two eyes and a mouth. Then the rest of the room was bathed in reflected light.

Peering at the monitor, Robert was the first to react. "Crikey, that looks just like a face! It's just like the letter said."

"It's computer screens," Raj said, his voice firm with authority.

"I never saw an oval computer screen," JR answered, referring to the two 'eyes' above the square light. It was the shape of them that most fed the impression of a face.

"That's because you never saw an Eighth Cycle computer," Daniel responded.

"Where are the controls, then?" JR challenged.

As they stared, no one could see any sign of anything looking like a controller for the device. No keyboard, no mouse, no joystick - nothing. But Raj had spotted something else. On a table in front of the face in the wall rested a small metal box. "There's the user manual," he said, again with high confidence he was right.

No one challenged him. There it was. Now, how were they going to safely bring it out?

Chapter Forty-One

THE SKYWALKERS

Day 3 to 4 - the Rossler Foundation

While Sarah and Rebecca worked together to handle ordinary Foundation business, Salome turned over all security matters to Luke while she continued her research to find out who was behind the two pharmaceutical companies that were inexplicably buying up pathology labs. She had a feeling it was more than just buying companies to generate losses for tax purposes.

As Salome tracked down the companies behind the two pharmaceuticals, she saw some names that were familiar to her. These same shell corporations had turned up before, but there were roadblocks now in updating their holdings. Drilling down to the last level to try to get the names of the people hiding behind the company masks was more difficult than ever. Had her previous searches alerted someone?

It was a tedious and slow process, made all the more so because Salome had come to rely on Raj's genius with data queries, rather than her own skills. She could do it, of course. She was just rusty.

After that, the computer had to work through mountains of data to get down to the levels she wanted. And then there was still quite a bit of manual processing, instinctual lines of inquiry that as far as she knew no computer could be programmed to do. Even so, she wished more than once that Raj was there to throw more computing power at this, to speed it up.

Day 4 - the Canyon

Once the mini robot had done its job, Roy sent in a bigger robot. This one was not only equipped with 'arms' to manipulate and pick up objects, but it was capable of cutting its own hole big enough for it to move through. As soon as Roy programmed it with the coordinates that would avoid the electromagnetic fields, it went to work.

In no time, it had retrieved the metal box, with no apparent alarm from the beast. In fact, Daniel would have wondered if the face in the wall was actually the beast, as quiet as it seemed to stay after activating upon detecting movement in the room. That is, he would have wondered if it hadn't exactly matched the description in the letter. Now the question was whether the processing unit, for it was clear this thing was a computer of some kind, was large or small. The robots hadn't shown them anything that looked like it could be a CPU, so he assumed it was behind the wall. But, they'd soon know if they were right in believing the metal box contained the specs and operating instructions.

The Skywalkers

Raj put his computers to work extracting the sound files, but he didn't have all the server power he had back at Foundation headquarters. Furthermore, he had to keep pausing the process to change the batteries, requiring a trip outside each time. With the computers working at 100% capacity, they churned through the batteries much quicker. Changing them more often meant that sometimes Raj had to wait for an hour or more for a full charge.

The process was painfully slow. It took until the following morning to get the first of the files to Joseph to begin translating.

Between changing batteries, Raj was constantly making backups of all the files on all of the computers, Joseph's and onto the handy little nanotech version of USB sticks that Roy made for him a few years ago. About the size of his thumbnail and equipped with a special connection device he'd modified the computers to accept, each could store approximately fifty terabytes of data. He could, and often did, put dozens of them in his pocket at the same time.

Now that the beast had been activated, Daniel banned further exploration until they knew what they were dealing with. This left too much time on their hands for men of action, especially JR and Robert. At least most of them had phone calls with their wives back home to occupy part of their downtime. Taking turns on that secure satellite phone so kindly provided by Brideaux, they updated everyone back at the Foundation about their progress.

Brideaux also accompanied them out, both for phone call breaks and every time they went out to swap batteries. No one thought anything of it. He had his own phone, and lots of interests and companies to stay in touch with even while he was here.

Day 5 - at the Rossler Foundation

Early on the morning of the fifth day of the expedition, Salome finally hit pay dirt with the first one of the names of the real owners behind the companies she was investigating – John Brideaux! It shouldn't have been a surprise. She knew the slimy bastard was up to no good from the first moment she met him. However, it was a shock. Salome knew immediately she had found something significant, but she couldn't quite put it together, even with Luke's help.

She also knew she needed more. If she'd seen his name before, she could have warned Daniel. What had she missed? Did he have his fingers in all the other pies she'd been watching? How powerful must he be, to remain hidden so well? And, what about his associates?

Before she started the task of rooting Brideaux out in the other industries, Salome consulted with Luke. Who should she tell, with Daniel away, and when? As a result, a hurried meeting was called with Sarah, Rebecca and Sinclair.

"Friends," she began, the look of grave news on her face alarming them. "I've discovered something disturbing. I don't know what it means yet. Normally, I'd take it straight to Daniel, but Luke and I wonder if that's the best course of action at this time. So, you're here to help us decide."

Sinclair, unable to restrain his curiosity any longer, interrupted. "Well, spit it out, lass! What is it?"

His outburst broke Salome's tension a bit, and she gave him a half-smile. "I'm getting to that Sinclair. There's no easy way to say it. I have evidence that John Brideaux may not be the unselfish benefactor he seems to be."

The anti-climax startled a laugh out of both Sarah and Rebecca, which in turn startled Salome. She turned a look of confusion on them. Sarah explained. "He 'may not' be? Salome, please explain why this required a meeting."

Salome regrouped. "Oh, I see I needed more background for you."

She proceeded to explain her Spiderweb, omitting the fact that she had been instrumental in constructing the top-secret government project it was based upon. They didn't need to know that. Once she'd explained its function, Rebecca remained a bit confused about its significance, but Sarah got it. She remembered her conversation with Salome a few days ago.

"So, you've been monitoring people who are, through wealth and influence in major financial and industrial areas, capable of shifting power in any number of ways."

"To put it in a nutshell, yes," Salome replied. "My major concern is the influence on social behavior worldwide. Finances, industry and political power. Those are the three legs on which society functions. It's just like the concept of our government – separation of powers. When one person or a handful of people dominate all three of those pillars, we're in trouble if that person has nefarious motives. In fact, we're in trouble anyway. No one should have that much power. Not even a Mother Teresa."

"Amen," Sarah breathed. "This *is* disturbing. Thank you for bringing it to our attention."

"Of course," Salome replied.

"However," Sarah went on, "I don't think this is the time to spring it on Daniel. Or any of the others. They have a dangerous job to do. Putting more stress on them with little to back it up and no idea what Brideaux may be up to just doesn't seem productive to me."

"I agree," replied Rebecca. "JR's so much better now than he was five or six years ago, but he can still be volatile if something sets him off the wrong way. Let's wait until we know more."

With Sinclair and Luke in agreement, Salome bowed to the majority. Nevertheless, she had a sinking feeling it was the wrong decision.

Day 5 - the Canyon

Meanwhile, in the Canyon, Joseph got an early start on the first sound files and worked as fast as he could. The first file was like an introduction to the rest, a table of contents.

From that first foil they quickly learned what they can expect to find in the foils. His first report to the group was to let Raj know that in the first foil, he'd find diagrams of the beast, which may need to be handled differently than the text. Joseph didn't know of any way to translate a diagram to speech.

The diagrams would show how the beast was constructed, critical knowledge if they were to dismantle it.

Next would come detailed descriptions and code for how the beast communicated with something he translated as 'skywalkers'. Joseph didn't stop to analyze what skywalkers must be, but as he spoke his translation into the microphone of his computer, Raj had arranged it so a speech-recognition program would pick it up and broadcast to a streaming file for the others to read if they liked, in real-time. As Joseph continued, JR, Robert and Roy gathered around Daniel at his computer and discussed it.

"It's got to be the same as the 'birds' in the letter," JR said.

"Maybe." Daniel sounded doubtful. "We can't jump to conclusions."

"Whether it's the same or not, I'd lay odds it means satellites," Roy said.

"No takers," said Daniel. "I think you're right."

By now, Joseph's next translation was rolling down the computer screen. JR looked at it and jerked his head toward Joseph in his corner. It took Daniel a moment longer, but both of them recalled hearing Navajo legends at their grandfather's knees. How did Joseph mean this? JR strode over to Joseph's corner to question him.

"Joseph, can you stop a minute? We need clarification."

Joseph looked up. "Yes?"

JR assessed his demeanor. Most Navajos, even 'modern' ones who'd been completely assimilated to mainstream American culture, would be a little shaky at the mention of 'skinwalkers'.

"Can you come over to Daniel's desk?"

Joseph got up and joined the others. "What's the problem?"

JR hated to even say the word. Not that he was superstitious, but he didn't want to offend Joseph, and he certainly didn't want to have to delay the translation for a ceremony.

"This word," he said, pointing to it on the screen. "Did you mean a witch, or is it literal?" He waited with apprehension for the answer.

Joseph laughed. "There are no witches. This is exactly what the sound file said."

Relieved, JR asked the next logical question. "So, what do you think it means?"

"Isn't it obvious? It has to be the device the letter

described, the thing everyone had implanted at birth to control their health and diet."

Joseph's interpretation was so matter-of-fact and practical that JR was ashamed to have thought he'd be superstitious.

Joseph went on, though. "Is that all you got out of that section though?"

"Well, it was the first thing that jumped out. What else did you notice?" Daniel asked.

"It isn't just the beast that's connected to those 'skywalkers'," Joseph said. "The 'skinwalkers' are, too."

A ripple of uneasiness went through everyone around the computer, as each began to get an idea of how the beast had managed to kill people. Unconsciously, more than one rubbed the back of his right hand and felt relief when they found no 'skinwalker' embedded there.

Chuckling and shaking his head, Joseph went back to his corner. Next thing he knew, they'd be asking him to do a rain dance. Foolish white people thought all Navajo were backwards. If it hadn't been so funny watching JR try not to offend him, it would have been an insult.

As the long day went on, Joseph translated untiringly. Details emerged about the nanotechnology, which kept Roy engaged and the others horrified at the level of control over the general population it gave the beast's operators.

Finally, Daniel asked Joseph to skim the table of contents for what really mattered; how to shut down the beast, and how to dismantle it if necessary.

That evening, as Daniel spoke to Sarah, he told her they had decided not to make it a two-stage expedition. Rather than bringing everything back to the Foundation, it would be safer and just as easy to shut the thing down right where they were, assuming they could quickly find the foil that contained the shutdown instructions. It should be straightforward; the table of contents indicated the foil was included in the user manual.

Once they identified it, Joseph would translate it, they'd do the shutdown and get out of there. The only challenge was to find that specific foil in the box. Raj was supposed to find it tonight, as soon as he'd spoken to Sushma on their nightly call.

Day 6 - at the Rossler Foundation

Salome had gone along with the decision not to alarm the guys on the expedition, but she couldn't shake a feeling that they were in as much danger from John Brideaux as from the beast. For that reason, she had pulled an "all-nighter" to dig more. As a result, she'd come up with a handful of names. These were people who could be Brideaux's associates based on mutual business interests. After narrowing it down to a group of six who had business interests one hundred percent aligned with his, she employed one of the most secret and powerful aspects of The Prophet, a complete history of the cell phone movements of a select group of wealthy and powerful men and women in the world. With it, she was able to track the movements of four of them. The report revealed that those four had been together a few times the last few weeks for an hour or so at a time.

Even though John Brideaux was not on the list, there was a strong possibility he and the other two men she'd identified as his associates had been with the others. If not, it didn't prove they weren't involved in some sort of secret cabal. Only that the others very likely were.

It almost looked like they had become careless in the last few weeks, because there was no trace in the records that these people were together before. At least, not for the past twelve months prior to that first meeting she'd found out about, which was as far back as she looked.

Based on their holdings, when they'd acquired them and how the stock had behaved both before and after their acquisitions, she had no doubt they'd been associates for years, though. The only conclusion was that they had a secure method of communication and ordinarily had no need to be in each other's physical presence. It worried her that they now gathered in the same place, that the frequency of these meetings seemed to be accelerating, and that all of them, to the last man, were buying up pathology labs as fast as humanly possible.

Luke received a call from his old friend Sam Lewis early the same morning with an invitation to lunch. Sam was on his way from a fishing trip in Wyoming to a balloon festival in Santa Fe, New Mexico and would like to swing through Boulder to catch up. Luke was enthusiastically on board. He hadn't seen Sam since he retired right after the Sword of Cyrus near-miss. It would be good to have a beer and talk about old times.

Without saying so over the phone, Luke thought it would be a great idea to fill Sam in on some of the peculiar goings-on within the Rossler Foundation as well. He trusted Sam more than one hundred percent. In a back corner of a little tavern between Boulder and Limon, Luke and Sam

The Skywalkers

had enjoyed a good meal and talked about shared memories until the place cleared out from the lunch crowd and the two old friends were alone except for the bartender.

It was then Luke turned serious and began to tell Sam about the Eighth Cycle site, the beast, and why they could not go to the government with this. Finally, he got around to Salome's project. Sam knew of The Prophet, but was shocked when Luke showed him what Salome could track and learn about people's personal stuff these days. He laughed when he said he was glad she was an exceptional case, but still, it was a little scary.

"You should see the report she ran on me to convince me of all this, Sam. On second thought, you shouldn't. Too much very private data on there. Almost lost my temper with the girl when I saw it," Luke said.

"I'm glad I'm not in the job anymore," Sam replied. "I'm enjoying my retirement and catching up on all the fly-fishing I missed all those years. I don't mind telling you, I'm just too old and tired to handle all of the demands of the job. And these days, the total lack of privacy is too much for me. "

Luke's interested expression encouraged him to go on.

"You know, just the other day I was talking with one of my old operatives who's still at the Agency – don't think you knew him, Luke. Anyway, just as an example of what you're talking about and what I don't miss about the job.

"He told me that a major breach in computer security happened a few weeks back. When security audits were done to see what the hackers got, they found that all medical data from the president down to every high ranking government officials, top brass military, FBI and even CIA were copied or hacked into."

"No kidding," Luke said.

"Nope, not at all. It was a good week after the break-in before they discovered it, too. The guys who are supposed to keep a lookout for this sort of thing twenty-four-seven were fast asleep at the wheel! Even more embarrassing, it happened in other countries at the same time."

"So, what happened?" Luke asked. "Why didn't anyone hear about it?"

"Oh, a few heads rolled. Nothing was given to the press, because it was a limited number of people, even though they were very important people. It was just too embarrassing to admit their screw-up in public."

"I can imagine," Luke deadpanned. The two had a good chuckle and agreed it certainly was much better to be in retirement, even though Luke kept getting pulled back into the Rossler Foundation business.

"You'll have to escape and go fly-fishing with me sometime, buddy," Sam said. "But right now I have a date with a hot-air balloon. Always wanted to fly in one of those things. Now I've got time, it's something to cross off my bucket list."

"Well, have fun," Luke said. He hoped Sam would get to cross off a few more things on his bucket list before all hell broke loose, but since he couldn't say when that may happen he didn't say anything but goodbye.

Luke waved Sam on his way and then drove over to Foundation headquarters to look in on the girls. He poked his head into Sarah's office and found her deep in conversation with Rebecca, so he just waved and went on to see Salome in her office. She was staring into space, but gave him a warm welcome, so he sat down to tell her about his lunch with Sam Lewis, who sent her his regards. Then he related Sam's funny story about the security breach.

As he talked, though, Salome's face changed. She was white with shock... what had he said?

While Luke was talking, the light dawned for Salome. Thanks to Sam's story, which wasn't at all funny, she finally saw the connection, why this group of men, through the guise of their ownership in pharmaceutical companies, had been buying up pathology labs.

It all fell into place; the merger with the company that had perfected GENTS, the pathology labs, even the reason for the theft of medical data belonging to highly-placed officials in government and the military. Worst of all, the connection to the beast, and the reason for John Brideaux's presence at the site.

As Luke became more alarmed, Salome finally spoke. "I've got it, Luke. That was the last piece of the puzzle. Our target group has been buying pathology labs so they can build up a genetic profile of every person on the planet!"

"Why would they want that?" Luke asked, still not seeing it.

"Because the beast operates on some sort of principle related to a person's genetic profile. Their blood, Luke! Remember the letter. The beast knows my blood, he said. The death from the sky is programmed specifically to a genetic profile. It's probably a highly targeted poison or designer illness, delivered by something too small to see."

"You're thinking of Roy's nano-bots."

"Of course I am. And remember, the Sword of Cyrus wiped out a couple of villages with targeted diseases. Whoever controls the beast has the power to wipe out entire populations or target just one person. Luke, Brideaux made that connection long ago. It's why he's at the site. He's there to take control of the beast, and once he has it, he and his group could take over the world.

"Salome, calm down. That's a pretty big leap on circumstantial evidence."

"Oh my God Luke, we're in trouble! We're too late, and our husbands will be killed there in the Canyon. Brideaux has everything he needs literally to take over the world."

"Maybe not. They haven't finished translating the manual, have they?"

"This is what they have. I took notes when I talked to Roy this morning, and Daniel told Sarah the same thing last night. They were going to have Joseph start the first thing this morning with the section on shutting down the beast, but the rest of the manual tells how to build one."

Salome handed him her notes, where he read the bullet points one by one, becoming paler with each point.

Luke looked up. "You're right, they're in extreme danger and we have no time to waste. One of us should get to Sarah immediately, and the other should round up Rebecca and Sinclair."

"I'll go to Sarah. Get Rebecca first and send her straight there. I don't know how Sarah will take this, she may need medical attention."

Luke snapped his fingers. "Wait, I saw Rebecca in Sarah's office just a few minutes ago. Hurry there, and page me if she isn't there still."

Salome literally flew to the other end of the hall, where Sarah had taken over Daniel's office while he was gone. Later, she wouldn't remember her feet hitting the floor, and it seemed she'd arrived before she left. Out of breath, she saw with relief that Rebecca was still there.

Her appearance in the doorway startled the other two

women, who looked up with alarm as she slid in on one foot and then bent over, breathing heavily. Sarah stood with a cry and Rebecca went to Salome to discover what was wrong. Salome held her hand up.

"I'm...all...right. Give me...a minute...to catch...my breath."

Just then her pager went off with Luke's report that he was on his way with Sinclair. Only a little recovered, Salome turned the device so Rebecca could read it.

"Come sit down," Rebecca ordered. "Sarah, there's evidently some urgent news, but Luke and Sinclair are on their way. Let Salome catch her breath until they get here."

Sarah nodded, her eyes still wide. Whatever this was, it couldn't be good. Once Luke arrived and Salome had explained her conclusion and its basis, apologizing that she'd frightened them with an unexpected panic attack; the group shook off their shock and began to brainstorm a plan.

On the surface, it was simple. They needed to work out what they could do before the next time one or more of the expedition members called. Of course, they needed to warn them, that is, if they were still alive and in a position to call. If everything was still okay, that should be this afternoon, about three hours from now, when they come out to swap batteries. Before the Headquarters group could determine what to say, they needed to brainstorm to figure out Brideaux's plan. The facts as they knew them were these. He could make his move now if he has not done so already or he could be waiting to get the translation or maybe even until the beast is disabled. With no information to the contrary, they concluded there was really no reason for him to wait any longer. He undoubtedly had what he needed and therefore he and his henchmen could take it from there.

But, what purpose would it serve to kill them? Unless he had a specific reason, there was a chance – a very slim chance - that he may just take all he needed and leave them there. None of them had done him any harm at all, ever, and he had no reason to kill anyone. But they know, and that may be enough reason. Salome's opinion was that he was as evil as Hitler or Stalin, anyone who'd ever been responsible in the past for the deaths of millions, and maybe all of them rolled into one. But Sarah held out hope. Brideaux and Daniel had always been cordial. Maybe he would spare the Foundation men because of it. After all, even Hitler had had friends for a while.

They had to believe that their men were alive, that Brideaux had made no move as yet. And with that belief came the necessity of doing *something* to keep them that way. Should they try to send a rescue team? If so, who could they send? Also how could they get there quickly?

Sinclair volunteered that if they had a private jet, they could get to Flagstaff in under an hour. From Flagstaff by helicopter it would take maybe a couple of hours. The real delay would be gathering a rescue unit and equipment.

In spite of the long odds, they had to try. While Rebecca went to search JR's office for contact information, the others took a break and Sinclair and Luke went to the canteen to get everyone some coffee. It could be a long night, and Salome was already running on sheer adrenaline, not having slept the night before. Sinclair took a detour for his bottle of Jameson's, in case anyone needed fortification as the meeting wore on.

While they were gone, Rebecca reminded Sarah that the

owner of the security company responsible for the building was a friend of JR's, an ex-Marine.

"That's right – Daniel likes him, too. They all get together for coffee every now and then when he comes to check up on his crew."

"They've been known to have a drink or two, as well," Rebecca remarked, just as Sinclair came in with his Jameson's. He perked up.

"A drink? Who are we talking about?"

Sarah rolled her eyes at him. "His name is Mark Bryant. A friend of JR's and now Daniel's. We've just remembered he's an ex-Marine, and I think some of his crew are, too."

By now the others were filtering back into the room. Sarah and Rebecca filled them in on what they'd remembered about Mark, that he was an officer, a captain Rebecca thought, in the Marines. JR had persuaded Daniel to give his fledgling company a shot at the Rossler security contract when he started it up in Boulder.

They will contact him and see if he can mount a rescue attempt. That is all they can think of now. The cops and the FBI and the CIA - all of them - are out.

Salome was convinced. "Luke, could you contact him to organize it? Excuse me," she said to the others. "I'll be right back."

As soon as they'd cleared the door, she said to Luke, "I haven't brought this up yet, and I don't want to spook the girls until we can discuss it, but it's clear to me we're going to have to activate Enigma. I'm thinking we offer him, his employees and their families' sanctuary at the Rabbit Hole when this is done, one way or another."

"Good idea, but I'm going to bring him back here. You can tell him yourself."

"All right. Do you agree, about Enigma?"

"Yes, on both counts. Activate. And, we haven't had a chance to organize security, which we'll need anyway. I'd say it's a win-win."

"Okay then, I'll raise the subject and we'll have a plan by the time you get back. Thanks Luke, you're the best."

"No, Salome, *you're* the best. This wasn't even on my radar, and you nailed it. Okay, gotta go. I'll be back as soon as I can."

"Where are we? So, assuming Mark agrees, rescue will be on the way, let's say in four hours. The guys are going to be calling in less than three. What do we do?" Sarah was asking for input but Salome needed to think it through.

The guys were indoors most of the time. They wouldn't know anyone would be there to help them, and they'd be back inside the facility before the rescuers got there. If it came to a firefight, they wouldn't know what was happening. They had to be warned.

"We have to tell them to be careful of Brideaux," Sinclair said. That was obvious, but how? Would he be close enough to anyone who was calling to hear the warning? Would it put the guys in immediate danger?

"Oh, my God," Salome said. "The phone they're calling on… Brideaux supplied it. They could have been listening in all along. We have to assume there's no way to warn them without alerting Brideaux's people."

"We can't talk on it anymore, then," Rebecca said. The thought of never speaking to her husband again if things went wrong overwhelmed her before she could finish her thought.

"No, that's wrong," Salome replied. "If we don't answer, the bad guys will definitely know something's wrong. We have to think of a way to warn them without listeners catching on that we know anything's up."

"What if we just blurt it out, tell them we've discovered John Brideaux is a monster and they should take him captive and wait for JR's buddies to get there?" Rebecca said, taking hope again, knowing that she could hear JR's voice one more time."

"It's worth discussion. Sinclair? What do you think?"

"I think we should ask Luke, frankly. Unless any of you have any kind of secret code you've used before? Sarah?"

"Oh, gosh, Sinclair, it's been years," she said, causing Rebecca and Salome to look at her with interest. "Daniel and I used to have a code worked out so we could talk with the Orion Society listening in and sound like the conversation was about nothing at all, when really we were conveying secrets. But, I don't remember much of it, and even if I did, I don't know if he'd remember. Plus, I'd have to alert him to it being code."

"Do you remember any of it?" Salome asked.

Sarah blushed. "Well, just one exchange, for when we wanted to, er." She looked at Sinclair, who gave a broad grin.

"Made love over the phone," he supplied.

Rebecca was startled into a laugh. "You did what?" she asked Sarah.

"Oh, it was just a silly game. He'd text 'RUR' for Are you ready? And I'd answer RWA. Then we'd tease a little more. I remember one time we Skyped and I had him believing I was going to be wearing a sexy negligee. You should have seen his face when he saw my flannel nightgown, buttoned up to my chin, long sleeves and all."

The whole group had needed something like that, and the tension relief when they all howled at the story.

Then Salome asked, "And what did RWA stand for?"

"Ready, willing and able," said Sarah, now laughing at the story herself. That set them off again.

When she'd caught her breath, Salome asked. "If you said that to him, would he be alerted that there was a second meaning to anything that came after?"

Sarah thought for a moment. "You know, he may."

"Then it's worth a shot. Sarah, you have to remember anything you can about your old code. And then you have to let me do the talking. I'll tell you why in a minute."

With Sarah's brow wrinkled in confusion, Salome had to look at the others as she explained some other things she'd considered. The first was that there was a very good chance Brideaux had already deployed people to come to their building and take over the libraries. His reasoning would be that he could never be safe, even in control of the beast, as long as someone else was in possession of them. Because there may be knowledge in them that could neutralize his weapon. If it hadn't been put in place yet, it was only because Brideaux felt safe in the knowledge that no one knew of him and his plans. It was safer to believe they were in imminent danger of attack, and plan a response to that

If their worst fears were true and Brideaux had already killed their husbands or was about to, he would not hesitate to kill them and everyone at the Rossler Foundation to get what he wants.

The Skywalkers

Before they'd come to the crux of the matter, Luke was back with Mark.

As quickly as possible, Salome filled him in, sharing the details of the discovery and what they feared.

"So, you don't even know at this time whether they are alive?" he asked, his face grim.

"We don't have any reason to believe otherwise."

"Then you don't need to say any more. Once a Marine, always a Marine, and Marines don't leave anyone behind. How many are there, and exactly where are they?"

Mark made notes on a little spiral notepad he pulled from his pocket as Salome gave him the coordinates of the slot canyon. Luke disappeared for a moment and came back with a data stick with the layout of the facility, a map of the area with the lift entrance marked, and directions for opening the doors and operating the lift.

"Anything else I need to know?" he asked.

"Yes," said Sarah. "You may be walking into a very dangerous situation. We have to warn our guys when they call, and that may be before you get there. It could be a mess after that."

Mark grinned. "Cleaning up messes is what we do best, ma'am. Your husband gave me a chance, and now it's time to return the favor."

"One more thing," she answered. "We've prepared a contingency plan. We call it Enigma. Without wasting time on detail, it's a hiding place for our people, to ride out what we think is a disaster that's coming as soon as this John Brideaux and his colleagues get hold of the beast. We're going to activate Enigma, so we won't be here by the time you get back. Your family and those of anyone you take with you to rescue our guys are welcome to come with us. And we'll need you to bring our men there."

Luke interrupted. "The coordinates for there are also on that thumb drive."

"I don't want to delay getting to your men. Can someone brief our families and help them get ready?"

"We'll take care of it."

"Then I'll take care of your men." He hesitated. "I don't want to borrow trouble, but... if we're too late?"

Fighting tears, Sarah looked at Rebecca and Salome, who nodded. "Then bring them to us anyway. They belong with us, dead or alive."

"Yes, ma'am. I'd better get going. I'll let you know when we're ready to leave, probably within three hours."

The few people remaining in the room had a responsibility to get their families, employees and friends – and now the families of the rescue group - out of harm's way and to the Rabbit Hole. For that, they'd need help, because the plans were incomplete. Woefully short of younger men to help with the heavy lifting and organizing, the women did what they did best – they organized and improvised.

Chapter Forty-Two

EXODUS

Sarah called her dad to come and help after briefing Luke what they'd been up to. Daniel's parents and Aaron were still at Bess's, helping her deal with all of the details that seemed to crop up after the death of a spouse and waiting anxiously for the return of their other two sons. She called and asked Ben to come to Daniel's office for some very important information.

When he got there, she took longer than she wanted to explain exactly what was going on and that she needed him and Nancy to get Bess, Martha and Sinclair to safety. Aaron she needed to stay and help. Ben proved to be as smart and resourceful as his sons when he took it all in stride and told her to leave all that to him. What else could he take that they may need?

Sarah was closer to Daniel's grandparents than his parents, but his calm acceptance made Ben look like a knight in shining armor to her. She threw her arms around him for a hug, and asked him to take little Nick to her mother, who would take him and Aunt Sally to the Rabbit

Hole. That would leave her mind free to do what needed to be done here.

Salome had informed her the ones who remained here would have to pack Raj's servers for him as well as Roy's lab. Luckily Raj had showed her how he had marked the most important servers. In addition, his assistant Stuart Harding has been briefed and was on their list of people to go to the Rabbit Hole with them. She paged him next to ask what kind of help he needed, then sent her dad to give it as soon as he arrived.

Stuart, who had no girlfriend or family to worry about, knew what to do and had it organized by the time Ryan arrived to help him load it all into an unmarked van. Stuart showed Ryan where he'd put a little red paint dot on the back of each of them. While Ryan began the task of loading, Stuart retrieved all of Raj's backups from the company vaults.

Meanwhile, Salome had found Roy's lab perfectly organized and already packed neatly in toolboxes and the shelves before he went on expedition. They will just have to clear it out completely. She was carrying one box at a time to the garage and packing it into another of the unmarked vans when Ryan and Stuart finished their task. They returned with her to the lab to help get that out before Stuart headed out in his vehicle for the Rabbit Hole.

If Sarah hadn't seen it with her own eyes, she'd never have believed that they could empty the building of anything of use to the enemy and cleared it of people in a matter of two hours. But now, it was time to concentrate on the message of warning to the man who was her whole world. If she lost Daniel, how would she go on?

Meanwhile, Mark Bryant contacted two of his employees, ex-Marines, as he'd promised Sarah. In a closed-door meeting in his office, he briefed them on a "need to know" basis. Both agreed to go, for all the reasons he had agreed to take on the mission. The Rossler Foundation was indirectly responsible for their good jobs; they owed the head of the Foundation a favor, and his ex-Marine brother their loyalty.

"Okay, get out of here. Tell your families to stay home and wait for the Rossler people to come and tell them what's going on. You can tell them to be ready to pack for an extended trip. The Rossler people will tell them what they can take."

Bryant booked the private flight to Flagstaff and the helicopter in his own name so it couldn't be traced back to the Rossler Foundation.

Four hours after Mark met with Sarah, he picked up his men and drove them to the airport to take the private flight to Flagstaff.

Day 6 - the Canyon

Joseph had reached the chapter that talked about how to disable the beast in his translation efforts. It was going slowly but they were making progress, and as he worked, JR, Daniel and Robert studied what he'd translated so far.

John Brideaux was sitting in his corner working on his tablet. He hadn't fully decided on the right time to make his move. With the beast identified and all the sound files already created by Raj, he could actually do it now if he wanted to.

His people were on standby to come in and take everything - kill all of them if necessary, except Joseph, whom he needed for the rest of the translations.

But, he reasoned, it would be so much better if he had the full translation and the beast had been shut down before they move in. Let someone else take the risk of the shutdown. That way, he'd be able to move the beast, set it up in another place and activate it again when he was ready.

First, he'd need to launch satellites through some of the private space companies in which he and his Eligo Rarus group had invested. They'd load the beast with the DNA they'd stolen along with what they were now already collecting through the labs, and in a matter of a few weeks he'd be ready to take over the world.

Once the satellites were up, they can just keep on uploading data as it came in. Brideaux actually liked this Rossler outfit. They were an intelligent bunch of people and he could have used their brains in his empire. But, the biggest problem with them was that they had moral values. He didn't need that.

He didn't really want to kill any of them, especially Daniel, but it wouldn't bother him at all if he had to kill them all. A good leader knew when it was time to sacrifice a few for the common good of all mankind, after all. His conclusion was that he'd like to do it as cleanly and as quickly as possible, but it was better to wait a bit longer until the translation was done and the beast deactivated. Then he'd call in his soldiers and take over.

Meanwhile back at Rossler Foundation

After the frenzied activity, the girls, Sinclair and the reinforcements of Aaron and Ryan had kicked off everything they could. Aaron wasn't happy that he hadn't been included in the rescue team. Those were his brothers in trouble, after all. But Rebecca was right when she pointed out his lack of experience with that kind of thing.

Enigma was implemented and everyone but this group would be on their way to safety within hours. The Canyon rescue team were on their way as well. It only remained to have a final chat about what to do when one or more of their husbands were expected to call in an hour. Salome calmed Sarah and Rebecca with the observation that everything they'd done was undercover, and there was every reason to believe their husbands, or some of them, were still alive. If the call came, it would confirm that. It was the reason they were sending people out in small groups; family members first, as they'd be the least likely to be watched.

Sarah and Rebecca weren't trained for this type of situation, and their emotions were on edge. Rebecca was actually doing better than Sarah now, first because of her medical training to handle a crisis with calm, and second because Sarah now regretted not having a chance to kiss Nick goodbye before Daniel's parents delivered him to her mom. At least Mom and Aunt Sally were already on the road and would be among the first to arrive to safety. With a gulp, she resigned herself to the idea that if anything happened to her, or to Daniel, God forbid, Nick would be raised by four loving grandparents and an uncle and aunt who adored him.

Sarah was actually taking pride in how she and Rebecca were handling their stress. Rather than being paralyzed by it, it had galvanized them to action in getting the exodus organized. The biggest issue they had was being unable to use any phone or the internet to make any arrangements at all. Everything had to be done in person. In fact, she was about to send Aaron to Raj's house to collect Sushma and the baby with no warning. She didn't envy him the task.

If the phone call they were waiting for came through as expected, they'd have to wait only long enough for the report of success by the rescue team. With their husbands' safe, they'd do all the rest of their moving under cover of darkness tonight and not alert too many people about their moving. The waiting, though, was excruciating.

Salome and Luke had gone over the Canyon situation again a bit more rationally after the initial shock and finally had come to almost the same conclusion as John Brideaux had, of course, unaware that he'd done so. It would probably be better and more efficient for him to wait until the group had the full translation and had deactivated the beast before he made his move. So, having considered all the risks and options they decided they had one chance at this and that would be when that phone rang with one of the boys on the other end still alive.

Sarah hadn't come up with anything except the RUR/RWA question and response for codes - she'd just been too busy to think. Salome told her it was okay, probably too complicated to pull off anyway. As the experienced

FBI agent, she wanted to handle the conversation, afraid that either Sarah or Rebecca would get nervous and give away the game somehow. They agreed, although Rebecca wasn't happy about not getting to talk to JR if it was him. Salome assured her that if there was a chance to do it, Rebecca or Sarah could get on the phone after she – Salome - had conveyed the critical information.

The plan was this. Salome would answer and direct the conversation as if she were the wife of whomever called. They would have to take the chance of talking in the open and tell him what is going on, using misdirection as much as possible. She wouldn't mention Enigma, and if Daniel or JR mentioned it, she'd deflect it and try to pass it off as something else, hoping the caller would get the picture. Brideaux's outfit must not know about it under any circumstances.

She also wouldn't mention the rescue mission. If the theory she and Luke were counting on were correct, then Brideaux was waiting to make his move. And if that were the case, she didn't want the ex-Marines running into an alerted ambush. Let them be the surprise factor.

To be as prepared as she could, Salome jotted down a script of sorts, with suggestions from the others. They were all gathered in the small conference room again, where they gathered to take their turn at talking when the men called every afternoon. As the time approached, Sarah kept looking at her watch every few minutes and Rebecca stared out the window or paced. Salome hoped the call wouldn't be delayed. She could have cut the tension with a knife.

Chapter Forty-Three

THE END GAME

When the phone rang, it was Daniel. Salome thanked Providence that it was he, whom she assumed would catch on to the ruse more quickly, having been through it before.

"Daniel, it's Salome. Listen very carefully, and above all, act normally. We've made some discoveries. I want you to say hello honey, or whatever you usually say to Sarah. Ask about Nick. And then, just listen. Don't say anything else until I can give you some instructions.

Daniel's voice sounded strained to her, but maybe it was just the effect of the phone signal having to bounce off the satellite.

"Hi, sweetheart? How are you? How's Nick?"

Salome breathed a sigh of relief. He got it. Even if there were listeners, he and the others would be alerted before Brideaux could get reinforcements there. With any luck, the chopper with JR's friends would get there first.

"Don't say anything until I tell you to. Here's the situation. I need to know if John Brideaux is nearby? If he's there and can hear you, say 'I'm sorry to hear that, but don't worry, we should be back in a few days.' If he can't hear you, say 'We're almost finished.'"

"I'm sorry to hear that, but don't worry. We should be back in a few days."

Damn, luck wasn't running with them so far. But she was prepared.

"Ok, yes or no to this one. Is everyone still alive and well?"

"Yes?"

The upward inflection let her know he wanted to understand what was going on. She'd get to it as quickly as she could.

"OK, if the answer to the next question is yes, just say yes, but don't make it a question this time. If no, say 'We're just finishing up.' Here's the question. Have any other people arrived?"

"We're just finishing up."

"Okay, I'm going to tell you what's going on. When I pause, just say anything that you might say to Sarah. Act like this is a normal conversation."

"Of course, sweetheart."

"Good. Daniel, John Brideaux isn't who he seems to be. I've turned up evidence that he and a handful of colleagues are on a mission to take over governments on a world-wide basis. He's after the beast, and he doesn't intend to destroy it. He wants to use it. Say something."

"Darling, you can't be serious!"

"Excellent. Believe it, Daniel. It's not just me saying it. I've showed the evidence to everyone here. They agree. You're in danger."

"Well, I'm surprised, but I left you in charge, sweetheart. I'm sure you'll do the right thing."

"Can you handle things from here on? We're concerned that he'll act sooner if he knows we know what's up."

"Yeah, no problem."

"Okay, Daniel, I'm out. We all love you all… be careful."

"Bye, sweetheart."

"Wait, Daniel, Sarah wants…" But the line was dead. Salome turned to Sarah. "I'm sorry, hon, he got away."

"At least I know he's alive," Sarah said, a forlorn note in her voice. At the window, Rebecca was weeping.

Daniel had tried to move away from Brideaux as soon as Salome had asked about his proximity, but every time he moved, Brideaux followed. There had been a time when he would have thought nothing of it. Now he was convinced Brideaux was trying to listen in. Thank goodness Salome had planned for that contingency.

Continuing his charade, Daniel went to swap the batteries. He picked up the charged ones and inserted the spent ones into the charger.

All the while he was doing his normal outdoor tasks, Daniel's mind was racing, while at the same time he was wishing he had the others to help him. Raj had stayed behind in case Joseph needed him, Robert and JR had been playing cards, and Roy had been asleep. It would be up to him.

He must try to overpower Brideaux. That shouldn't be a problem, since he was younger, taller and stronger. He'd do it in the lift as soon as it moved, while Brideaux was hanging on for that horrifying ride down. Daniel was sure that

Brideaux didn't have a clue what he knew, and he would take him by surprise.

While Daniel was busy with the batteries, Brideaux got another call, but because he was out of earshot where Daniel couldn't hear, he didn't notice.

When it was time, they made their way to the lift and got in. The moment the lift started to move, Daniel lunged toward Brideaux, but to his surprise, John had a big smile on his face and a big gun in his hand, pointing it at Daniel's head.

"Rossler, you must be thinking I am stupid. I know all about it. Now if you want to come out of this alive and save your friends, you will do as I tell you."

Brideaux had almost smiled when his operative called right after Daniel ended his phone call. The man had gone on and on about how this call was different, how it's usually all sexy stuff, men talking to their wives, until Brideaux had told him to get to the point. Then he'd dropped the bombshell. This time it wasn't Rossler's wife he'd spoken to, though from what Brideaux had heard, it seemed to have been. The predatory look came over his face when he heard what had really gone down, but he'd smoothed it over again by the time he and Rossler got into the lift.

He was ready for Daniel's attack, which had been bad news for Daniel. Now the lift was opening, and he was ready for that as well. Who else it was bad news for would be determined in the next few minutes.

Daniel walked out of the lift, with Brideaux right behind him. JR and the others, all but Robert, were gathered around Joseph's computer, but at the sound of the door opening, he looked up and shouted, "Hey Daniel, how are the girls back home…?"

He stopped abruptly when he saw on Daniel's face there was something wrong. He started to get up, but hadn't made it out of the floating chair when Brideaux gave Daniel a shove from behind, knocking him over one of the chairs. He lifted the gun and shouted at them to all get up and away from Joseph's computer. Raj who was sitting behind his own computer, got up quickly, turning to conceal it as he pulled out the mini-flash drive and shoved it into his pocket.

Brideaux was over-excited. He shouted at them to put their hands in the air, keep them there, and to move out and away to a corner. Just then, Robert who was out in one of the side corridors, appeared in the doorway. He had heard the commotion, heard everything when he cautiously approached, and decided to sneak up on Brideaux and overpower him from behind.

Now, at the door behind Brideaux, he was about five yards away and preparing to lunge across the gap when Brideaux heard something. He whirled around and shot Robert between the eyes, killing him instantly.

Daniel was stunned. In the moment it took him to start for Brideaux, JR yelled "You bastard!" and lunged for Brideaux himself. Brideaux fired, hitting JR in the left hand.

He smiled coldly. "I suggest you don't take any more chances. I can shoot the eyes out of a rat at ten paces on a full gallop. I have no intention of killing you, but I also have no issues whatsoever to do it if you give me any more shit. I am not going to tell you again to move to the corner and keep your hands up."

As they shuffled into the corner, he looked at Roy and sneered. "If it wasn't for that blond fuckin little slut of yours mingling in my affairs, this could have ended very well for

The Skywalkers

all of you, including your dead friend over there. But now I have to change my plans slightly."

Roy heard nothing but the insult to his wife. Ready to kill this man with his bare hands, he started to move forward, but Daniel caught him and held him back.

"Good move Danny, you just saved that boy's life. All of you listen very carefully, I would have killed him as well because I have a very itchy trigger finger on this gun at the moment. I have no use for him, and in fact I have no use for any of you. So this is my second and final warning. I have no problem killing you all. Do as I say and you live; try any of that heroic fuckin shit and you are dead."

No one moved or opened his mouth, but if looks could have killed, Brideaux would have been dead on the spot. He smiled again. It didn't matter to him; he was now in control, and there had never been a more satisfying feeling.

He said, "Okay, now Joseph, go over to my bag there on that table. Take out the cable ties and tie up these motherfuckers so I don't have to kill any more of them." He was enjoying this moment so much that he became even more obnoxious with his rhetoric. "You must see it as a lifesaving mission Joseph. Make sure you tie them up good. If anyone of them gets out of their ties and I have to shoot him, you are responsible for his death – you understand me? Ok do it. I'll be watching your every move." Waving the gun carelessly, he added, "I have no issues shooting you as well - there are plenty more translators where you came from, so get on with it."

Daniel listened to this braggadocio and couldn't believe the man had fooled him for all the years they'd been associated. How could he have been so blind?

Brideaux supervised as he directed Joseph to tie them up with their hands behind their backs and then their feet.

When they were trussed like Thanksgiving turkeys, he had Joseph drag them apart so they couldn't talk to each other without him hearing.

Now he had one last direction for Joseph. "Okay, now sit your ass down at that computer and carry on with that translation and finish it. And let me give you a few tips that concern your health and the health of every one of your friends. I'm in a hurry now. I want that translation done in the next two hours. Search for the part that says how you shut that fuckin machine down and translate it. I'm setting the timer on my watch and this is how it's going to go down.

In the next 30 minutes, you will find that part and start translating it. If I am not happy with your progress, I'll shoot one of those boys. Every 30 minutes I'll shoot another of them until you have the whole thing done. So health wise it will be good for you and the boys if you stick to my time management plan here. Comprende?"

Joseph, a respected elder of his tribe in his late sixties, swallowed. A man of peace, he had never been treated like this. If it never happened again, it would be too soon.

Brideaux, satisfied he had the lot of them cowed and ready to follow orders, walked over to his bag and took out a bottle of his favorite drink. If the others had been interested, they would have noticed it was a very, very expensive cognac. Then Brideaux took a crystal glass from a little box in his bag and poured himself a stiff drink, He sat down to wait for Joseph's results.

Joseph, too upset to focus, tried to concentrate, but 30 minutes later he had not been able to find the shutdown routine. As soon as the alarm sounded, Brideaux walked over and asked Joseph to show his progress. Wordlessly, Joseph shook his head, pointing to the screen, which said "Your search showed no results."

Brideaux said nothing. Instead, he walked over to Roy and without ceremony shot him in his lower right leg. Roy howled in pain, but the bullet had not hit bone and passed through.

Before anyone could say anything, Brideaux remarked, "It must be that cognac. I aimed for his head. But I think I will keep on shooting until I hit the target." As they watched in horror, Brideaux pretended to take careful aim, pulled the trigger and hit the wall. He laughed. "Shit, that stuff I'm drinking is really potent. It's fucking up my aim completely."

He took another wild shot, this time showing that he'd deliberately missed Roy.

But, by then, Joseph was begging him to please stop and blubbering that he'd try harder. Brideaux reloaded the magazine and said, "Okay, I'll give you another 30 minutes. But Roy, you will really have to talk to Joseph. He has to move his ass or I will have to come back for more target practice in 30 minutes."

Daniel spoke up. "He needs something to stop the bleeding, you asshole, before he bleeds out."

Brideaux looked at him with contempt. "He's not going to bleed out in half an hour. But if Joseph hasn't made some progress by then, I'll put some more holes in him and speed up the process."

Moaning, Roy still managed to shake his head at Daniel. There was no bargaining with a madman, and no use in getting himself shot, too.

Somehow Joseph got control over his nerves and emotions and found the strength to go on. He ran another search, found the right text and started translating and writing it down. On the hour he had translated a huge chunk of it and Brideaux rewarded him by not shooting anyone. At the ninety minute mark, the lift door opened and five heavily armed men walked into the great hall.

Brideaux greeted them happily, quite drunk by that time. He waved his glass vaguely in Roy's direction and told one of them to see to his wound for now. The man had cleaned it and was wrapping it in sterile gauze when, five minutes before the two-hour mark, Joseph announced he was done.

It took a little while longer for the men to read and understand the directions, and for Roy to give them directions for operating the robots. Once they were ready, though, entering the room, running the shutdown routine and removing the beast was surprisingly quick. They packed up all the computer equipment and took it out, leaving Brideaux to do as he wished with his prisoners.

Brideaux had finished his bottle of cognac and started on another, celebrating his victory in style. Although still almost falling-down drunk, he staggered over to where Daniel sat on the floor and stood over him, reeling.

"Goodbye my friend! Thank you for all your help to get this done. I could not have done this without your help."

Though his words were slurred, they burned into Daniel's mind. If it was the last thing he did, Daniel would remember this and take his revenge – but Brideaux was still talking.

"Now jus' a few health tips for you as well, Dan'l. I'll be in control of the worl' soon. In fac' I am awready. But it will be goo' for you and your love-y Sarah and little Nicky to be goo' ci'zens. I'm gonna be fair and jus' king. Goo' health, wealth, happiness and prosperity and a long life to ever'one.

Don' come after me. Don' hate me. Just be nice and quiet and I leave you alone. All you mother otherfuckers here as well. Oh, I almos' forgot. My guys are on their way to pick up those 10th and 8th Cycle Libraries a' your place righ' now. We jus' can't leave 'em in your hands anymore. You guys are just not capable of managing it prop'ly – you fuckin idiots almos' destroyed the worl' twice 'cause you can't manage it."

While he was rambling, Daniel caught JR's eye and lifted his eyebrows. Had JR managed to get loose yet? They needed to rush this maniac while he was distracted. But JR shook his head. No way to get out of the cable ties.

Brideaux was still making his speech. He'd put his gun hand over his heart, and was making some kind of pledge.

"I promise I will protec' it and make sure all that comes out of it will be used for the common good of all mankin' an', an' womankin' an' you guys here. Sorry about you frien' over there JR," pointing to Robert's dead body, " bu' maybe he died to let you all know you don' fuck around with me."

He turned to go. Daniel said, "John, you've won, but at least cut us loose."

Brideaux looked at him with surprise. "No, I don' think so. Okay, goo'bye. I hope your lovely girls come and look for you and take you all home." He turned to Joseph and said "Ol'timer, get your stuff and le's go. You will be living with me for a while. I've decided to hire you."

Leaning on Joseph, he left, while Daniel shouted, "John Brideaux – I will have my revenge – in this life or the next." Brideaux had one parting thing to say. "Dan'l. Dan'l my ol' frien' you din' listen. Don' hate me. This is for the goo' of all mankin'." Somehow, he regained his feet and clearer speech as the lift doors closed. The last thing Daniel heard was, "I have the same ideals as you. We are not that different." Daniel didn't respond. Even if he'd still been within earshot, he was not going to talk with this evil man anymore. It was not worth his breath.

JR lifted his wounded hand in a wave and said, "We will see you again John."

If John Brideaux knew what those words meant he would have killed JR and everyone else then and there but one and a half bottles of very expensive cognac had clouded his thinking.

Meanwhile at the Rossler Foundation

As soon as the call was over, the girls got moving again on their assignments.

Most of the families of the selected Rabbit Hole coterie had been briefed as the Enigma plan was developed. A 'phone tree' except without the phones sent a cascading message to them that the time was at hand. Sarah delivered the message to the first family, who notified the next, who notified the next until everyone was ready. Now all she needed to do was gather Mark's family and those of the other two ex-Marines and get them started.

The plan had been simple until the extras were added. Each family would make its way to a rendezvous point where a large van would be waiting. They were staggered in different meeting points and at two or three hour intervals so as not to create suspicion.

Since there were no more than two or three routes to the Rabbit Hole, and at least one was considered too far out of the way to be practical, they would stop in different towns along the way and wait to proceed at pre-determined intervals designed to keep them from becoming a convoy of white, unmarked vans that would surely attract notice. Once each group was delivered to within walking distance of the Rabbit Hole, the van driver would drive to the Billings airport and abandon the van, making his way to a place where the next one would pick him up – a different place each time. It was the best they could do, but it should work.

Each family had been given a list of what to bring, allowing as much as practical, including keepsakes and children's cherished toys, but leaving behind everything large and bulky. More than one woman mourned her Keurig coffee maker or a favorite piece of heirloom furniture, but they all understood the necessity. All cell phones and other electronic devices were collected and thrown in a bin to be destroyed.

It would be like going into witness protection. There would be no contact with anyone left behind, ever. For the good of the Rabbit Hole Gang as one of them dubbed the group, as well as the good of friends and extended family left behind. The latter would be as safe as anyone, as long as they knew nothing of where the Rossler Foundation had gone.

The last to be sent on their way were the Canyon rescue party's families. They needed the most time, since they hadn't been prepared ahead of time. Sarah was the most impressed with their discipline, though. When it came time to destroy the electronics, there were no protests from teenagers over their Gameboys and Playstations. In fact, they'd left them behind. She only hoped her mom and Aunt Sally had as easy a time of it with little Nick's game. He loved that thing.

Aaron was to drive the van that would take these families to the Rabbit Hole. Sarah stopped by to make sure he would be able to find it.

"Don't worry, Sis," he said. "I'm good with a GPS."

"How did your mom and Grandma Bess take the news?" Sarah asked.

"Mom's good as long as Dad's with her. And Grandma was amazing. She took her clothes and Grandpa's ashes and nothing else. Said she was glad to leave all that clutter behind, because it just had to be dusted."

"I love your grandma," Sarah said, smiling.

Just then, the first of the three ex-Marine families arrived and Sarah introduced Aaron as their driver. The two helped get the families settled and their possessions stowed, and Sarah hugged Aaron goodbye. She would be the last one out of the Foundation building if she had anything to say about it, and would be the one to pick him up after he abandoned the van. The two of them would have to hike for several miles to their final destination at the Rabbit Hole to throw off any followers.

Back at the canyon

With Brideaux and his gun gone, not to mention his henchmen, Daniel and JR had scooted together and managed to get their cable ties off. They were attending to JR's hand and Roy's wound when the doors slid open again. They froze. Had Brideaux changed his mind and come back to finish them off as well?

JR recognized Mark first. "Hey, are we glad to see you guys!"

Mark answered, "We heard you might have had some trouble. Where are the bad guys? We'll take care of them."

"Gone," Daniel answered. "You must have missed them by minutes. Did Sarah tell you what was here, what's at stake?"

"Yeah. I guess they got that beast thing, too?" Mark answered.

"They did. We need to get out of here and get our people to safety."

"Already done, my friend. That's one efficient wife you've got there. She told us to bring you to the Rabbit Hole, dead or alive. I assume you want to get there alive?"

"That would be my choice. JR?"

Daniel's dry humor made the others laugh as JR answered, "Oh, I guess."

Then they sobered, remembering Robert. "He has no family here," said JR. "His mom is in Australia. Should we take him with us?"

Daniels voice was gentle as he made his regrets to his little brother. "We won't be able to contact her, JR, and she won't be able to come and get his body. I think it's best we leave him here, outside in the canyon. We'll bury him before we go."

Later, as they stood in a circle around the cairn that marked Robert's grave, they swore again to avenge his death, sometime, somehow, even if they had to follow John Brideaux to hell to do it.

"What's the range on this thing?" Daniel asked, as the seven men climbed into the chopper. "And what the heck is it?"

"This is one of the Lynx Mk9 choppers out of the UK

that were modified for conditions in Iraq, back in 2010," Mark answered. "A buddy of mine bought it when it was decommissioned, for use out here. He ferries actors from Flag to sites out in the desert for filming. Or, he used to. It belongs to the Rossler Foundation now."

"Cool!" exclaimed JR. Daniel supposed it didn't matter. If they had no further use for it after this mission, it represented money they'd never use again anyway, probably.

"So, what's its range?" he asked again.

"Oh, 400 miles or so, depending on weight. With our current load maybe 250," Mark said, grinning.

Daniel thought fast. The chopper had already flown from Flagstaff to here. They could probably make no further than Farmington, New Mexico on the remainder of the fuel.

He called Mark, who was still trading good-natured insults with JR, to come back and talk to him, and asked him how they could make it to either Billings or Bozeman, in Montana. It would take several hops, but Mark had a surprising number of friends along the way who could help organize refueling and overnight rests inconspicuously and without asking questions.

It was settled - they'd fly as close to the Rabbit Hole as they could get. Mark said if they chose Bozeman, he knew a man who would store the chopper in a place where no one would question it.

Within a few minutes, the remainder of the expedition and their rescuers were on their way across the Navajo reservation on their way to Farmington. Daniel hoped Brideaux would treat him well. He had no idea where to even look for Joseph for a rescue attempt. One more friend left behind among many. He knew they couldn't save everyone, but this one hurt more than any other.

Just after midnight of the 6th day at the Rossler Foundation

Just after midnight on the same day, two helicopters with FBI insignia on them landed on the lawn in front of the Rossler Foundation building and ten men, all dressed and armed as FBI SWAT team members, jumped out. At the same time, two FBI incident vans stopped at the front gates. Two "FBI" agents got out, walked up to the security guards and shot them at short range with silenced guns. Afterward, they drove the vans right up to the front door.

As soon as the fake FBI agents stormed through the front door, the two security guards inside jumped up and were killed as well. With no one left to stop them, some fifteen operatives raided the place. They broke into the server room and took all the servers, collected all the computers and documents and anything else they could lay their hands on throughout the building. An hour later, they were done and moved out the front gate, with no one in the city any the wiser.

Brideaux was waiting for them in a warehouse in Denver, with Joseph under guard at his side. He watched, at first in triumph and later in a growing tantrum, as his experts got everything set up and started working through his prize. None of the computers would boot up. Brideaux railed at the fake agents. "Don't you know the difference between an operational computer and one that's been stripped of its hard drive?

His experts calmed him. There were still the blade servers. This was a job for their hackers. But, when they booted up the servers and hacked into them, they found

Raj's little joke - a welcome screen on each and every one of them with a photo of his hand showing a middle finger! Beyond that, there was nothing but movies and games on them. Now they understood the blank spots in the racks. The missing Rosslers must have taken the important ones with them. In the boxes they'd taken from the vault, they found only rolls of toilet paper. This last insult sent Brideaux into such a fit of rage that he had to be sedated. When he woke, he directed his crew to find the missing Rossler employees at any cost and make them talk. Where had those sons of bitches gone with his libraries?

Those of the Rossler Foundation people who had to be left behind had each found an email in their home computers the next morning, after the bug-out. With no other explanation, they'd been given regretful severance notices and told to check their bank accounts, which had been enriched by several thousand dollars in severance pay for each. A few of them received frightening and painful visits from FBI agents – they didn't know the difference – who demanded to know where the Rosslers and a few other key employees had gone. After finding that even under torture the ones left behind had no knowledge of the others, they went back to Brideaux with the report.

It seemed that they'd vanished into thin air, clearing out the building before they left. The agents found no one at the houses of Daniel, JR, Sinclair, Luke, Bess, Luke, Ryan or even Daniel's parents in North Carolina. Some of the Foundation employees were also missing.

They had gone, disappeared with no word to anyone. The neighbors didn't know anything, hadn't seen anything, they had no idea. Brideaux went mad. Waving his gun to prevent his people from sedating him again, he was swearing like no one had ever heard a human swear before.

He knew he had a problem. Although his plan had worked out exactly as anticipated up until now, he knew he'd never know peace again as long as the Rosslers and their brilliant scientists had access to the Tenth and Eighth Cycle libraries. Until he could find them and those libraries he would always have to look over his shoulder.

With his future and that of the world at stake, Brideaux deployed all of his resources. He put out contracts on them in the crime world. He let police in every likely jurisdiction, the FBI, the CIA and a handful of other alphabet-soup agencies know – they were wanted for heinous crimes. He called in his NSA stooges to track cell phones, land lines, internet activity; every possible lead or trace. He had to find them.

Chapter Forty-Four

UTOPIA HAS ARRIVED

New Delhi - The G20 summit

It didn't take long for Brideaux to demonstrate his new power in an even more sinister manner. A week after putting a price on the head of every missing Rosslerite, at a G20 conference held in New Delhi, among the usual protesters were a handful of men with backpacks. Seeing nothing but what appeared to be computer equipment, security officers allowed them to remain in the roped-off area where the crowd was gathered. Inside, the twenty representatives to the conference as well as some dozen or more heads of state of the delegate countries were seated for lunch in the Emily Eden Room.

The delegate from the United States rose as if to give a toast and the conversation quieted. Rather than a toast, however, the delegate had an announcement.

"Ladies and gentlemen, please be advised that when I call your name, you will be required to leave, with our thanks for your service, which is no longer needed. I represent a group of individuals who will now replace selected members."

A buzz of conversation ensued, with some laughter as people decided it was a joke, although in poor taste. However, when the man began calling names, the buzz turned to angry shouting. "Ibrahim bin Ibrahim. Yoshi Yamaguchi." Before he could utter a third name, other delegates rushed him and seized him.

"What's the meaning of this? Are you drunk?" demanded the delegate from Germany, in impeccable English.

"Not at all. Let go of me or suffer the consequences." His hand slipped into his pocket and the delegate from Canada moved to restrain him and draw it out. In it was a small device that looked much like an old-fashioned pager. This started a stampede among those near enough to see it, as they assumed it was a trigger for an explosive device. Instead, it signaled the men outside, who each brought a hand-held microphone from their pockets and began to speak in a language strange to the passers-by and protesters in the square.

There was no hue and cry, as the crowd was polyglotted anyway. When nothing of note happened, they turned their backs and ignored the men with the backpacks. Once those had intoned their lines into their microphones, they melted away into the crowd and eventually left the area.

Inside, however, was chaos. The two delegates whose names had been called were the first to collapse, followed by several other delegates and a few heads of state. By the time others realized they were dead, those others, too, were desperately ill, some fighting for breath, others exsanguinating from all orifices or expiring after clawing at their eyes. A few only were left, and a few heads of state, when the horrifying scene simply ended with perhaps two-thirds of the participants lying dead.

Those few walked out of the conference room and convened in a smaller room, where they proceeded to calmly hear the report of the US delegate, now the de facto head of G20, which had abruptly gone back to G8.

News media personnel on hand to report on the doings of the conference erupted in excited shouting as the delegates dropped, but by the time the carnage was complete were also divided into two camps--the living and the dead. One head of a media corporation was later heard to remark it was a uniquely efficient way to complete a reduction in force. The few reporters and photographers who lived were those who, whether warned ahead of time or simply quick to analyze what was happening, cut their feeds as soon as the first delegates fell dead. Those followed the remaining delegates to the smaller room and calmly reported that a new era had dawned. The theme to emerge would be an end to poverty, hunger, environmental waste and crime.

In a matter of weeks, worldwide, Utopia was becoming a reality.

Cooperating heads of state declared military rule to quell the riots that occurred when announcements of various restrictions began. No one seemed to understand what had happened, except some unfortunate news analysts who mysteriously dropped dead as soon as they attempted to communicate 'subversive' thoughts. None of them had been present at the meeting where they might have witnessed the fate of their late colleagues and learned where their bread was buttered.

Most shocking, however, was the near-universal capitulation as participants on social media outlets began praising the way their governments had responded to crisis. Curfews were such a good idea, so that violent criminals couldn't use cover of darkness to terrorize good citizens. Everyone knew that mass transportation was superior to individual vehicles, most of which had been confiscated. An easy and anonymous way to inform on your neighbor's antisocial behavior was quite conveniently offered. It was all so pleasant, not having to put up with air pollution, noisy neighbors and crime anymore.

Chapter Forty-Five

WE WILL HAVE TO DO IT

Sarah and Aaron had arrived last, as planned. Salome had warned her that there would be no way of knowing the fate of their men until they, hopefully, walked into the Rabbit Hole safe and sound. But, after two weeks, hope was beginning to make way for uncertainty. Rebecca reminded her of the first Antarctic expedition when they all turned up alive on the day of their funeral.

"Remember, they have to keep a low profile," she urged. "We have to keep hoping."

Sarah would keep hoping, then, for another week or two or a month. After that...she would... no there is no other way – they must be alive and will get here. Meanwhile, there were almost fifty people in this place, and plenty of work to be done to keep them hidden, safe and fed.

They all agreed - they had three things in their favor; Nicholas' prophesy on his deathbed, the 10th and 8th Cycle libraries and the hope that Daniel, JR and the rest are alive and are making their way to their new home.

The Skywalkers

They all remembered, not too long ago, when JR said, "You'll see, we will have to do it."

Next in the Rossler Foundation Mysteries Series

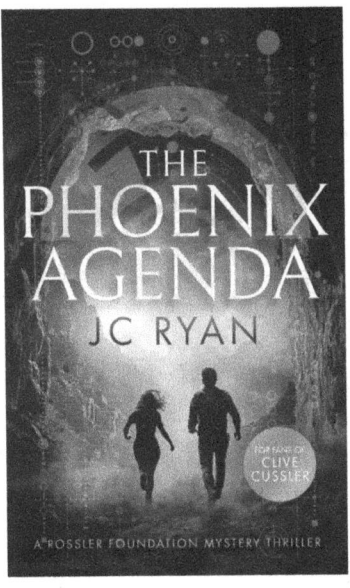

vinci-books.com/phoenix-agenda

A fight for freedom against the One World Supreme Council.

In a world teetering on the brink of tyranny, the Rossler Foundation faces their most formidable challenge yet. From the depths of the Grand Canyon to the halls of power, they must thwart John Brideaux's plans of establishing a new world order.

Turn the page for a free preview…

The Phoenix Agenda: Prologue

"Big-Mac, Big-Mac, this is Two-One Alpha. Can you read me?"

"Two-One Alpha, This is Big-Mac. I read you, over."

"Big-Mac, where are you? Serious shit over here! Heavy fire! Can't move our asses! Two casualties! Over."

"Two-One Alpha, you'll see me in 2 seconds. Mark the LZ, I'm close. Over."

"Big-Mac, roger, roger. Out."

John 'Doug' MacArthur tightened his grip on the control. His feet were shaking faintly on the tail rotor pedals as he took in the scene below him when his chopper broke the horizon over Hill 39 in the Shah-i-Kot Valley in Afghanistan's Paktia province.

"This valley's been a hellhole the last few months," he muttered. "Now this! Damn it!"

He curved the chopper around over the soldiers, surveying the scene rapidly before pulling away once again out of firing range.

Ten Marines, pinned down behind rocks and in shallow

ditches, were firing at an invisible group of thirty-odd Taliban fighters on the hill above them. Open ground in front with no cover behind. They were sitting ducks. Tracers and bullets from AK-47s, ancient British Lee-Enfield rifles, and a Russian RPK machine gun, created a blanket of instant death over the pinned-down soldiers.

Luckily, the Taliban fighters were not known for their marksmanship, and they didn't always understand that the skill of the person holding the weapon was what made the weapon useful. Most of their shots were missing their targets by several yards because they didn't understand that the fundamental principle of shooting downhill requires dropping your aim down. Nevertheless, some of their fire was hitting the target, and it was obvious the boys down there were in serious trouble.

"Big-Mac this is Two-One Alpha. I see you - putting out smoke now. Tell me the color!"

"Two-One Alpha, this is Big-Mac. Green?"

"Big-Mac, Two-One Alpha. That's it."

The unmistakable trace of smoke left by the rocket from an RPG 7 racing down the hill caught the co-pilot's eye. Leo McKenzie said, "Oh shiiiiit. The bastards have an RPG!"

The rocket exploded about 20 yards behind the soldiers, sending a chilling sensation through John's spine. He knew all too well how devastating an RPG could be. Even in the hands of an untrained person it could create havoc on the receiving end and was a very simple but deadly effective weapon against a helicopter. The US military learned the dire lesson in 1993 during the Battle of Mogadishu. Somali militia fighters, basically untrained armed civilians, successfully shot down two Black Hawk helicopters with RPGs and damaged three others - a battle that saw 18 American soldiers killed and 73 others wounded.

Over the past 18 months, John had survived many evac missions, also known as a DUSTOFF, the backronym for Dedicated Unhesitating Service to Our Fighting Forces. He knew what it was like to be under fire. He'd seen a few tight situations in his time here in the war zone, but this one in front of him now made the others look insignificant.

John knew there was no time to waste. He had to make the decision, land the chopper and risk the ten soldiers on the ground and the three of them in the helicopter. It was that, or get out and wait for help, which would almost guarantee the death of those on the ground.

'Unhesitation' was exactly what was happening when he shouted into his helmet's intercom system. "Those boys are in serious trouble down there. We better get them out and fast. With all that metal flying around it's a miracle they're not all dead already."

Tony, the third crew member and gunner, turned the door gun on the enemy positions and started firing. Some of their fire turned to the chopper but became sporadic very quickly when they experienced the business end of the machine gun.

"We can't wait for reinforcements. If we don't get them out now, they'll all be dead. I'm going in to put her down, Tony!" he shouted to the gunner as he maneuvered the chopper down to land. "Just keep those bastards on the hill down. And while you're at it, make sure that RPG isn't pointed at us."

"Roger that. I'll keep 'em busy - you can bet your ass on it," Tony shouted back.

"Two-One Alpha, ready for you. Move it. We're in kind of a hurry to find a quieter place!"

The Skywalkers

Two wounded men were hauled to the helicopter first by four of their buddies, with the rest strafing the hill to keep the Taliban heads down. The fright and panic in the eyes and faces of the soldiers were clearly visible. Their screams rose above the thundering noise of the engines as they pushed the wounded in and then took up position outside the chopper to provide covering fire for the remaining men to get in.

"All in. Let's get out of here!" Leo shouted.

"Grab tight. It's going to be a rough ride boys!"

John pulled the chopper into a steep climb while banking away from the hill. With no fire coming from the doorgun to keep them down, the full force and frustration of the enemy was now directed at the chopper and its occupants. They saw their prey escaping out of their hands right in front of their eyes.

A burning pain shot through John's back and legs as the body of the helicopter shuddered under the power of the two Rolls-Royce Gem turboshaft engines at full throttle. Smoke started to billow from the starboard engine. *I have to get over that hill three miles away. Why am I dizzy? I have to get these boys out of trouble. I have to level the chopper and save power. I must get over that hill. I must get out of the reach of the bullets.*

"Doug! Doug! Can you hear me? What's wrong man?" Leo screamed in a high-pitched, panicked voice. "Oh my God, you've been hit! Are you ok? Shit man, put the chopper down now. You'll crash and kill us all!"

"That hill ... I have to get over it ... out of range ... I must get us there ..." Doug stuttered.

"What was that? I can't hear you. For God's sake put the chopper down!" Leo shouted at the top of his voice.

"Going down, going down ... radio for help!" John whispered, a few seconds before everything went dark.

The Phoenix Agenda: Chapter One

THE NIGHTMARE AND THE MATH

Doug paid little heed to his passengers as he banked away from the canyon rim. Max was back there to help them. Doug had plenty on his mind, between the flashback to his crash in Afghanistan and wondering when whoever had shot two of his passengers would show up and try to shoot the chopper down here and now, over the Grand Canyon. Not to mention nursing the aging machine to do his bidding.

Within minutes after takeoff from the canyon site, lying in the back of the chopper, JR and Roy were oblivious to their surroundings due to the morphine injection administered to them by Max Ellis – an ex-Marine medic and the third member of the Rossler boys' rescue expedition. Others on the chopper had more on their minds.

Raj was in his own world, eyes closed, wondering about his wife Sushma, their child, and the future. He and Sushma were not the outdoors adventure and camping types – living in a cave with other people was going to take some getting used to for them. They both grew up and had lived in the city all their lives. How was this going to work out for him and his family and, for that matter, for all of the Rosslerites?

Ever since the Rosslers, with his help and that of others, had discovered the wealth of ancient knowledge hidden in the Great Pyramid of Giza, It seemed no matter what good came of these discoveries, there was always a megalomaniac, or a group of them, who wanted to exploit it for their own nefarious reasons.

It was brought home to them over and over again that they could never rest. Whether their discoveries led to a fabulous hidden city in Antarctica or a way to micro-miniaturize the most sophisticated of electronic marvels, someone had designs on it and it was up to the Rossler Foundation and its leadership to thwart the evil-doers' plans. This time, it seemed they may be too late to foil the latest maniac.

Raj could not make up his mind immediately. What was worse, being ruled by a resurrected Persian Empire or by this psychopath, John Brideaux? They were now living in the new world of John Brideaux. There was no choice. From what he'd seen so far, he was sure neither he nor any of his friends were going to like it. He was sure they were not going to accept it either. He was not going to walk around with a chip in his body that controlled his life; he had never been controlled by anyone ... except perhaps by Sushma, he thought, as a smile played on his face.

Although Raj was uncertain about the future, he was very sure about a few other matters. He was definitely going to stay with the Rossler Foundation. They would rely on him – and he on them – to bring this new world to a speedy end. They had always relied on each other in the past to overcome adversity, and this time was the same. The second thing he was determined about was that he was going to find a way to seek out and activate his underground network and bring their full force down on John Brideaux. That lunatic was going down, and he fully intended to be there to witness it.

Max Ellis was wondering what the future held for him and his wife. He'd seen a bit of action in the last days of the Afghanistan war, before the troops were withdrawn. Returning to the States, he'd joined M&J Security Company in Boulder. He married Jenny a few years ago. She was a kindergarten teacher, and lately he'd been working part-time as a security guard while studying for a computer science degree.

Uncertainty and unknowns about what would happen to him and Jenny in the days and weeks to come made him nervous about today's events. He trusted Mark and John, or 'Doug' as everyone called him, though. They'd been good to him over the years, had encouraged and supported him to take up his studies. They'd also made it possible for him to work part-time so he and Jenny could still make ends meet while he studied.

Daniel, the only one in the back with his headset on, was startled by Mark's voice.

"Earth calling Doug! Doug, can you read me? ET calling Doug. Come in Doug. Anybody home?"

"Huh, what was that?"

Mark smiled. His best friend must have been deep in thought, as he hadn't responded to his chatter for the past few minutes. "Buddy, where have you been? I thought you fell asleep behind the wheel?"

"Ah man, that frickin' nightmare paid me a very unwelcome visit. This chopper and all the stuff today, wounded men and all, aren't good for forgetting memories you don't want to have."

"You ok, my friend?"

"Yea I'll survive. I'm ok."

"Nightmare? What nightmare, John?" Daniel asked.

"Long story Daniel, long story. A horrible start but a good ending."

"Hey Mark, why'd you call him Doug? I thought you introduced him as John. You are aware we have a military hero by the same name. Related, John?"

John smiled. "Yes, but I have to explain it to you."

Mark chipped in before Doug could say anything further. "Another long story, Daniel. If you understand it, you will be the first. He claims there's some relationship to General Douglas-Old-Soldiers-Never-Die-They-Just-Fade-Away-MacArthur. He's tried to explain it to me and many others many times, but none of us got it - at least not yet. Therefore, instead of listening to his complicated genealogical descriptions, we decided to call him Doug. It seems to make him happy and spares us the pain of listening to his explanation!"

John, a very good-natured person, was having a good laugh at the jokes at his expense. "Let me put it this way, Daniel - my nickname will be as close as I will ever come to fame and power."

"Doug, I'd surely like to hear your stories someday, both the nightmare and the math."

"Sure, Daniel. As soon as we can get a campfire going and get a few stiff shots of Scottish Aqua Vie under the belt, I'll tell you."

Grab your copy...
vinci-books.com/phoenix-agenda

About the Author

JC Ryan is a bestselling author renowned for his intricate espionage, archaeological thrillers, and conspiracy mysteries. With over 30 acclaimed novels, including the popular Rex Dalton K9 Thrillers, Rossler Foundation Mysteries, and Carter Devereux Mystery Thrillers, Ryan has captivated readers around the globe.

Drawing from his diverse professional background—as a military officer, lawyer, and IT manager—Ryan creates compelling narratives that skillfully blend historical accuracy with thrilling adventure. He is celebrated as a master storyteller, known for crafting riveting plots, meticulous historical details, and engaging, multidimensional characters. Ryan's meticulous research lends authenticity and depth to each story, immersing readers in richly constructed worlds filled with intrigue, suspense, and adventure.

Fans of David Baldacci, Lee Child's Jack Reacher, Tom Clancy's Jack Ryan, Nelson DeMille's John Corey, Vince Flynn's Mitch Rapp, Mark Greaney's Gray Man, Gregg Hurwitz's Orphan X, Robert Ludlum's Jason Bourne, Daniel Silva's Gabriel Allon, Brad Taylor's Pike Logan, Brad Thor's Scot Harvath, James Rollins' Sigma Force, Steve Berry's Cotton Malone, and Dan Brown's Robert Langdon will find JC Ryan's novels equally compelling and unforgettable.

When not writing, Ryan enjoys spending time with his college sweetheart, whom he married in 1978. They are proud parents of two daughters, have two sons-in-law, and are grandparents to two grandchildren.

www.ingramcontent.com/pod-product-compliance
Ingram Content Group UK Ltd.
Pitfield, Milton Keynes, MK11 3LW, UK
UKHW020045211025
464173UK00003B/117